DISPUTE

DISPUTE

JUDGE, JURY, & EXECUTIONER™ BOOK EIGHT

CRAIG MARTELLE

MICHAEL ANDERLE

DISRUPTIVE IMAGINATION

Copyright © 2020 Craig Martelle and Michael Anderle
Cover by J Caleb Design, Typography by Jeff Brown
Cover copyright © LMBPN Publishing
A Michael Anderle Production

LMBPN Publishing
PMB 196, 2540 South Maryland Pkwy
Las Vegas, NV 89109

First US edition, January, 2020
ebook ISBN: 978-1-64202-686-3
Print ISBN: 978-1-64202-687-0

THE DISPUTE TEAM

Thanks to our Beta Readers

Micky Cocker, James Caplan, Kelly O'Donnell, and John
Ashmore

Thanks to the JIT Readers

Jackey Hankard-Brodie
Nicole Emens
Peter Manis
Jeff Eaton
Rachel Beckford
James Caplan
Diane L. Smith
John Ashmore
Dorothy Lloyd
Misty Roa
Micky Cocker
Larry Omans

If I've missed anyone, please let me know!

Editor
Lynne Stiegler

We can't write without those who support us
On the home front, we thank you for being there for us

We wouldn't be able to do this for a living if it weren't for our readers
We thank you for reading our books

CHAPTER ONE

Wyatt Earp, Interstellar Space

"Pizza." The word hung in the air with a nearly physical presence. Six faces stared at the small big-headed Crenellian.

"No. I'm not going to use Federation assets to bring you pizza." Ankh crossed his arms. Groenwyn snuggled up next to him. He tried to shy away, but she wrapped her arms around him with a speed the eye could not follow. The wombat, Floyd, climbed into his lap and sniffed his face.

Rivka, Red, and Lindy leaned toward Ankh. The big bodyguard, Red, licked his lips.

Sahved, the bald and gangly Yemilorian, stood behind the group, growing more excited by the magical food item called pizza. He looked forward to his first slice.

"I know you," Ankh said in his even, emotionless tone. "If I do it once, it will be a forever thing."

"Give me the power, and then you won't have to worry about it. On my authority as a Federation Magistrate."

Rivka crossed her arms, mirroring Ankh's pose. "Or you could do it just this once as a technology demonstration."

"I already know the technology works," Ankh replied.

"We're going on vacation—a real vacation—and there's no better way to kick it off than with a taste bud celebration." Red thought he was more convincing than he sounded.

Floyd and Groenwyn continued to snuggle the slight alien. Ankh looked like he wanted to be somewhere else.

Anywhere else.

"What kind of vacation is it where we all go together?" Ankh asked.

"We're friends. We don't really trust anyone else. We'll have some people come visit us, maybe. In case we get recalled, we don't have to scour the galaxy for runaways."

"Runaways?" Ankh was confused.

"Maybe a poor choice of words. Then again, maybe it's exactly what I meant. Think about it—us not bugging you because our mouths are filled with the cheesy deliciousness of an All Guns Blazing pie."

"You're not going to leave me alone until I say yes, are you?"

"You already know the answer to that one," Groenwyn whispered into his ear.

"Fine." Ankh held out his hand and Rivka put her datapad into it. "What do you want?"

As if she'd spent all day memorizing the menu, she blurted, "Five moonstokle pies, seven pepperoni, four bistok sausage, eight bistok and pepperoni, five vegetarian, and two with the five-cheese blend."

"There are only ten of us on board," Ankh said without looking up.

"You're right, so change from two cheese pizzas to ten, plus everything else. We can add some stuff to spruce up the leftovers." Rivka glanced at her team, receiving appreciative nods in return.

Ankh tapped a series of commands and let his finger hover before pressing the final button. He handed Rivka's pad back to her.

"You're my new hero, big man," Red said, grinning broadly and standing to stretch. Lindy pushed away from the conference table and joined her husband, and they left *Wyatt Earp*'s conference room.

Rivka watched them go before turning her attention back to Groenwyn. "Sticking with the platinum green?" she asked, pointing at the young woman's shining hair.

"For now." Groenwyn twirled a strand of hair around one finger and smiled mischievously. "I think a glittery forest green is coming soon."

Rivka chuckled and leaned back, crossing her arms to take in the scene. Vacation. Off the grid. She wasn't sure what she'd do with herself, but the entertainment had already begun.

Floyd kept lunging at Ankh's face as he tried to hold the wombat at arm's length, but she was too heavy for him. He settled for wedging her between the table and his body.

The conference room door opened and the small dog-like alien ran in, yipping to announce his presence. The big orange cat, Wenceslaus, appeared out of nowhere, jumping onto the table and strolling casually to the middle, where he flopped to his side and rolled over the holoprojector, blackening the image of space outside the ship where they expected the drone with the pizzas to appear.

Sahved poked his three fingers toward the cat. Wenceslaus ignored him.

"We need to get you into the Pod-doc." Rivka unfolded her arms and jabbed a thumb toward Sahved but looked pointedly at Ankh.

He blinked slowly, his face emotionless. Rivka looked from one alien to the other.

"That means you need to program it. First order of business is to settle his stomach. If he pukes again on our ship, I'm sending him out the airlock in interstellar space."

Ankh didn't move. Groenwyn poked his cheek with her finger.

"May I say something?" Sahved interjected. Ankh couldn't push Groenwyn's hand away since he was occupied with keeping Floyd out of his face. The small dog-like alien bounced behind his chair, nipping at the back of his shipsuit. Ankh twisted in his seat.

"When did Ankh become Doctor Doolittle?" Rivka asked.

"He's got a gift," Groenwyn said before leaning over to pick up the barker. The creature calmed instantly.

"I think a couple of someones have a gift." Rivka smiled at the look on Groenwyn's face. Simple joy, the kind people rarely enjoyed in the company of others, but the faeries had given the young woman the gift of clearing her soul. The burdens of her past life had disappeared. She had been a happy spirit from the time she joined Rivka and her crew, but nothing like the freedom she enjoyed now. "Does he have a name?"

"May I say something?" Sahved asked again, leaning across the table to get closer to the others.

"He doesn't, but I've been thinking, maybe Titan, or Maximo."

"We should probably take him back where he came from," Ankh deadpanned.

"No." Groenwyn met the Crenellian's gaze. He looked away after a few moments and struggled to lean far enough forward to push Wenceslaus off the projector. Groenwyn tickled the cat's paws until he rolled over. The drone was there and being guided into the cargo bay.

"Pizza!" Rivka declared. "Chaz, can you give me ship-wide broadcast, please?"

"Yes, Magistrate," the ship's artificial intelligence promptly replied. The system popped to life.

Rivka cleared her throat before speaking loudly. "The pizzas have arrived, straight from All-Guns Blazing. All hail Ankh and the first intergalactic pizza delivery. May his Galaxy Eats business flourish, but let it be known it was done first right here, right now."

Red's muffled cry came from the corridor outside the conference room. "Pizza!"

Ankh started rubbing his temples. Floyd, no longer being held in place, stood on his lap and nipped his chin before jumping down and heading for the door. Wenceslaus ran after her.

Groenwyn leaned close to Ankh and examined his face. "She drew blood. What did you do to her?"

Ankh looked up at the young woman, his expression blank. "Humans are the strangest creatures in the galaxy. Your denial of logic boggles my mind. If it weren't for Ted,

I would have lost faith in your species long ago. Now, if you'll excuse me, I'll retire to my workshop."

"No dinner?" Groenwyn asked.

"Well, since it's here."

The little creature started to wiggle when he realized Ankh was leaving. Groenwyn tried to soothe him. "We won't let him get away, Tiny-Man Titan, and yes, that is his name."

Ankh hesitated before letting his chin drop to his chest.

Rivka took the opportunity to insert one more pin into Ankh's psyche. "You know we're going to eat that order in its entirety in about a day, and three days from now, you know we'll want more. If you hand over the keys to the pizza delivery drone, we won't bother you."

"Not a pizza delivery drone," Ankh replied evenly, still looking at the deck.

"Red?" Rivka asked, looking at the table where the microphone pick-ups were located.

"Magistrate," Red acknowledged through the overhead speakers.

"Is there a drone in the cargo bay?"

"You know there is. The pizza delivery drone has arrived."

"Chaz, would you be so kind as to program a maintenance bot to paint 'Ankh's Intergalactic Pizza Delivery' on the side of that drone."

Ankh lifted his head and faced the Magistrate. His expression was neutral, but he threw his hands up in frustration. "You win," Ankh mumbled.

"Belay that last, Chaz."

"I had a logo and everything," the AI needled.

"Save it. We might be able to get some use from it. It's not about winning. It's about doing what's right by those who love you most." Rivka finally hopped up from her seat, motioning for Ankh and Groenwyn to go first. Groenwyn wrapped her arm around the Crenellian's shoulders and they walked through the open door side by side. Titan nestled into the crook of Groenwyn's elbow and closed his eyes.

Ankh rested his head against her chest as she led him to the galley, where Red and Lindy were bringing the loot. Rivka stopped and watched the tender connections between her crew. A tap on her shoulder broke her out of her reverie.

"You are the most magnificent of ship's captains," the Yemilorian started, using superlatives, as his race did.

"I'm sorry, Sahved. You wanted to say something?"

"What if I don't want to go into the Pod-doc?" he asked.

"Then you don't have to. It's your choice." She shrugged indifferently. "The Pod-doc has saved all our lives and helped us better survive the violence done to us in the course of our duties. It's still your choice, but I want you to make an informed decision. Ankh has not upgraded anything in his body with the nanos, but he does have an implant in his head where Erasmus lives."

"Erasmus?" Sahved scratched his face with his three fingers before the lightbulb came on. "The AI. Yes. I would take an AI, I think."

"There's the rub. AIs now have full rights, so such a taking could be considered kidnapping without a proper contract in place that clearly states the rights and responsibilities of both parties. A contract with proper considera-tion and acceptance."

Sahved's head bobbed in a parody of a human nod. He ducked slightly to keep from banging his head against the ceiling. "I will think more about this. When do you need an answer?"

"Before our next case, which means after the rest of us take a vacation. You'll remain on the ship and study Feder-ation law. I've put together a course of instruction I want you to follow if you're going to be on my team. If you have any questions about nanocytes and what they'll do to you, ask Chaz. He'll have the answers." Rivka pointed toward Red and Lindy, who were entering the galley, guiding two bots loaded high with pizza boxes, before turning back to Sahved and gesturing that their short conversation was at an end. "After all we went through to get those delivered, I would hate to let them get cold."

CHAPTER TWO

Wyatt Earp, **Interstellar Space**

Red stifled a belch. Tiny Man Titan was upside down in Lindy's lap. His soft snores made her giggle. He'd been passed from person to person until Lindy finally gave in and fed him half a slice. His little stomach bulged from eating too much.

Floyd had had her pizza, too. As one, they had all celebrated, everyone getting a share of the booty. The wombat filled Groenwyn's lap as she snoozed in silence. The young woman was the only one who'd demonstrated any self-control. Everyone else had feasted mightily.

"Where are we going again?" Red asked, slurring his words while his eyelids started to droop.

"A remote getaway on Tanglewood. At least, that's what the ad called the planet," Rivka replied. "No connectivity."

"What genius thought that was a good idea?" Red perked up, turning his head to stare at Groenwyn. The others, even Ankh, shared the same look.

Groenwyn steeled her features and threw her shoulders

back in defiance. "You people need to get back to nature and revel in the roots of your existence."

Red looked confused. "Say what?" Lindy shook her head.

"I won't be leaving the ship," Ankh said. "I have work to do." Wenceslaus rolled around on the table in front of the Crenellian and found his furry body in the middle of Ankh's plate. He tried to shoo the cat off to wipe the sauce from his fur, but the big orange feline was having none of it and swiped a paw at Ankh's hand. The Crenellian barely dodged the exposed claws.

"You don't need to leave the ship." Rivka stood and called for calm. She rested one hand on Groenwyn's shoulder. "I approved the vacation. If you have a terrible time, you can blame me. Until then, fun is mandatory. We'll be able to fish, relax, get some natural sun, and drink fruity drinks to our heart's content."

"No one shooting at us?" Red asked with a laugh.

"Of course not." She faced him and clearly enunciated, "Va-ca-tion."

Clodagh raised her hand.

"You don't need to do that." Rivka smiled at her chief engineer.

"All of us get to go ashore?"

"Everyone. Aurora, Ryleigh, Kennedy, and even Alant Cole." Rivka nodded to each as she said their names. "Not you, though. You have homework."

Sahved twirled his fingers in the air. "I know. Master Vered said I was on double-secret probation."

"Damn straight, probie," Red shot back.

"No one's on double-secret probation. What the hell is that, anyway?" Rivka glared at Red.

He picked up a slice of pepperoni and shoved it toward his mouth but couldn't finish the job. "I can't eat another bite," he admitted and put the slice back in the box.

Lindy nudged him. "Like anyone else will eat it after you've touched it."

Red raised one eyebrow as he faced his wife. "Give it three days and everyone else will want it, no matter who touched it." Lindy looked from face to face. No one shook their head.

"He's not wrong," Alant Cole, the Bad Company warrior, suggested. "Let's put it in the fridge and find out."

Clodagh removed a pen from her coveralls and marked the box with Red's piece. "Let's get this cleaned up. We're burning vacation time sitting out here in the middle of nowhere. Chaz! Fire up the Gate engine and prepare to take us to the sunny beaches of Tanglewood." She turned to Alant. "Bring your swimsuit."

"Who needs a suit? We're all friends here." He smiled broadly at the three young pilots.

"I can kick his ass for you," Lindy offered.

"No one wants to see your junk." Clodagh crossed her arms and stared.

"Maybe we should ask..." he started.

"No. One." The two stared, unblinking.

"I'll be in my workshop," Ankh said softly and walked out.

"And there we have it!" Red declared loudly. "Suits for everyone. No suit, no vacation."

"Hear, hear," Rivka agreed.

Alant stood and hugged Clodagh. "I'll get our stuff ready," he whispered into her ear. She nuzzled his head before pushing him away.

"We have a ship to fly," she told the trio of pilots. "Ryleigh on the stick. Aurora on nav, and Kennedy in the engine room, as soon as you three get this place cleaned up. Chop, chop!"

The young women started gathering boxes and remnants. Anything that wasn't eaten was shoved into the one refrigerator. The refuse was set aside for the cleaning bots to recycle.

"Take us to Tanglewood, Lieutenant. The ship is yours." Rivka parodied a salute that drew a snicker from Private Cole. "If I see you without your suit, I'll send a report directly to Colonel Walton."

"No, ma'am, although I answer to a higher authority than him." He pointed at Clodagh.

"And don't you forget it," she replied. Alant winked, and together they headed out, with the three pilots on their heels.

Sahved watched in rapt fascination.

"What do you think?" Rivka asked the Yemilorian.

"I do not think I understand the human language very well. Your words suggest you are engaged in mortal combat, but your actions tell me you are friends. We would never think to tell anyone they are less than the absolute best."

Red snorted. "One of the most fucked-up things I've ever seen was when the perp on that last mission exploded her own head. I've seen some shit, but that took the cake."

"I'm not sure what language you are speaking." Sahved

leaned closer to better concentrate on what the big body-guard was saying.

"My point is that if it weren't for the good people I was surrounded by, that might have gotten to me. I might have wanted to ask why and how, but the Magistrate shrugged it off."

"End of the case. She was judged and found wanting. Justice was served." Rivka's tone suggested the event was well behind her.

"A quick break of the neck, but exploding her head? I think some of the blue crap went in my mouth."

"Don't go into a rat's nest with your mouth open," Rivka noted.

"Sage advice, Magistrate." Red finally stood. Lindy handed Titan to him. Red held the tiny creature in one hand. "How does shit like this happen? Why do we have a tiny dog?"

Groenwyn struggled to stand, keeping her arms wrapped around the wombat. She closed on Red and motioned with her chin. Red deposited Titan into a small gap between Floyd and Groenwyn's chest. "Because we love them," she said.

Red opened his mouth, but Lindy elbowed him in the ribs before he could say his piece.

"Yes, we do," Lindy agreed.

"We have the space," Rivka suggested. "And they make the ship a little homier."

"Our home..." Groenwyn contemplated. "Yes."

She waddled out the door.

Red brushed his hands off on his pants and flicked away a strand of hair that tried to cling to his finger.

"We're going fully armed," he said casually.

"Vacation, Red," Rivka shot back.

"Do you know everyone down there? Are you confident you're safe? Well, I don't, and I'm not." He put his foot down to emphasize his point.

"Fine." Rivka threw her hands up in surrender. "Always on the job, but make sure you do something for you and your wife while we're down there. Consider it your honeymoon."

"I will not," Red countered. Lindy looked from her husband to her boss and back again. "You owe us a proper honeymoon, and you cannot get yourself killed while we're away."

"I think I can agree to that." Rivka held out her hand, and Red shook it.

Lindy gestured toward the door. Red took the hint and strode boldly out.

Rivka waved at Sahved. "You have law to study. You better start now. It isn't going to study itself."

He tried to salute but jabbed himself in the head with his fingertips. He looked unkindly at his digits for their betrayal.

"Carry on," Rivka told him and headed for her quarters, biting her lip to keep from laughing.

Gating to Tanglewood in the Abkhaziyan Sector

"The star in the nearest system has gone supernova," Chaz reported after the Gate closed and active sensors came back online.

"And?" Clodagh asked with a shrug. "When was that?"

"Two years, three months ago. The reason you need to know that answer is because the shockwave is already in this system. Our shields…"

Clodagh waited, but Chaz didn't finish.

"Shields are down," Ryleigh shouted over her shoulder.

Ankh's voice came over the intercom. He was not his usual calm self. "Gate us out of here right now!" His voice still sounded small, but the urgency with which he spoke changed nothing. They were not capable of leaving.

"Gate drive charging," Ryleigh stated before adding, "Not gonna make it."

"Hang on!" Clodagh yelled over the shipwide broadcast. It was the only warning that could be given. She held onto the captain's seat for all she was worth as a tidal wave of energy rolled over *Wyatt Earp*, tossing the heavy frigate like a balloon in a hurricane.

"Engines at maximum," Ryleigh reported loudly as if the sound of the hurricane was inside with them. She bounced in her seat despite being belted in. "Engines stalled. Thrusters at maximum." She tried to keep her voice calm, but it warbled—maybe from the teeth-rattling vibrations, maybe from fear.

Artificial gravity went out. Red spewed a high volume of imaginative profanity from somewhere in the corridor outside the bridge. The ship's nose-over-tail spin exaggerated the pressure the restraints exerted on Clodagh's body. Ryleigh grunted as she fought to tap the controls.

The ship stopped tumbling, and artificial gravity returned. Loose items that had floated away to be pressed against the ceiling fell. A cup banged off a console, while the coffee within, which had floated away as a brown cloud, came down with the force of spring rain, splattering Aurora and her nav station.

Report, Rivka asked using the internal communication system.

Ship's coming back to life, Ryleigh replied. *But the engines are still out, and we're caught in Tanglewood's gravity.*

Ankh. Rivka sounded calm but was using her angry voice. *What did you do? Never mind that. Get our power back on right fucking now.*

Ankh's reply was curt. *Soon.*

Clodagh activated the shipwide broadcast. "We have gravity and environmental control, but not much else. Alant, get to the hangar bay and check on *Destiny's Vengeance.* We may have to use it as a lifeboat."

Footsteps pounded down the passageway. Rivka appeared in the open hatch. A cut on her head was already closed, but the blood that had flowed still traced a line down her face.

"Get us out of here!"

"Can't," Clodagh answered, finally unbuckling herself from the captain's chair. "That shockwave did us up nasty. Whatever the hell Ankh was doing cut our shields, so we took the full force of it on the unprotected hull. I'm surprised we're not glowing."

"Or dead," Ryleigh added.

The ship jerked sideways and lurched forward, nosing down toward the planet. Rivka bounced off the bulkhead beside the hatch, then steadied herself. The planet now filled the main screen.

Red had his left arm tucked against his body while using his right to support Lindy.

"Okay?" Rivka asked.

"Broken bones. We'll be fine in a bit." Lindy's eyes remained unfocused, the bloody patch in her hair telling the tale of her gravity gymnastics.

"Chaz, give me the intercom." Rivka started. "Everyone aboard *Destiny's Vengeance*. Abandon ship. All hands abandon ship. Chaz, that means you, too."

"If the engines come back online, I'm sure I can get *Wyatt Earp* out of here." Ryleigh frantically tapped her screen.

"We can get another ship." Rivka gasped as the ship twisted violently. "We can't get another you. Abandon ship. That's an order."

"Ladies!" Clodagh shouted. Ryleigh and Aurora were slow to respond as they both fought to steady the ship. Clodagh Shortall, who was taller and bigger than her bridge crew, physically yanked Ryleigh out of her chair and propelled her toward the hatch. Aurora didn't wait to be next. She tumbled from her seat and followed. Rivka led the way down the corridor, with Red and Lindy staggering behind.

The two pilots worked their way up next to the bodyguards to help the injured keep moving. Clodagh took one last look at the bridge before turning away from the others and running for the engine room.

Rivka hammered on doors as she passed. "Abandon ship!"

Sahved stepped into the corridor and pointed back toward his room. "Get to the hangar bay," she yelled in his face.

Groenwyn was already on her way, carrying Titan and

shuffling behind the terrified wombat to keep Floyd going in the right direction.

"Railguns," Red grunted as he snapped his forearm into place and sighed in relief.

"No time," Rivka replied.

"I'll be right back." Red handed Lindy over and bolted before Rivka could stop him.

"Don't you die!" Lindy screamed in a lucid moment before her eyes rolled back in her head and her body went limp. Ryleigh and Aurora caught her between them and struggled to move with the much heftier woman holding them back.

Rivka waved them off, shouldering Lindy's mid-section and hoisting her bodyguard over her shoulder. "Let's go." Ryleigh ran ahead to help Groenwyn. She picked Floyd up, stuffing her nose under her arm to shield her from the flashing emergency lights. The wombat calmed, and Groenwyn hurried ahead.

Destiny's Vengeance filled most of the cargo bay. They didn't have to walk more than a couple of steps before entering the open side hatch, the one they'd breached when they'd secured the ship from the pirates. Groenwyn and Titan entered first, with Ryleigh close behind. Rivka went through sideways to protect Lindy's head. She moved carefully into the small ship and rolled Lindy into the top bunk. There only two, plus a small galley and a cockpit with one seat. They were going to stuff ten people into the ship.

Sahved ducked to get through the hatch and stood once inside, only to savage the top of his head on an exposed frame. He staggered and fell, filling the small space with his long legs, skinny torso, and stick-like arms. The ship jerked with the buffeting that threatened to tear *Wyatt Earp* apart.

Rivka and Aurora maneuvered close to pick up the unconscious Yemilorian. Much like trying to carry an uncoiled rope, they half-carried, half-dragged him into the sleeping quarters, which was little bigger than a closet, and stuffed him into the bottom bunk.

"Where the hell is everyone?" Rivka demanded. "Chaz, update, please."

The ship's AI replied immediately. "Red, Clodagh, and Kennedy will be here momentarily."

"What about Ankh?" The AI did not reply. Rivka switched to her internal comm system. *Ankh, you get your ass down here right now. I am not going to let you and Erasmus crash into this planet.*

Working on something. You need to get off the ship now. If I'm successful, I'll come get you.

"Ankh!" Rivka yelled out loud, jumping over Floyd to get to the hatch but stopping when Clodagh and Kennedy forced their way in. Red squeezed in behind them. He was wearing full gear, and his arms bulged since he carried half the armory. He dumped the weaponry and ammunition into the corridor, completely blocking the passage. Kennedy dashed toward the cockpit.

The hatch started to close.

Clodagh yelled through the opening, "Follow us down!"

"Cole?"

"He's in his mech suit."

The ship accelerated backward into space and flipped upside down when it hit the turbulence of the planet's lower atmosphere. It took Kennedy a few moments to level the vessel, but *Destiny's Vengeance* continued to accelerate toward the planet.

Rivka gasped as she tried to get past the weapons in the corridor. "Dammit, Red!"

"You'll thank me later," he replied with a wry smile. "That gear will save our lives. If we survive this, I bet we'll need it."

"Hang on!" Kennedy yelled over her shoulder. Rivka groaned as she stretched her body across the corridor to brace between two bulkheads. Red tried to lie across the weapons to keep them from flying around the corridor.

Destiny's Vengeance screamed in pain as she hit a tree. Or a mountain, or something that didn't need to be hit. Then the engines died, filling the ship with silence and dread. Kennedy didn't bother to shout another warning.

The ship slammed into more trees, ripping off branches before hitting something that refused to give. The ship came to an abrupt stop, tipped backward, and fell a few meters to the ground before twisting sideways to land upright as if it had meant to do that all along.

"Status," Rivka said in a normal tone. She reached to open the hatch, but Red caught her arm.

"Let me make sure it's clear." He dug through the weapons until he found his railgun, checked the loadout and power, embraced it, and let his hand hover over the hatch access. "Check on Lindy for me?"

When Rivka nodded, he hit the button and crouched over the barrel of his weapon. He headed out slowly, his aim following where he looked to lessen his response time should he need to shoot.

The jungle was quiet, but only for a moment before bird and animal cries returned.

"Chaz, tell me you got off a distress signal," Rivka pleaded.

"Comm was down. I was not able to broadcast a distress signal, nor launch a buoy."

"How long before they come looking for us?"

"Your flight plan was for two weeks. On the fifteenth day, the High Chancellor and Grainger will begin to wonder. On the sixteenth day, we will have company. Our beacon is already transmitting. Once inside the atmosphere, they'll locate us quickly."

Groenwyn hugged Floyd and started to cry.

"What about the resort? Shouldn't they be looking for us?"

"We can only contact them through a relay satellite, but this planet is not so connected. We're here because someone wanted to disconnect."

Rivka bit her lip. "That was me." She hung her head for a moment before kneeling to comfort Groenwyn. "It'll be okay. We just need to survive for a couple of weeks. The jungle should provide everything we need until they pick us up."

"But Ankh and Wenceslaus?" Tears rolled down Groenwyn's face.

"Kennedy, did ship's systems track *Wyatt Earp*? Where did it go down?"

Rivka jumped over the weaponry in the corridor to get to the cockpit.

Kennedy held her hands up as Chaz took over and replayed the systems. "*Wyatt Earp* was tumbling but seemed to regain control over this small mountain range. We came down on this side. They should be on the other side. When I left, Erasmus took over ship systems."

"Did they not crash?" Groenwyn asked from the short corridor.

"Unknown," Chaz replied.

"We'll take that as a 'no.' Get them on the horn, Chaz." Rivka crossed her arms and leaned against the bulkhead, trying to think through their options.

The ground shook when something heavy hit next to the ship. *Honey, I'm home.*

Clodagh appeared in the corridor and managed to get an arm out the hatch to wave.

"There is no comm signal," Chaz reported.

"From them or us?" Rivka was tired of playing twenty questions. "Tell me if you get anything. In the interim, we're going to see what we have. This is supposed to be a vacation spot, so let's vacate."

Kennedy looked up at the Magistrate, brow furrowed. "I'm not sure that's how it works," the young pilot said.

Rivka grabbed Lindy's railgun and headed outside.

CHAPTER THREE

Tanglewood, Unidentified Sector, Deep Jungle

"Next time, let me know when you're inbound, and I won't have to shoot you." Red poked a finger at the mech.

Cole turned his sensors toward the ship's structure. "Chaz, link up with me so I can show you what's going on out here."

The AI connected with the mech and started receiving the data stream with images and sensor data.

Destiny's Vengeance sat in a small clearing, barely larger than the ship. Besides paint scrapes along the sides, it looked to be intact and without structural damage. Scans and physical checks would determine if it was possible to fly the ship out of there.

Rivka walked to where Red was watching the jungle. "What do you see?"

He scanned the shadows between the trees. "We're not alone out here."

"Besides that." Rivka squinted at shapes on branches high in the canopy overhead. Leaves and other branches.

She listened. The wildlife was returning after a brief departure following Cole's thunderous arrival. "Ankh…"

"He made it," Red said dismissively. "Because he had to. As much shit as I give him, he sends it right back, but orders of magnitude greater. That bullshit with the mayo instead of ketchup." Red chuckled before looking at the ground. "We need him."

A breeze drifted by, reminding them that they were sweating. The heat and humidity were higher than they were used to. "We better find water." Rivka slapped Red on the back and returned to the ship.

Alant had parked his mech and was climbing out the back. "If you haven't reentered the atmosphere in a mech suit, you should try it." He slapped at a bug that appeared on his arm before smiling broadly. "Once."

"Not up for a replay?" Rivka poked.

"Once is plenty. Please don't make me do that again. Suit's spent. Needs to recharge."

"I didn't make you do it the first time. I think *you* made you do that because you didn't want to leave your toys behind. Just like Red. Men and their toys."

Alant crossed his arms and leaned back, looking thoughtful. He rubbed his chin and shifted his feet before answering. "Not toys. Weapons to protect the people we love."

He looked at her from hooded eyes.

Rivka smirked and shook her head. "*Toys*," she said clearly.

"Maybe just a little, but we have jobs to do, and without our *toys*, we might not be able to do them."

A bird screeched nearby. Rivka crouched and brought

her railgun up, scanning the trees for an enemy. She waited for a few moments.

"I better get used to this place. Looks like we're going to be here for a couple of weeks unless Chaz can figure out a way to fly us out of here."

"Not so much. Nothing wrong with the ship. This thing was built tough, but the engine is in disarray, it appears. To fix it, we need something we don't have."

Rivka sighed and handed him the railgun. "Coordinate with Red to keep watch. I'll put together a scavenging party to find food and water." She mumbled to herself on her way to the ship's hatch.

"Red's probably not going to like that," Alant offered, smiling as he walked away.

"You're probably right," Rivka said softly over her shoulder.

The Magistrate climbed back into the ship to find Lindy moving the weaponry into a storage area under the lower bunk.

Sahved squatted in the small galley, one hand on his head.

Rivka leaned over Lindy. "How are you feeling?"

"I'm fine. Took a tough shot to the head, but the nanos finally kicked in. Looks like Sahved got it worse than me." Lindy then gestured with her chin toward the young woman in the corridor, who was carrying both Floyd and Titan. "Groenwyn caught me up on our situation."

"What's your take?"

"We're in the middle of nowhere, and out of contact. Ship's broken. No food or water, ten people, and it'll be a while before anyone comes looking. Ankh and *Wyatt Earp* are missing." Lindy arranged the last of the weapons and ammunition in the storage cubbyhole. When she dropped the bunk back down, a couple of blasters, grenades, and a railgun lay on the mattress. Lindy checked the loads and geared up.

"I think you've captured our predicament perfectly. We need to find food and water—enough for a couple of weeks. Red says there's somebody out there, so I guess we had better be on our best behavior. Don't shoot any of the locals. We'll probably need their help."

"You know Red," Lindy remarked, tapping one of her blasters and smiling.

"I do. Maybe you can convince him to keep the peace."

Lindy holstered the two handheld weapons, clipped the grenades on her pistol belt, and hoisted the railgun. "Keeping the peace is what we do best." She winked on her way out.

Rivka watched Lindy go—a restaurant server turned trusted ally, warrior, and friend. "The universe is a strange place," she said.

"Yes, ma'am," Ryleigh agreed, stepping into the corridor from the cockpit. "Orders?"

The pilot looked at both Clodagh and Rivka for clarification. Rivka moved into the galley to see if the Yemilorian needed help. He had been mostly forgotten as the crew went about their duties. She stopped just inside the doorway, taking his soft moaning as evidence that he was okay.

Clodagh deferred, looking at the Magistrate for guidance.

Rivka took charge, locking eyes with her engineer. "You stay to fix the ship. Do you need an extra pair of hands?"

Clodagh nodded. "Aurora has some mechanical skill. She can help me, but there isn't much I can do without the transwarp flux capacitor."

"The what?"

"I'm kidding. We need a special part, though. Without it, we're not going anywhere." Clodagh was confident in her assessment because Chaz agreed.

"What do you need to keep the other systems running, like climate control, food processing, and sensors?"

"We're good with those for the time being. Should outlast our stay by quite a bit."

Rivka nodded. "Ryleigh, Kennedy, Groenwyn, and if you're able, Sahved with me. We need to find food and water."

Floyd bounced past them and out the door.

"Is she going?" Rivka gave Groenwyn a hard look.

"Floyd's a wombat. She's comfortable in nature. She'll see and hear things before any of us, so yes, she's going, and she'll take point."

Sahved groaned as he stood up.

"Watch your head," Rivka warned. He ducked instinctively. "There's your testimonial for going in the Pod-doc and getting juiced with the nanocytes, especially if you're going to keep hurting yourself. For the record, I can't have that. I need my team intact. If you want to consider that undue pressure for you to modify your body, then so be it. No one can hold us back. If you can't agree, then we will simply return you to Yemilore."

Sahved's eyes cleared as he met Rivka's gaze. "I don't feel pressure, just a headache. I know you always do your best for the most right that can be done."

The Magistrate's expression remained blank. She heard the words but couldn't determine whether Sahved agreed or not.

"Make your decision when you're comfortable. I have to run my team as I do because the last thing I want is to bury one of our own. It's just like putting your armor on."

"But I don't have any armor. It looks like you don't either," the Yemilorian noted.

"We just abandoned ship," Rivka started before shaking her head. "Are you physically capable of going with us?"

"I am the most capable," he proudly replied.

"Of course you are." Rivka took a quick headcount. "Shall we?"

Ryleigh and Kennedy snapped to attention while Clodagh returned to the cockpit for continued conversations with Chaz about repairs to the ship.

Rivka led the way out. Sahved walked with his hand over his head to prevent further injury. The two young women moved lightly with a spring in their steps.

"Where are you going?" Red called from a short distance away.

Rivka stopped and looked at the sky for a moment before answering. "Food and water."

"You're not going alone. Do you have Reaper?"

"No chance to get it from my quarters."

Groenwyn choked and started to cry.

"It's just a neutron pulse weapon. I'm sure it can be replaced." Red strolled toward the group, stopping amidst the angry glares.

Sahved watched with as much interest as he could muster.

"It's not about Reaper," Rivka explained. "It's about Ankh and *Wyatt Earp*." Floyd started to whimper.

Red looked indignant. He motioned for Alant Cole to take his place on the perimeter. "I already told you he's fine. There's nothing to cry about." Red waved his hand dismissively.

Groenwyn sniffled and looked at him through red and puffy eyes. "How do you know?"

"I just do. And you know it, too." Red stood tall, chest out and confident. "I'll take point."

"With Floyd," Groenwyn said with one last wipe of her face. Red didn't acknowledge the wombat, who was instantly happy with Groenwyn's return to emotional peace. The rotund creature bounced a few steps ahead and stopped, unsure of where they were going.

Rivka pointed toward the hill where they'd last seen the heavy frigate. Red nodded once.

"Might as well. At this point, one direction is as good as another. Water first, then food. That way, Floyd." Red gestured with his arm, hatcheting toward the low point between two hills in the distance where the growth appeared denser than where they stood.

Chaz had called it a clearing. Compared to what they could see ahead, he was right.

"There's something out there. Stay frosty," Red told Lindy and Cole.

Tanglewood, the Deep Jungle

Floyd moved ahead, her chubby body able to navigate below the branches and heavier undergrowth. Red forced his way through, breaking limbs and shredding leaves and fronds. The others were strung out behind him.

Rivka wished she had brought a knife.

Red stopped and held up his fist. The two pilots continued blundering forward. Rivka stopped them with a look and held a finger to her lips.

Titan began to give out with his high-pitched yip. Groenwyn tried to calm him, but his little hackles were up as he vibrated and snarled between barks. He focused like a laser on a lower branch of a larger tree. Red cleared an area around himself and leveled his railgun at the area. Rivka moved behind her bodyguard, not to hide, but to watch the other direction.

Floyd scurried through the brush and came back to the group. Red jumped but settled quickly, returning his focus to the trees.

Rivka caught the wombat and lifted her into her arms.

People. Lots of people, she cried.

"We got company," Rivka said out loud.

"We heard," Red said. "I can't see anything in the trees, but I trust Floyd and Tiny Man Titan. I'll be damned. Groenwyn and her zoo came through."

"Friends! Not a zoo," the young woman with the platinum-green hair shot back while keeping a firm grip on Titan. She looked more proud than angry.

Rivka took a deep breath. "Listen up, people. Nobody kills anyone until we figure out who they are. We're on their turf, so, their rules. We'll play nice for as long as we can but keep your heads down."

"Boss?" Red said to get Rivka's attention. The trees came alive.

A group of humanoids flowed through the bushes and branches. Titan picked up the pace of his barks until he ran out of air, then huffed for a few seconds before starting afresh.

Rivka tried to step in front of Red, but he held her back. She reluctantly submitted, allowing him to loom over her like an overprotective mother hen.

"Howdy," Rivka called. "We seem to be lost."

The locals' clothing blended with the undergrowth as they walked lightly, without a sound. The pale green of their skin also helped them to blend in. They carried light arms, rifles mostly. A couple had backpacks, but they generally remained unencumbered.

When they spoke, the translation chip in the heads of the Federation party instantly recognized and interpreted the sounds.

"We are Yindle, from the border village of Keosh. I am Master Dee. Which side do you fight for?" He could have been older or younger. The Yindle all seemed to be the same age, or their bodies didn't reflect their age like other races.

"I am Magistrate Rivka Anoa. We are of the Federation and fight on that side, no others. We are here on vacation, but our ship lost power, and we crashed. We would greatly appreciate your assistance in helping us out of here. We need to get to the other side of Tanglewood. Can you take us to a transportation facility?"

The dozen Yindle chuckled before the previous speaker answered, "We cannot, not out of a lack of desire to help, but there is no such thing where we live." He looked at his fellows and back to Rivka. "Whose side are you on?"

The question was final. The group raised the weapons. Red had never lowered his. In the silence of the jungle, she heard two clicks as Red ticked his weapon off safe to single fire mode and once more to rapid-fire.

Ryleigh, Kennedy, and Sahved shuffled nervously, freezing when Rivka glanced their way.

"We fight for the Federation of which this planet is a member…" Rivka started.

Master Dee waved his hand. Hers was not the right answer.

"You either fight for Yindle or Yangor. There is no in-between."

"There is always a third option," Rivka said in a low and dangerous voice. "Please, talk to us about your situation, and we will see what we can do. I am a Magistrate and have a great deal of authority."

"You are lost in the jungle, Rivka Anoa," Master Dee stated. "You have no authority here, nothing beyond what we grant you."

CHAPTER FOUR

Tanglewood

"I could argue your responsibilities under Federation Law, but you don't care about those because you didn't sign the treaty. I expect you had no say whatsoever, and this is probably the first time you're hearing such a thing applies to your planet." Rivka waited for the Yindle to confirm her suspicions, but they gave nothing away. "So, let's talk about the right thing to do. We have very little with us, but we can trade for information and help. I know you don't trust us. We'll have to earn that over time."

"You could start with that," Master Dee said, using his rifle barrel to point at Red's railgun. "It would go a long way toward earning our trust."

"It would go a long way toward facilitating our deaths. Sharing advanced weaponry isn't something we'll do. Consequently, we'll have to pass." Rivka crossed her arms and looked sideways at the Yindle. "To negotiate, one must always negotiate in good faith, but then again, if you don't ask, you'll never know what the answer is. Now that we know, what else might we be able to do for you?"

The master shrugged in a human way. The group remained in place, their rifles leveled at Rivka's party.

Tiny Man Titan was spent, his energy reduced to a small growl every few seconds. Groenwyn rhythmically stroked his head as she slowly stepped forward. "I am Groenwyn. The jungle and its living creatures are of great interest to me. Can you feel what I feel?"

Master Dee stepped toward her, earning a single bark from the small dog-like alien. He focused intently on the Yindle leader.

"I can feel the jungle, stranger. And I can feel you." He bowed slightly to her and motioned for the others to lower their weapons. "Thank you for choosing our side. We don't want to fight, but the Yangor leave us no choice."

Rivka clenched her teeth.

"We do not take sides in local squabbles," Groenwyn reaffirmed dismissively. "That is your business. We can help end your fight so no one need take sides."

"With weapons like that," Master Dee nodded toward Red, "the war will end quickly."

Rivka stepped up. "I already said we wouldn't trade our weapons, but Groenwyn is right. We can arbitrate your dispute. It's what we do. It's what *I* do."

"We will consider it." Master Dee pointed in the direction the Federation group had been going. "If you keep going that way, you will run into the Yangor. They will be far less accommodating than us. You will probably have to fight them. Don't hesitate. Kill them all."

"I have high hopes that we'll be able to get them to talk.

We are strangers in your world, crashed, looking for food and water to sustain us until we can complete our repairs. We are looking for a second ship that might have crashed somewhere on the other side of that ridge. We will not abandon them, and will do everything in our power to recover our friends and our spacecraft."

"A leader's loyalty to her people is a laudable quality, but it does not change the fact that you will have to fight the Yangor. May your aim be true." Master Dee turned his back on Rivka and her team and faded into the jungle, and the rest of the Yindle from Keosh disappeared with him.

"We'll see them again," Red muttered. "We never did get to see the group up ahead."

"Probably the rest of the village come out to see the weirdos. We might be in a zoo and don't realize it—all of us on display for the locals to gawk at." Rivka's attention was torn between where they were going, where the Yindle had gone, and where *Destiny's Vengeance* was.

"I'm hungry," Sahved said as he looked greedily at the leaves on a nearby bush. Groenwyn stepped close to him and let Titan sniff the Yemilorian.

Lindy, can you hear me? the Magistrate tried.

Loud and clear, the bodyguard replied.

The locals know we're here. I don't know if they are hostile or not, but they are armed with slug throwers. They blend into the jungle, so you probably won't see them unless they want you to. They have not agreed to help us, so draw the security perimeter in, and if you're not on watch, stay inside the ship.

Roger. I'll draw back to the ship and have Cole suit up and go on standby.

Rivka nodded. "It's nice to see that something works

like it is supposed to." She took stock of her team. "Ryleigh and Kennedy. What is your estimate of their technological level?"

The pilots looked at each other. Ryleigh tipped her chin, and Kennedy spoke up. "Based on their clothing, I would have said primitive, but their weapons and a certain savvy suggest they are modern, but possibly choose to live in an austere fashion."

"I don't think they are telling the truth regarding the Federation. I think they know but choose to ignore the law," Ryleigh added.

"I agree on both accounts. Well done, ladies." Rivka laced her fingers behind her back and started to pace.

Red cleared his throat. "We're not getting any closer to *Wyatt Earp*, Ankh, food, or water by standing here," he said softly.

"Your point?"

"You can pace going in one direction, and we might get where we want to go."

"I want to see the ship, know that Ankh is alive," Groenwyn suggested, not sounding confident.

"Me, too," Rivka agreed. "Floyd? Can you take us to Ankh?"

The wombat started to cry. *I don't know how!*

Groenwyn looked shocked. "No, little girl. All you have to do is keep going that way and look for food and water. We'll watch for Ankh. Deal?"

Deal, the wombat replied in her happy voice. She bounced into the brush, and Red moved after her. The team fell into line, trundling through the jungle toward the ridge where the Yindle cautioned them not to go.

But it was the one place they had to.

Destiny's Vengeance Crash Site

"It's not charged up. Barely a few percent above critical," Cole argued.

Lindy watched the jungle, refusing to be distracted by the private. "Then sit there quietly and use the sensors. It can do that without using more power than it takes in, can't it?"

"It can, but minimal air conditioning means it's going to get pretty hot in there."

"Drink lots of water." Lindy had learned her sympathy skills from Red. "Stop fucking around and get in there."

Cole understood the tone of the message along with the words. There was no doubt who was in charge.

"It sucks being the lowest guy on the ladder."

"Somebody has to be," Clodagh said, leaning against the hatch inside the ship, her arms crossed. "We need the sensor systems live. Why are you complaining?"

"This was supposed to be a vacation, and all of a sudden, it's a mission, like life or death. We're in a tropical paradise, but everyone is jumping through their butts." Cole lifted his chin in defiance despite the inanity of his argument.

"If a warrior isn't complaining, he isn't happy," Lindy joked before turning serious once again. "Get in the mech and fire up the sensors. I need to know what's out here."

"Aye, aye, ma'am." He climbed through the back and secured himself inside, then fired up minimal systems to keep the solar charging unit providing more power than the mech was using. He expected they would need all of the suit's capabilities in due course. *Sensors online. Infrared is showing a bank of heat; everything outside this immediate clearing has blended into each other. Switching to ultraviolet. Now cycling through to active millimeter wave scans. Whoa!*

What do you have? Lindy asked.

A dozen, no fourteen locals in the trees, watching us. He switched between IR and MMW. *Their body temps are exactly the same as the ambient. IR can't distinguish, but the active scan sees them,* Cole reported.

Don't let them know that we know. Start tracking and send the map of their positions to Chaz. We need to be ready in case they turn hostile.

They're just sitting there, watching us. It'd be creepy if we didn't have the firepower we have.

Reminds me, where's your mech-sized railgun? Lindy raised her eyebrows. She knew the answer. *Never mind. It's still on* Wyatt Earp, *along with everything else we own.*

And all that glorious pizza.

Lindy blew out a breath as if she'd been gut-punched. *Why'd you have to bring that up? Reminds me that I'm hungry, even though it wasn't that long ago when we ate. It doesn't matter. Keep an eye out for the Magistrate and her party. No sense in staying out here when we can't see anything. Let me know if anything changes.*

Changes, he thought. *Like being marooned on a jungle planet?*

He chuckled to himself as the sweat started running down his head.

. . .

Tanglewood, the Deep Jungle

Birds called and insects buzzed; the norm of the deep jungle returned. Floyd stopped to sample a small plant. Satisfied with the first bite, she consumed the whole thing, nipping it off neatly at ground level. She hummed with pleasure. Soon, her entire effort at leading the party devolved into finding more plants to eat.

As an herbivore, Floyd preferred plants, but her diet had adjusted on board the *War Axe*, and later with Rivka's team. She'd weathered it all well, owing to the nanocytes that helped her digestion and overall health.

"Red." Rivka didn't have to say anything else. Red moved in front and picked up the pace. Groenwyn was already carrying Tiny Man Titan, who seemed terrified of the jungle. He jumped back into her arms each time she put him down.

The magistrate caught Floyd and hauled her in to cradle against her chest. "You've had it too good, little girl. You need to go on a diet."

No die! Floyd howled over their internal communication system.

"You need to eat less," Rivka clarified.

Floyd grumbled for a few moments before falling asleep in Rivka's arms. "She needs to take it easy on the food. She's almost too big to carry," Rivka complained to Groenwyn. The platinum-green-haired woman looked away, acting as if she were taking in the sights.

Sahved lumbered along, taking long, easy strides in the relatively low gravity of Tanglewood. It was comparable with Earth standard, so the others walked normally.

The challenge they faced equally was the heat and high humidity.

"Doing okay, Red?" Rivka taunted. "I don't want to have to carry you again. My arms are already full. It's like wearing a fur coat."

Having the wombat pressed against her wasn't helping her stay cool.

"We need to find water," Red stated. "Before anything else." He looked intentionally uphill to the low pass between two higher points.

Beyond that was where they'd last seen *Wyatt Earp*.

Rivka raised one hand in the air. "If Ankh made it, he's going to have to get by for a bit longer. The Yindle came from over there, so let's go this way back toward the valley and loop around to *Destiny's Vengeance*. We need to get back before nightfall. We'll head out again early tomorrow morning, retrace our steps, and see if we can get over that hill."

"There's no doubt we can get to the other side," Red said softly. "What will we find when we get there? That is the question."

Rivka nodded and pointed in a direction away from their line of travel, abandoning their secondary mission of looking for Ankh to focus on survival. They needed water.

CHAPTER FIVE

Rivka slapped a bug wading through the sweat running down her arm and licked her dry lips. Her nanocytes would keep her alive even if she was horribly dehydrated, but her body would eventually consume itself without fuel to keep the tiny machines working.

Fuel in the form of food and water. Floyd was back on track, leading the team. She was positive there was water up ahead.

The pilots stumbled along. They had not been through the Pod-doc, nor had Sahved.

"I think I made a mistake bringing them," she whispered.

"It'll be fine if we find water. A little crisis and suffering are good for the soul. Helps them grow hair on their chests," Red replied over his shoulder.

Rivka smiled at the big bodyguard. "I'm sure they have no desire to grow hair on their chests."

Red held a finger to his lips before turning and running.

Floyd was at an all-out sprint. Rivka ran after him, with the others jogging and staggering along the path Red blazed.

Floyd never slowed down when she reached a small but serene pond, little more than a catch-basin for a trickling stream on one side before disappearing into the jungle on the other. She hit the water, her rotund body slicing across the surface. She sighed as she floated like an arrow toward the other side.

The water surged and a creature came out, jaws wide, teeth like daggers. Floyd froze.

The railgun thundered. The jungle absorbed the echo, but the blast continued to ring in the group's ears. The creature's head disappeared in a red spray that painted the opposite bank.

Floyd turned and swam back toward her friends. She came out of the water and ran straight to Groenwyn. Titan continued to whimper from the loud sound. Groenwyn pulled Floyd into her arms and hugged both her friends.

Red lowered his weapon. "Never trust a pond in the middle of nowhere. Next thing we know, a woman will be giving you a sword and telling you to rule the country. Fresh water on that end." Red pointed with the railgun barrel toward the tiny waterfall feeding one end of the pond.

"Drink up, ladies," Rivka ordered. She stepped forward and prepared to dive into the pond.

"What the hell are you doing?" Red asked as he grabbed her arm.

"I'm going to drag that carcass out of there. If my bearings are right, we shouldn't be far from the ship. This is going to be our favorite spot, so we had best clean it out."

Red wanted to argue but couldn't. He was thirsty, too.

"Fire in the hole," he warned, and Groenwyn dove into the jungle. Red set his railgun to automatic and stitched a pattern back and forth across the pond before gesturing for the Magistrate to go ahead. "Be my guest."

Rivka decided not to dive in. She waded into the cool water instead. "So nice," she muttered before diving to the bottom, which was no more than a couple of meters down. She grabbed the rough-skinned creature and dragged it along with her as she walked out the far side. She forced it onto the bank, then climbed out. The Magistrate stood over the remains of the creature, which was a solid two meters long. She dragged the carcass a few steps and tossed it into the trees.

"What if that was some sacred god the Yindle worshipped?" Red asked while waiting for his turn to get a drink.

"Then we'll be in deeper shit than we're already in." Rivka made a slow three-sixty, scanning the trees both high and low. "Do you think they're following us?"

Red glanced into the trees and back at the water. "No doubt about that."

The pilots lapped the water like dogs, their faces immersed in the trickling stream. Sahved took a few steps upstream and tried to make a cup out of his hand, but three fingers wouldn't hold much water. He gave up and plunged his face in all the way to his ears.

Groenwyn appeared, still holding Floyd and Titan. The green-haired young woman spoke softly to her charges. "Rivka and Red made the water safe. Are you okay to get down and take a drink?"

Okay, Floyd agreed. Groenwyn put her down, but she hesitated until the young woman sat on a root that hung over the narrow shore and dangled her feet in the water. Groenwyn looked at Red for reassurance, and he gave her a meaty thumbs-up.

Rivka walked around the pond to join the young woman on the tree root. Titan finally decided to get down and make his presence known; he barked at the water before taking a drink. After sating himself, he looked at the trees and growled.

"I'm sure they're out there," Groenwyn softly remarked. "I think we're going to have to get used to them being around."

"Wouldn't it be nice if they talked to us?" Rivka shook her head.

"Only if we choose sides." Groenwyn was not amused. "We cannot pick a side. I won't sell out to survive."

"Don't worry, Groenwyn, we won't take sides." Rivka looked at the trees and shouted, "Did you hear that? We won't take sides!"

"If we had a fire, this looks like it could be edible," Red said, having worked his way to the carcass. "I think we should butcher it."

"Of course, you do." Rivka patted Groenwyn on the shoulder. "Is Tiny Man Titan an omnivore?"

"Judging by the way he attacked that pizza, I'd say yes." Groenwyn looked around until she found the wombat eating a small bush. "Floyd, not so much. She likes the cheese and crust, but not all the toppings."

"Our pizza," Red moaned. "Now I'm hungry again. Magistrate?"

Rivka stood as Red prepared to throw her the railgun. She held out her arms, and he tossed his weapon the short distance over the pond. The Magistrate caught it and slung it over her shoulder, letting it rest easily, combat style, under her arm. Red produced a larger-than-normal knife and started methodically carving up the pond creature.

"Not only are we going to kill your water god, but we're also going to eat him," Groenwyn mumbled. "We'll end up fighting somebody, and it'll probably be our fault."

"If only we could get them to talk. Speaking of which, I need to let the ship know we're on our way in."

Alant Cole, can you hear me? Rivka asked, using her internal comm chip.

Loud and clear, Magistrate. I have been tracking your progress by pinging your chips. You are less than two kilometers from the ship on a bearing of forty-five degrees to the left of your previous course, Cole replied.

"Everyone got that?" Rivka looked from face to face. They had all heard. "Looks like we're fifteen minutes from our home base. Red, when will you be ready to roll?"

"Skin's a little tough on this bastard, but I'm getting there. Give me another ten." Red continued working on the creature, grimacing while looking confused at the same time. He caught Rivka and Groenwyn watching him. He smiled and held up something from inside the beast. Entrails? Groenwyn quickly looked away.

Titan barked, and his little tail wagged furiously.

"Now's the time to fill up your flasks, people," Rivka told the crew. She and Red had not brought water flasks. They had limited supplies on the ship, which was never intended to be a lifeboat. They brought what they could, but they would find more containers to augment the small ship's recycling system. Made to support three crew, ten would stress it beyond capacity.

We're being watched, ma'am, Cole interrupted. *I forgot to mention that earlier. They blend in on IR and visual, but the millimeter-wave system highlights them like luminescent fish.*

Can you see where we are?

No, ma'am. System peters out about halfway between us because I have the suit running on low power while I'm trying to recharge it. It's not much good when it's out of juice.

Thanks for the update, Cole. We'll be along shortly.

"Aha!" Red declared with a final split of the rough skin, exposing everything within. He finished cleaning the kill, wrapped a small cord around it, and hauled it onto his back. "Ready to go when you are."

Groenwyn remembered that she had not yet had a drink and hurried to the stream to satisfy her thirst. Floyd lapped at the water beside her, along with Tiny Man Titan. Floyd stuffed her face into the water, pulled it out, shook, and repeated the process until Groenwyn was soaked. Titan barked at the wombat with each new spray, loving the water game.

Sahved was sound asleep. Rivka nudged him with a toe. When he opened his eyes, they rolled around in the sockets, remaining unfocused. She waited until his senses returned. He stood and started to hold his stomach as if he was going to puke. He closed his eyes and forced himself to breathe slowly until his insides stopped heaving. He opened his eyes and nodded before twirling his fingers in the air.

Ryleigh and Kennedy watched sedately.

"Are you two in shock or something?" Red asked tactlessly.

"It's been a long day," Ryleigh countered, breaking her reverie.

"Day's the same regardless. It's how you invest the time that matters. We are alive, and before anyone says it, so are Ankh and that orange cat. And now we have water and food. Everything we needed to do today, we did. I'm ready to start a fire, chow down on some pond beast, and get a little shuteye."

Kennedy laughed but not in a funny way. Ryleigh touched her arm and looked with concern.

"We're in the middle of nowhere, sweating off our bajoolysnackers, and he's blasting everything in sight so we can drink the same water that's filled with alien blood!" Kennedy shifted from one foot to the other and back as she looked frantically from one face to another.

"What would you have us do?" Rivka asked.

"Get out of here! I want to go back home," the young woman pleaded before breaking down and starting to cry. Titan relieved himself on a nearby bush before sniffing Kennedy's leg and looking up at her.

"He needs you," Groenwyn told her, then approached, tipped Kennedy's chin up, and repeated herself. She was answered by a blank stare.

Groenwyn picked up Tiny Man Titan and pressed him against Kennedy's chest. She instinctively took him.

"He needs you. Take care of him, please. I have my hands full with this one." Floyd bounced by before Rivka intercepted her and pointed in the direction of the ship.

The wombat sniffed the air and headed in the undergrowth.

"This way, boys and girls. Stay close. It gets thick up here." Rivka followed Floyd, using the railgun to part bushes and break small branches. She thought she could hear Red wince with each use of the railgun as a club.

It didn't take long. Red plowed past her and used his knife to cut his way through. She had to back away from the stench of what was destined to be their dinner.

CHAPTER SIX

Destiny's Vengeance Crash Site, a Clearing in a Tangle-wood Jungle

Sahved held his blaster in both hands while his gaze darted randomly across the jungle.

"Do you think this is a good idea?" Rivka asked.

Red leaned close and whispered, "It's not loaded." He stood up straight. "He has to learn sometime. We have limited assets right now, so he gets a turn in the barrel."

"What about the pilots?" Rivka asked. She knew what the answer needed to be but had to hear it to be sure.

Red looked around before dropping his voice. "Them too, but not Kennedy. She's on the precipice staring into the darkness below. I don't want to be the one to push her over."

"Or me," Rivka agreed. "Minimal shifts. We can't see the Yindle except from the mech, so everyone else is superfluous."

"Except in attitude," Red replied. "I think everyone needs to know they are contributing to your safety and

49

your team's. Give them something to do, even if that something is standing around trying to look menacing."

Rivka gestured with her head toward the Yemilorian. He was attempting to figure out how to stuff his three fingers into the blaster's trigger guard while holding the weapon with his other hand.

"Maybe that wasn't such a good idea." Red strode toward Sahved. "Give it to me." He snapped his fingers, and the alien handed it over. Red drew the knife he'd used to clean the pond beast, flipped it, caught it by the blade, and offered it to the Yemilorian.

Sahved took it with a big smile. "This the largest knife I have ever beheld, truly magnificent. I shall carve out a new world with its greatness." He stepped back and slashed it through the air, beaming the entire time.

"Don't cut yourself or anyone else. Save it for the enemy."

"We are having an enemy?"

"Anyone who shoots at us is an enemy," Red explained.

Sahved looked confused. "No one has fired their weapons at us on this planet of Tanglewood."

"That's because they know you are here, and dangerous as all get out. No one wants a piece of you." Red nodded confidently.

"A piece of me?"

"What?" Red replied. "Just keep watch. Don't let any bad guys get too close to the ship."

"How will I know if they are bad guys?" Sahved asked.

"They're the ones who aren't us." Red touched his nose and headed into the ship before Sahved could ask any more questions.

Rivka shrugged and stepped into *Destiny's Vengeance*. Lindy and Clodagh were waiting.

"Holy crap, it's hot in here." Rivka fanned her face with a free hand.

"We need to button it up and cycle the systems to cool things down. This heat isn't good for anything." Clodagh reached for the button to close the outside hatch.

"Stay close!" Rivka yelled at Sahved and Red before the engineer cycled the hatch closed. Cold air immediately started blowing from the ship's small air ducts. They took a moment to enjoy the respite.

"Comm seems to be functional, but we can't raise anyone," Clodagh said.

"Which suggests it's not functional," Rivka countered. "Any ideas?"

"Chaz and I have run through the list, and the only thing we can think of is that it's external, like a dampening field." Clodagh threw her hands up.

"Our internal comm chips worked perfectly."

"They work on a different band. Both the ships' systems piggyback on the Etheric, a little modification Ankh made to *his* ship."

"We gave it to him to keep him on the team. I need him. *We* need him and now," Rivka looked around before lowering her voice. "He might be dead."

Clodagh motioned for Rivka to follow her to the cockpit. Once squeezed inside, they closed the door. "Ankh was running an experiment that shouldn't have interfered with anything, but with the gamma burst from the supernova, it started a cascade of failures. That should not have happened, except many of the safety protocols had been disabled because of the experiment."

Rivka stretched her neck to relieve the tightness. "So, Ankh *was* the reason we crashed? I thought so."

"Pretty much." Clodagh puffed out her cheeks with the revelation. She felt like the school gossip. "But we would have been fine, perfectly normal without the gamma burst. One in a million chance, but it only takes that once."

"Although I want to wring his neck, I hope to hell he survived." Rivka twisted her mouth into a half-smile. "I was growing fond of that ship, too."

Clodagh leaned back and crossed her arms. "*Wyatt Earp* felt like home. As odd as it sounds, I thought we were making a good life on board. We had everything we needed."

"The world's our oyster. We just have to get through these next two weeks. We're on vacation, so enjoy it!" Rivka smacked the engineer on the shoulder and opened the hatch.

"For the record, Magistrate, going on vacation with you sucks."

"I don't think you'll find any dissenting voices," Rivka replied as she kept walking. "I better check on Red and our dinner."

The Magistrate opened the external hatch and waded into the wall of heat and humidity. She secured the ship before continuing to the edge of the clearing, where Red lounged against a tree, nursing a fire with his pond beast on a spit above it.

"It smells better now that it's cooking." The green

kindling belched heavy white smoke, forcing Rivka to stand to the side.

"I had a hunch," Red replied with a big smile. "I love me some vacation."

"We crash into a jungle and lose all contact with the outside. We have ten people in a ship built for three, and here's you, having a good time." Rivka sat on the ground, watching the fire spark and dance. "You're making it feel like a vacation."

"It's a gift." Red chuckled. He jabbed a stick into the coals and stirred things up. The wet wood popped and snapped, sending sparks outside the depression Red had dug. The jungle-like conditions were not conducive to building great fires.

"How did you get the fire started?"

Red tapped a blaster at his side. "I encouraged it properly." He held a finger to his lips and whispered, "If you train your eyes to look away from what you want to see, you can make out our visitors. There's one in the branches over my head."

Rivka jumped to her feet and looked up. "Hey!" she shouted. "I see you. Come down here and talk to me."

"That's not exactly what I had in mind," Red said.

The figure overhead stepped away from the tree's trunk and foliage, appearing as a vague shape. The individual leapt from the branches and dropped the five meters to the ground, landing lightly by flexing her knees. She faced Rivka with her head up, mouth set.

"That's better. We don't want to be here anymore than you want us here. If you could help us, we would get out of your hair."

The slightly built Yindle woman instinctively reached up and ran her fingers through her curls. "There is nothing in my hair," she said.

Red poked his stick into the cooking meat, acting like he wasn't paying attention to the Yindle, but he was laser-focused, with his hand resting casually on his blaster, loosened in its holster and ready for action.

"Can you help us contact our people on the other side of the planet?"

"No. We do not have the means to do that."

Rivka studied the Yindle. Slight, with a green tint to her skin and hair, barely over a meter and a half tall, no more than forty-five kilograms. Her clothing blended naturally with the surroundings. Up close, she seemed young, sporting no wrinkles from the rigors of age.

"Why are you watching us?"

"You should not be here. You could be Yangorian spies."

"Do we look Yangorian? And if we were spies, would we be so keen on getting out of here, which is all we want, by the way?"

The young woman's expression remained the same—hostility edged with curiosity.

"Can you tell me what that thing is? It tried to eat our wombat." Rivka pointed to the hunks of meat hanging over the fire.

"A kinga. Very dangerous. I applaud your ability to kill it with one shot."

"News travels fast." Rivka held the Yindle's gaze. "Can you tell us what else we should be wary of? We didn't come here to fight or die. We're supposed to be on vacation."

"Yangor. Beware the Yangorians." The woman turned

and stepped into the jungle, disappearing almost immediately. Rivka forced herself to not look directly at the Yindle, and her eyes picked up the figure moving gracefully through the brush.

"Does that mean she doesn't think we're Yangor spies anymore?" Rivka wondered.

"Sounded like it to me. You might have swayed our first ally." Red used a small knife to carve off a piece of meat. He popped it in his mouth and chewed slowly. "Tastes like processed chicken. Is there any salt in the ship?"

Rivka didn't know. She held out her hand for a piece. Red obliged.

She chewed, pleasantly surprised by the texture and flavor. "I have to note that she wasn't armed," Red said, cutting a bigger slice to slap into Rivka's palm.

"I saw that, too." She ate the second piece and was reaching for a third when she stopped herself. "We better get the others before I eat it all."

"Without technology, surveillance consists of the mark one eyeball. The ones watching us are just eyes and ears, no direct-action mission." Red sliced off another piece of the kinga and stuffed it in his mouth.

Rivka pointed at Red. "Slow down. Save some for everyone else." She hurried back to the ship, opening the hatch and yelling inside, "Dinner is served. You better get some before Red eats it all. Trust me when I say that you want some of this."

Sahved abandoned his position and hurried to the cloud of smoke that signaled the cookfire. The others gasped when they left the air conditioning. When Cole appeared, Rivka stopped him. "I need a quick check of the Yindle. I'd like to invite them for a taste of the kinga."

"Kinga?" Cole asked, looking wistfully at the fire and the line forming. But Terry Henry's teachings were to always make sure the non-military ate first, and then proceed from the lowest rank to the highest. "Roger, Magistrate."

"The pond beast is called a kinga, according to a Yindle we met. In any case, get me the locations of our watchers, and then join the others at the fire."

Cole didn't bother closing the suit behind him. He brought up the systems, bit his lip, cycled through a round of diagnostics, and then shut everything down.

"They're all gone, Magistrate."

"Well, now. That was unexpected." Rivka clasped her hands behind her back and started to pace. Cole waited for a few moments before excusing himself and joining Clodagh in the chow line. They stood hand in hand, watching the Magistrate talking to herself while walking back and forth in front of the ship.

"What do you think?" Cole asked.

Lindy stepped up. "I think when she's done, we're going to have a whole different mission."

Groenwyn nodded. "We've seen it before. The gears are turning." The young woman wrapped an arm around Kennedy's shoulders. "How are you feeling?"

"Better." The pilot tried to smile. "I don't know how you do it. Every planet we go to is something different, filled with surprises that could kill you."

"But we don't let them kill us, which is why you need to go into the Pod-doc, as well as Ryleigh, Aurora, and

Sahved. Help us to help you with some internal medicine." Groenwyn raised a hand to forestall Kennedy's obvious question. "I know. I'm the all-natural girl, but sometimes, we have to embrace the advantages technology has given us. Without it, we wouldn't be able to visit other planets and meet other cultures. Isn't it fascinating to see people who are one with the jungle?"

"I guess," Kennedy said, still clutching Tiny Man Titan while she looked down.

"Attitude is everything. Look at Titan. He probably thinks he hit the jackpot when he chased Ankh out of his house. Now he gets carried everywhere."

"If only our lives were so simple," Kennedy said softly.

"You would grow bored quickly." Groenwyn tapped her temple. "Expanding our minds is what makes life worth living."

She hugged the pilot until Titan started to squirm.

Floyd bounded across the small clearing and rammed into Groenwyn's leg. The young woman teetered but didn't topple. "Watch where you're going, little girl."

Sorry, Floyd replied, not sounding sorry at all before she bolted in the opposite direction. She bounded to a stop and ravished a small plant.

"It appears Floyd is enjoying our vacation," Clodagh remarked.

"She doesn't get around enough vegetation. Maybe she is at home. I don't know where wombats come from." Groenwyn shrugged. She enjoyed seeing Floyd happy.

"Terry Henry rescued her from a desolate planet of human slaves. Maybe she originally came from Earth, just like the others living on Home World," Red explained from the front of the line as he continued to carve slices from the kinga.

"Wouldn't that be something? Floyd is more Earth than we are."

Sahved stuffed the last of the meat in his hands into his mouth so he could twirl his fingers and make a series of gestures no one understood. The blank looks suggested he needed to explain. "Not me," he translated.

The laughter started and continued as he tried to explain each of the gestures. The humans tried to imitate the Yemilorian's finger twirls, to no avail. Human hands weren't knuckled the same way as the three-fingered race.

Private Alant Cole arrived at the firepit. He held out his hands and winked at Red. "A little something extra to keep the warrior's engine fueled?" he asked. Red tried to give a hard-ass look but knew where Cole was coming from. He'd already done that for Lindy.

"No," he said for public consumption before placing an extra slice in the warrior's hands. Cole smiled and joined Clodagh a short distance away. Red waited for Rivka, carving the rest of the meat and arranging it across the top of the creature's hard skin. One pond beast had equaled one meal. Red tried to get Rivka's attention. "Magistrate."

She stopped and looked at the sky before licking her finger and holding it up, turning it around to determine from where the slight breeze was coming from. Satisfied that she had it, she strained to see through the trees and into the distance. The saddle between two hilltops. It was the direction they'd last seen *Wyatt Earp* headed.

"Cole," the Magistrate started, fixing him with her working look, "is the suit powered enough for a full day of operation? I won't ask why we don't have an Etheric-powered suit."

"But it is. The colonel gave me the latest version to best protect the Queen's Barrister, but it's not working down here, so we have to count on the sun. I'll say that I think we charged it enough today," Alant replied. "Depends on what you need me to do."

"Come with us as we search for *Wyatt Earp*. Right now, everything else is a distraction. As long as the Yindle leave us alone, we can do what we need to do. If we can find our ship, we might be able to get out of here." Rivka walked toward the group, talking to all of them. "If Ankh is hurt, then time is of the essence. You Alant, Red, Lindy, and I will head out in the middle of the night to take advantage of lower temperatures. We're going straight over that hill," Rivka pointed, "into whatever lies beyond. I'm counting on the mech's sensors to help us focus. No flying or anything that chews through the power, just movement and scans."

"We'll hold down the fort." Clodagh looked at those who would remain behind. "We have Chaz and *Destiny's Vengeance* to protect us."

"And me!" Sahved declared, carefully removing the knife Red had given him and holding it out.

"And us," Ryleigh added, speaking for the three pilots.

Me! Floyd cried, abandoning her latest bush mid-bite and bouncing up to Rivka.

"You have to stay here and protect Groenwyn, Titan, and the others. They can't see the Yindle, but you can. Your little eyes, big ears, and boopable nose are better than anything they have. Keep your eyes and ears open and tell them if visitors are near. Clodagh and Chaz will take care of the rest."

The wombat stayed still for a moment as she contemplated the Magistrate's words before bouncing back to her last bush and renewing her attack on it.

"If only all of us were so easily convinced! I could run ahead and be back before you know it."

Groenwyn had great speed, able to run so fast that they couldn't follow her with the naked eye. But then she'd almost died.

Rivka handed the young woman a flask. "Can you run up to the pond where we found the beast and fill this canteen?"

"Of course." She accepted the flask and took off running. They watched her go. She tried to accelerate into the jungle on the path they had cut earlier in the day.

"Oh, no." She sighed, hung her head, and slowly walked back to the clearing.

"Ankh didn't tell you, did he?" Rivka asked. She knew the answer to that question. "When Ankh knew you would survive, he changed your nanocyte programming. Speed wouldn't save you, and he did not want to risk losing you. Your gift from the nanos is healing better than anyone else. You won't die. According to Ankh, all it will take is a little bit of flesh, and you'll be able to resurrect yourself. I'll take his word for it because I don't want to test it."

"Nor I," Groenwyn agreed and offered her the flask.

Kennedy held out Tiny Man Titan. "He *is* cute, isn't he?"

"He is the crew's protector. We know Wenceslaus doesn't care about people. That'll free you up to do your jobs." Rivka faced the others. "When we leave, it'll be up to you to make this clearing more like home. Collect firewood, find edible plants, and start bringing water. Everyone travels in pairs, and use your internal comm chips to stay in touch. We'll be back tomorrow sometime."

Rivka reached for the strips atop the kinga's carcass, snagging a handful. "Not bad, Red. I wouldn't have dragged that thing back here, but I'm glad *you* did."

"Somebody has to think about *your* stomach. This is a vacation, not a weight-loss-inducing survival program."

"I'm pretty sure this stopped being a vacation during our uncontrolled descent through the atmosphere." Rivka thought she had played the trump card.

"See? That's the difference between you and me, besides the lawyer thing, and that judge stuff—I'm always optimistic! Come over to the bright side, Magistrate. We have more fun." Red waggled his eyebrows.

"Red as the eternal optimist, the one who risked his life grabbing half the armory in case he needed to shoot something or level a town."

Lindy joined Rivka in looking down at Red, who took the respite to carve the last meat from the remainder of the kinga.

"Being pragmatic has nothing to do with staying positive." Red found a piece that was bigger than his thumb, cheered, and stuffed it into his mouth. When he finished chewing, he added, "I'm positive that if I need to shoot something, I can, like dinner, here. We wouldn't have Floyd with us, or dinner—two equally distressing outcomes."

Groenwyn joined the other women to glare at Red.

"What?"

"*Equally* distressing?" Groenwyn requested.

Red shrugged. "You guys better get some sleep. Midnight is going to come early to the garden of good and evil."

Lindy looked around the small clearing. "Who's going to sleep where?"

"There's the million-credit question," Rivka replied.

"I'll set up a watch with Sahved first." To the Yemilorian, he said, "I'm not sure your head's right, so you might as well stay up." Red pointed at the others, two at a time. "You'll get plenty of sleep, don't worry, but only in four-hour blocks. It'll do."

The pilots looked worried, not about the sleep, but about the security of the ship. None of their training had prepared them for that.

"I'm kidding. Once we leave, the rest of you will fit just fine inside the ship. Secure the hatch and ask Chaz if he'll watch things."

Kennedy laughed nervously, earning Red a stern look from the Magistrate. "Better get some shut-eye," he told her, standing and handing his fire-poking stick to Sahved. "Let it burn down, then cover it with dirt. We will not be the ones to start a forest fire."

"Environmentally conscious. Well done." Groenwyn clapped awkwardly while holding Titan.

"I don't want any more enemies than we already have, and we didn't do anything to earn those." Red smiled. "We're the good guys."

"I hope the Yangorians feel the same way when we run across them." Rivka waved goodnight and headed for *Destiny's Vengeance*. "Sleep fast, everyone. It's going to be a long night."

CHAPTER SEVEN

Cole climbed into the back of the mech and buttoned it up. He activated the systems one by one, bringing the suit to life. He flexed and stretched the suit, which was nearly three meters tall, humanoid-shaped, and bulky, but lean. The helmeted area where Cole's head rested had a variety of ways to "see." He usually went with the clear screen, using his own eyes, but tonight, he needed all the assets at his command: passive Infrared, ultraviolet, and the millimeter-wave scanner. He activated the heads-up display, the HUD, and took a few steps. From the outside, the mech was dark. No light seeped from within.

The inside view was that of a high-tech cockpit and the private played the role of an experienced pilot, driving the mech like a master. He activated the external speakers and then thought better of it and switched to the internal comm system. *Ready to roll on your orders, Magistrate.*

"Red, take the lead. Follow the path we took earlier, but move faster. Cole will let us know if the Yindle make an appearance. Until then, speed is of the essence." Rivka waved her blaster in the direction they needed to go. Red ducked as the barrel waved past his face. She holstered the weapon and locked it in before getting herself in trouble for poor weapon discipline. Red and Lindy carried their railguns at the ready.

Rivka's eyes had been enhanced to see better in the dark. They were slightly oversized, which no one seemed to notice. Red could see well enough in the dark, owing to his nanos, as could Lindy. There was nothing to hold them back. The jungle appeared to them as a pale gray in the darkness. Red moved out, walking quickly, but once comfortable with the trail, he started to jog.

The Magistrate moved in behind Red. Cole loped easily after her. Lindy brought up the rear.

Tiptoes, Cole, the Magistrate cautioned.

With a minor adjustment, the mech's steps sounded more like normal footfalls. They didn't need to wake the dead. Often, circumstances called for pounding the ground to instill fear into the enemy. This night was not one of those times.

The first few kilometers went quickly, with Red setting a fast pace. The trail was clear to the point they met the Yindle and turned away. Beyond that, Red slowed to a slow walk as he hacked through the jungle using a sturdy branch as a club.

Looks like we have company inbound, Cole reported. *Five bodies coming from our right. They'll intercept us in about ten minutes.*

Can you get past them? Outrun them? Rivka asked.

Yes. They are moving deliberately. That could change once we start hauling ass.

Time for you to blaze the trail, Cole. Let's see what you can do.

"Good," Red murmured. "Whacking bushes with a stick is bullshit."

Red stood aside, and Cole increased speed as he passed. With his active and passive systems fully engaged, he saw the path he needed to take, the Yindle, the long-distance target, and more. He plowed through the least restrictive brush. It didn't slow the mech, so Cole took that as an opportunity to accelerate.

Red jogged and then started to sprint. Rivka and Lindy kept pace, their enhanced bodies tailored for the rigors of physically demanding actions.

We've passed the Yindle. They are falling behind quickly.

We're making good time, so keep going.

The depth of darkness increased with dawn's approach. The starlight was chased away as the system's sun approached the horizon. False dawn's imminence left that part of Tanglewood dark and cool.

They're onto us. They are running along the trail I made with my smexy metal body, and they are gaining on us.

How long do we have? Rivka wasn't tired of running, but she wanted to open a dialogue with the Yindle. Maybe that's what the group was dispatched for.

Ten minutes, more or less, Cole verified, checking his instruments and letting the suit do the calculations.

Ambush, but no shooting. Continue cutting a trail, Cole, make a lot of noise but slow down. Red, Lindy, you know what to do. I'll be on this branch over the trail.

Lindy went one way into the jungle and Red went the other. They found hiding spots where they could see the trail behind and still maintain clear fields of fire. Red was in front of a huge trunk and Lindy behind, so they didn't accidentally shoot toward each other in case they had to light things up.

It wasn't long before the Yindle ran into view. Even in the dark, the jungle natives knew something was different. They immediately slowed and scanned the undergrowth.

Rivka shook a small branch to get their attention.

"Good morning," she called. When they looked up, she could clearly see their faces. None of them looked like the Yindle from the day before. "We haven't met. I'm Magistrate Rivka Anoa, and I'm hoping that we can talk about a mutual way forward."

The Yindle searched the jungle with their eyes. They knew how many people they were following.

"Red, Lindy, you can show yourselves." Rivka snapped her fingers as well. The bodyguards stood up and moved forward so they could be seen. Their railguns were leveled at the Yindle. "You can put those down. We're all friends here."

They let the barrels drop to forty-five degrees, but that was the farthest they'd go. The gesture of lowering them was ornamental since the railguns were less than a heartbeat from being brought into action. Rivka appreciated her bodyguards. The locals were not going to intimidate her or her team.

The Yindle's eyes flew wide when the mech appeared, walking slowly and not making a sound. Cole dominated the trail he had cleared. They didn't know he didn't have any weapons besides the rockets in his over-the-shoulder packs, but he was virtually indestructible by the weaponry available to the jungle people.

"Can you at least introduce yourselves?" Rivka asked. "We only want to get out of your jungle and off this planet. That way," Rivka pointed toward the hill ahead, "is where we think our ship went down. We need to know if anyone survived."

"That is Yangor territory. They would not let anyone survive. They hate life."

"And you are?" Rivka pressed, looking for a way to make a connection without making it about the conflict between Yindle and Yangor.

"I am Minor Yee," one of the Yindle said. The others deferred. Rivka could barely tell them apart. She noted a small necklace he wore that the others did not to distinguish him.

"It's nice to meet you. Are you from Keosh?"

"I am not," Yee replied. "I am from the village of Osheka."

Rivka dropped from the branch and stood before the Yindle. "We're from the Federation. We crashed on your planet and are looking for our ship, our friends, and a way out of here. Would you have any transport?"

"No." The Yindle was firm in his answer.

"What can we do for you, then? We're in a hurry to find our ship and our friend."

"Why did you not continue when you passed through earlier?"

"You *have* talked with the people of Keosh. Good. I don't have to explain myself twice. We were not properly equipped for the level of hostility that seemed to have come our way, so we adjusted our stance and are fully prepared to defend ourselves as we search for our lost ship. We would appreciate it greatly if you would help us." Rivka moved closer, but the Yindle remained out of arm's reach.

He also did not reply.

"Why are you following us?" The Magistrate hoped a direct question would encourage them to be more open.

"Because you are not guests of the Yindle. You are intruders."

Red growled, low in his throat like an animal. Lindy gritted her teeth.

"We are victims of a terrible accident. Did you know that the neighboring star went supernova? The star in your night sky that is no longer there after a horrible flash of light? We were caught in the radiation. Our ship should have been able to weather it but wasn't."

Rivka inched closer. The Yindle looked at each other and shifted nervously. "The brightest star in our sky is gone," the Yindle who had spoken previously stated. "We are still contemplating what it means. It could be a sign from heaven."

"It was indeed a sign from heaven that the star was spent and went out with a big bang. Will you help us now?" Rivka stepped forward while the Yindle were in disarray over the revelation and grabbed the leader's arm. "Why won't you help us?" she asked, concentrating on his thoughts.

The emotions rolled through the contact and into her mind. *A Yangorian trick. Distrust of all things not Yindle. Strangers! But they speak kindly.*

The Yindle removed Rivka's hand. "We don't touch each other here," he told her as if trying to teach.

A big step. "It won't happen again. Humans touch all the time. It is a regular thing in our culture, but please accept my apologies."

"The Yangorians touch, too, but they don't apologize," Minor Yee said, softening his tone. "We will go with you as far as Shelosha, the dip between the hills."

"Thank you." Rivka twirled a finger in the air. *Take us to Shelosha, Cole. I expect that's where we were headed. They'll tell us if we're headed in the wrong direction.*

Rivka walked at Yee's side, while Lindy fell in with the other Yindle and Red brought up the rear. Lindy introduced herself, smiling and nodding at her companions. They nodded in return but didn't speak. Cole continued blazing a trail toward the saddle between the two hills.

Yee seemed to wince each time Cole tore through a bush instead of sidestepping it.

"Would you prefer to lead the way? We're not jungle people and would love to learn your techniques for moving through the foliage and causing the least damage possible," Rivka offered.

Yee whistled and pointed behind him. One of the Yindle ran past the mech and continued moving deftly through the undergrowth. Cole stayed right behind the local, challenging his agility. The others closed in tightly behind him. The Yindle blazing the trail was hard to see as she moved in and out of the foliage in the darkness of pre-dawn.

Cole was hard-pressed to follow her using the scanning system overlaid on the HUD. He tried to miss the bushes, but he was about ten times wider than the slight native. The mech continued to widen the path as he shredded foliage and stepped on the living jungle.

"Maybe we should slow down," Rivka suggested. Minor Yee whistled and their trailblazer slowed to a walk. Cole almost stepped on her but was able to rein in the heavy machine.

"What is Yindle's problem with Yangor?" Rivka asked, avoiding making the Yindle defensive by saying the word "your."

"They are violent," he replied simply. "They are not us. They touch. They cut trees. But we hate them because they make war on us."

Rivka looked at her companion and breathed slowly, in through the nose, out through the mouth, before answering. "I have some experience as a mediator in planetwide disputes. I might be able to help."

"You'll find out soon enough," Minor Yee replied. The slope had increased as they climbed through the dense jungle. All of a sudden, the trees cleared, and they found themselves on the open ground of the saddle they'd seen from the ship. "Over that hill, you will find Yangor. We will remain here to carry your bodies back to your ship. We do this out of kindness."

Cole stomped his metal feet, shaking the ground. He wasn't sure there was a weapon on the entire planet that could stop the mech.

Lindy and Red smirked at each other. Rivka tried to signal for them to stop, but she couldn't disagree. The Yangorians had never seen anything like what the Magistrate was bringing. The Yindle had no idea what damage Rivka could wreak.

"I appreciate your concern," Rivka said tactfully. "I think we will be fine. Our only concern is for our friend, and we will travel the length and width of Tanglewood to find him. We shall approach the Yangorians as we did you, as lost strangers needing help."

Minor Yee nodded curtly, and the five faded back into the jungle.

"They really don't like their neighbors, do they?" Red asked.

"What do you think?" Rivka replied.

Lindy chimed in, "We'll find more of the same. Initial hostility, but they'll be curious. The Yangorians won't be as bad as the Yindle make them out to be."

"My thoughts exactly," Rivka agreed.

"And if they are, I bet we can get more of them than they get out of us." Red hoisted his railgun and shook it at the top of the rise before them. "It's not getting any closer with us standing here, Magistrate."

Lindy held up her hand. "What did you see when you touched the Yindle?"

"They don't appear to be a trusting sort, but we're growing on them. They come across as far grimmer than they are. My impression is that they don't get many visitors, so they don't know what to do when a pack of weirdos like us shows up on their doorstep, hat in hand."

"I'm sure we didn't have our hats in our hands. We only wanted them to stay out of the way." Red backed slowly up the hill, encouraging the others to join him.

Rivka and Lindy made eye contact and agreed with Red. It was time to go.

The Magistrate twirled her finger in the air. "Cole, on point."

Alant Cole headed up the hill and over the top. *All systems active, searching for* Wyatt Earp. *Nothing within a five-kilometer search. Expanding. Ten kilometers. Reducing resolution. Expanding. And there we go!*

"Where?" Rivka asked aloud, rushing forward to stand at the mech's side.

Thirteen kilometers in that direction. He pointed with a flat hand at a distant bump in the heavy jungle. *Ship appears to be intact. Hard to get particulars at this range because of the minimum resolution, but it's definitely* Wyatt Earp.

CHAPTER EIGHT

Tanglewood, Yangor Sector, *Wyatt Earp* Crash Site

Erasmus, are you okay? Ankh asked, his internal voice tentative. He tried to see where he was, but nothing was in focus. He tried to stand, but his left leg failed him. He fell to the deck, crying out in pain.

I am fine, my friend. The ship is in need of significant repairs, but I have already dispatched the maintenance bots. Current estimates suggest we will return to full functionality in just under nine months.

Ankh dragged himself across the floor of the engine room, stopping halfway to catch his breath while working through the pain. The Pod-doc was in the cargo bay. Too far.

Erasmus, please send a maintenance bot to carry me to the Pod-doc. I am not able to help you until my injuries have been repaired.

Internal scans show you are in danger, Erasmus replied. *A bot is on its way. We will repair the ship once you are well.*

Ankh remained where he was, grimacing with the

anguish of his injuries. He checked himself and found it was far more than just his leg. He lay back on the floor, moaning.

Why was there a cascade failure of the gravitic shields following the Gate transit? Ankh asked, trying to take his mind off the damage to his body.

My records are incomplete. Chaz has the information.

And Chaz is no longer on the ship, Ankh finished. *Will we be able to make repairs without the information?*

Of course. We will locate Destiny's Vengeance *and reunite with your ship and the crew.*

Ankh groaned when the maintenance bot rolled into the engineering space. He grunted through clenched teeth as he climbed onto its flat back.

Communications. Please relay our information to Ted so that a repair party can be dispatched. I have no intention of sitting here for nine months.

We do not have communications, Erasmus clarified.

How can that be? It's a shock-hardened portable system. The bot moved slowly to keep Ankh from sliding off. The ship listed five degrees to port. *Why is the ship leaning?*

The Etheric is dampened in this area. It may be a planetwide phenomenon, but without more information, that is only a guess as to why the communication system is non-functional. We are currently resting thirty-five meters above ground in the jungle canopy.

Are local communications operational? Can you raise the Vengeance?

I cannot, Erasmus confirmed. *We will discuss further after you've completed your biological repairs.*

As to that, please program the following parameters into the system...

Tanglewood, Border between Yindle and Yangor

Cole plunged downhill through the small clearing and into the trees. He dodged as much as he could but still left a wake of destruction, making it easier for Rivka, Red, and Lindy to follow. They ran after the mech on his beeline toward the crash site.

He slowed so quickly that Rivka had to put out her hands to stop herself from slamming face-first into the cold metal body.

We have company, Cole reported. *At least twenty natives with weapons, bracketing the path we're headed down. Your orders?*

Time to let them know we know they're there. Use your speakers and announce us if you would.

Cole continued until he was less than fifty meters from the welcoming committee.

"People of Yangor. Magistrate Rivka Anoa has crashed on your beautiful planet and respectfully requests your assistance in reuniting with her ship and any survivors who may be on board."

Where did he learn to talk like that? Red asked while performing a quick function check of his weapon.

I guess he pays attention when the right people are talking, Rivka answered. She stayed close to the mech, peering between its arm and its side, hoping to catch a glimpse of the Yangor. She had failed to ask the Yindle what they looked like, but that didn't matter. They'd find out soon.

I'm stopping here to keep them all in front of us. About thirty yards out at ten o'clock and two o'clock, I have bogeys in pairs.

Red and Lindy each took a knee and aimed outboard in the directions Cole had indicated. Let the Yangor wonder how the strangers knew they were there.

A group of slight natives appeared ahead. They had brown skin but were otherwise twins to the Yindle. They carried the same style rifles, but the natives stood at ease. They blocked the way without threatening the Magistrate's party.

Rivka stepped around Cole. Red appeared as if by magic on one side of her, and Lindy on the other. She took a position in front of the mech. That satisfied her bodyguards, who were ready to light up the Yangorians in case the conversation didn't play out as they hoped.

"You must be Yangorians," Rivka said. "Nothing like what the Yindle said you'd be."

"The Yindle!" One of the natives stepped forward and spat on the ground. He looked at his people, left, then right. They laughed together—a harsh laugh, mocking. "Whose side are you on?"

"Not that again," Rivka murmured before striding forward, much to the chagrin of her bodyguards. "We take no sides. We crashed in our lifeboat back there in Yindle territory, and our ship crashed over there." She pointed ahead. "We are on our way to check on our ship and our crew."

"Whose side?" the Yangorian reiterated in a deeper and louder voice.

"We are on the side of the Federation. Not Yindle. Not Yangor. The Federation. Can you help us get to our ship?"

Rivka changed her tone, not demanding now, but pleading.

"Why would we want to?" he countered. A couple of the group chuckled.

"Because we don't want to be here, and you don't want us here. Your help would be mutually beneficial to expedite our departure."

"Yangor is open to all friends of Yangor." He spread his arms wide. "I am Antwan, Keeper of the Barrier Peak, and these warriors are the Committed."

"Nice to meet you, Antwan." Rivka strolled forward, hands out to keep them in view, to show she was not a threat. She held out her hand. "It's a human custom. We shake hands as a greeting."

"What did the Yindle think of your *custom*?" he asked from behind a toothy grin.

"They expressed a certain amount of displeasure." Rivka laughed with the Yangorians.

When Antwan took her hand, she asked quickly, "Are you willing to help us?"

"Of course. I like you." Flashes of images in his mind, a way to *Wyatt Earp*. A feast with his people, a tour of the mech. No subterfuge, no anger.

His hand was smaller than hers. He looked at them, side by side, in comparison.

"You are giants!" He nodded his chin toward the mech. "And that is a magnificent monster. Can you show it to me?"

"In due time, Keeper Antwan. We have a long way to go, and it is already getting light. Will you accompany us?"

"We should talk first…" He let his voice drift off.

"Can we talk as we walk? Time is wasting, Antwan. We don't know if our guy is alive or dead, hence our urgency." Rivka started to edge around the Keeper.

"You need to know that not every Yangorian will be as welcoming as we have been."

Rivka stopped trying to encourage Antwan to move. "I'm sorry to hear that, but it doesn't change our mission. We need to get to that ship on the far side of this valley."

"I will escort you as far as the next enclave. The rest of my people will stay here, just in case the Yindle are following." He gestured and the Yangorians melted into the undergrowth.

They are spreading out and moving toward the saddle behind us, Cole reported. Red and Lindy watched the trees but couldn't see the Yangorians as they passed.

"You are very tall," Antwan said, looking up at each, but spending more time assessing Red. "And you are simply unreal."

"Thanks," Red deadpanned. "I've lost weight recently."

"What do you eat?" Antwan asked as they started to walk.

Lindy laughed. "What doesn't he eat?"

Antwan looked back and forth, smiling. "I like you, strangers." They continued to walk in silence. Rivka tried to will the Yangorian to go faster, but he maintained a steady pace.

"Do you have kinga over here?" Red asked.

"Of course. They are a blight on our jungle."

"They're good eating," Red added.

Antwan stopped. "You were able to kill one?"

Red tapped the railgun. "Oh, yeah."

"I should not be surprised since your weapons are beyond anything we have seen. Is there any way I could borrow one?" He started walking again.

Rivka replied, "I'm sorry. We need our weapons because we aren't always welcomed where we go. I'm a Magistrate. My job is to enforce the law, which means that we are always dealing with criminals of one sort or another. They don't take kindly to being caught and punished."

"Criminals. I don't know what those are. If you are talking enemies, we have those. The Yindle. They probably need to be punished."

"I'm not sure what for. They seem to be trying to live their lives, as you're trying to live yours. Crime and law are how we keep the peace and keep society stable so people can exist without interference. A common law establishes boundaries within which everyone works together. No surprises. If you buy something, it's yours. No one takes it, and if they do, they become a criminal and get to meet people like us."

"I see." Antwan chewed his cheek as he walked with his head down, deep in thought. When he looked back up, his eyes darkened. "I'm sorry, but this is all the farther I can go. Good luck with the rest of your journey."

He held out his hand, and Rivka took it. *Worry for the strangers. They would soon be attacked.*

Rivka didn't let him know she could read his thoughts. She smiled and nodded.

He thinks we're going to be attacked not very far ahead. Everyone stay frosty, Rivka told her team.

. . .

Destiny's Vengeance **Crash Site**

"Good morning, fellow castaways!" Chaz said cheerily over the ship's speakers.

Clodagh grunted. "Ugh. What time is it?"

"Time is a relative construct that varies from planet to planet, and sometimes across a single planet. I will inform you that it is light outside, so we'll call it morning."

"We will, huh?" Clodagh scratched her head. She was on the deck in the small passageway between the cockpit and the galley. At least she had a blanket. "I guess you're right. Time to get up. Did we have any activity overnight?"

"Nothing. I don't have the millimeter-wave scanners that Private Cole employs on the mechanized combat suit, but I have been able to cobble together a little something that can replicate the scanning technique. A small creature passed through a couple of hours ago. I think you would have called it a squirrel, a type of rodent. Besides that, we have plenty of birds and fresh air. Today will be as hot as yesterday, so if you want to be productive outside, you might want to get to it sooner rather than later."

The crew collectively groaned at the announcement.

"Up and at 'em!" Clodagh said loudly enough for all to hear. She licked her dry lips. "Chaz, how much water do we have, enough?"

"There isn't much water storage on board. Enough for two, but not five unless we're willing to allocate more power to the water recycling system," he replied.

"What do you recommend, Chaz?"

"That we don't allocate more power."

"First order of business," Clodagh stated while she stood. "All of us are going to get water. We're taking everything we can that will hold water, and we might as well wash up while we're there. You guys remember how to get to the stream?"

"I do," Ryleigh said, emerging from the bunkroom. She had slept head to toe with Kennedy, keeping her company while also getting some of the precious mattress space. Aurora had been in the top bunk, and Sahved had filled the galley with his lanky body.

"I'm not sure I can look at that pond again," Kennedy said softly.

Chaz came to her rescue. "I could use a pair of hands here to work through some diagnostics."

Clodagh started gathering the waterproof bags they had on board, along with the meager toiletries in the head. She gauged the amount of shampoo and looked at the three pilots' long hair. "Shit just got real."

Ryleigh and Aurora started to giggle. Sahved stood up carefully to avoid banging his head and leaned into the corridor. "It wasn't real before?" he wondered.

Groenwyn emerged from the cockpit with Floyd and Titan.

"Sahved," Groenwyn started but thought better of it. "You'll have to figure it out for yourself. Any word from Rivka?"

"I have not heard from them since they moved out of range," Chaz replied.

"That means they are enjoying their jaunt through the jungle, happily working their way toward *Wyatt Earp* and Ankh," Groenwyn replied.

"There is no data from which to draw such a conclusion." The AI sounded confused.

"Here's the deal, Chaz. As humans, we can choose how we want to feel in the absence of information. I worry, probably too much. But look at who and what went with her. If they can't protect themselves as well as find *Wyatt Earp*, if the ship is anywhere over that way, then we have lost all hope. Since we know they can protect themselves— woe to anyone who stands in the Magistrate's way—then the longer they go without contacting us, the more likely it is that they have found the ship. At some point, we'll hear from them. Between now and then, they are successful. Have you heard of Schrödinger?"

"Thank you for explaining, Groenwyn. Sometimes I'm too technically minded. Being with humans is such a breath of fresh air!"

"That's a good one, Chaz. Hold onto those talks and take good care of the ship while we're gone." Groenwyn leaned back into the cockpit and whispered, "And take care of Kennedy. Keep her busy with stuff that isn't busywork. She had quite a shock yesterday."

"All will be as you desire," Chaz told everyone in the ship. "We shall have it pristine for your return."

Clodagh stood at the hatch, ready to hit the button, trying to steel herself for the wave of heat and humidity that would assault her body. Titan started barking and worked his way in front of the engineer so he could be first out. He had to go.

Without further delay, she tapped the button, and the hatch cycled open. The corridor of *Destiny's Vengeance* doubled as an airlock by securing the hatches to the cockpit, the galley, and the bunkroom. On the planet, the corridor became another active space in which the group crowded, ready to go outside.

Like stepping through a curtain, the heat and humidity folded around each member of the group when they went outside. Floyd headed outside with the others and immediately ran for the bushes to eat breakfast.

"Eat fast, little girl. We have a short walk ahead of us before we can stop," Groenwyn told her. Floyd munched happily.

"Ryleigh, lead on. Sahved, you're behind her. Your job is to protect us all since you're armed," Clodagh explained.

"I will do my best," he replied proudly with his head held high. The engineer wanted him there so the others could easily see where they were going if anyone started to lag. She didn't bother showing him that she wore a blaster, and unlike the one he had carried the previous day, this one was loaded.

Ryleigh set off at a brisk pace toward the outlet stream's closest point, about a kilometer from the ship. Not far, unless you were carving your way through a jungle. Ryleigh did her best, but soon Sahved was in front, hacking his way through using Red's big knife. They stopped when they estimated they were halfway there.

Sahved panted like a dog with his mouth open and his tongue out. His strength wasn't the problem since he was used to much greater gravity.

Floyd seemed unfazed, bouncing through the gaps near the ground, finding her favorite plants and eating her way to the stream.

"How long have we been going?"

Clodagh checked in with Chaz.

An hour, and you're on the right path, but you're going to have company. The Yindle are waiting for you at the stream.

Recommendation? she asked.

You need water, don't you? the AI asked to answer her question.

I guess we'll see what they want, then. Clodagh shifted to speaking out loud. "You heard him. We're not going to change where we're going or why. Let's see what the Yindle have to say while we're getting some water."

Sahved continued carving a path through the jungle until the sounds of a small stream came from ahead. He pushed through the last bush to find himself in the middle of a group of Yindle who were aiming their weapons at him. Other natives descended on the rest of their group.

"We're here to get water, nothing more," Clodagh said when they were herded into the small open area.

One of the Yindle pointed at Sahved's knife and held out her hand. The Yemilorian gave up his knife without a struggle.

Two Yindle held Clodagh's arms as a third removed her blaster and took it away.

"You need to come with us." The leader announced, not bothering to introduce himself. "You are prisoners of the Yindle village of Ashkaar."

Sahved turned to Clodagh. "Did shit just get realer?"

CHAPTER NINE

Wyatt Earp Crash Site

"Erasmus, what is the problem? I should feel better than I do," Ankh mumbled from inside the Pod-doc. He blinked rapidly, trying to clear his eyes, but the fuzz remained. He decided to lie there until he felt well enough to sit up.

How long has it been since we crashed? Ankh switched to internal communication.

More than twenty-four hours. Your chip should have that information. Do you not have access?

One of many things that is not working as it should. Ankh groaned, then rolled onto his side and pushed himself upright. He looked for the maintenance bot to hitch a ride, but it was gone.

The maintenance bot?

Repairing the ship. We cannot have any downtime if we are to improve upon the nine-month timeline.

Concur, Ankh replied. *I will walk then.*

The Crenellian climbed from the Pod-doc and stood on shaky legs.

Is the ship moving? he wondered.

The ship is stable. May I suggest you lie down and sleep for a while?

Ankh shook his head, which sent a minor wave of nausea through his body. He stopped and held onto the side of the Pod-doc until it passed. *No time. We have too much work to do. I have no intention of staying here for nine months, although the company is exquisite, and the time away from the humans and their animals will be refreshing.*

Wenceslaus is still on board. He is currently sleeping in your quarters.

But he's all right? Ankh asked, worried about the cat's well-being.

He is perfectly fine, unlike you, who should join him.

Noted, Ankh replied tersely. *I'm going to get something to eat. I need energy for the nanos to finish their work.*

Ankh took one small step and then another, leaning and stumbling toward the frame of the entry to the cargo bay. He caught himself before slamming into the metal. He caught his breath and held on as he helped himself through and down the corridor to the small mess deck.

Are food processing systems intact? he asked.

Yes. Most ships systems are nominal. The main and Gate engines are offline with damage to the diagnostic system, and then there are the structural repairs, which will take the most time because we do not have the proper raw materials on board.

"Then we better acquire them. I'll look into it as soon as I get something to eat." In the mess, he found that some things had been tossed about. He ignored it all and went straight to the cooler. He found the pizzas intact and grabbed a few slices, then sat at the nearest table and saluted with a slice. "Here's to you, Red."

Tanglewood, Yangor Zone

Cole slowed, testing his systems before engaging with the enemy. The rockets were no good at close range but could intimidate an enemy who knew what they were. He could also use the suit to trample them and destroy any fortifications they might have.

Rivka slowed and let the mech move in front. Red and Lindy drew close, staying at her shoulders.

Update? Red requested.

Looks to be at least thirty with more coming in from the fringes of what I can scan. I think they called for all hands on deck.

Then we don't have to chase them down individually. Sounds like we have them right where we want them. Red wore the grim expression of a warrior ready for combat. He knew what he had to do. His muscles bunched and tensed as they prepared to respond to his demands.

Lindy rolled her shoulders and started to crouch as she jogged, limiting her profile.

Rivka pulled her blaster. *We don't want to fight them,* she reiterated, *but we're not giving up, either.* Wyatt Earp *is within reach, which means Ankh is there, too. I have to know that he's okay.*

"Me too, Magistrate. And I've got more stuff on the ship that I like, plus a mech-sized railgun for Cole. That would be all he'd need to take over this planet, Yin and Yang be damned."

Rivka thought for a moment. "That's why it sounded familiar! I'll be damned. Maybe aliens visited the Chinese and all that Zen stuff was alien wisdom." Rivka started to slow as her mind began to analyze the situation between Yindle and Yangor. "Let me think about how the two sides complement each other. That could be the balance I need to get them to talk. They aren't bad, just distrustful, and I don't know where their disagreement is."

Hold up, Cole. We're starting to lose the Magistrate.

The mech continued forward a few more steps before stopping and taking a position facing a gap in the jungle ahead.

They're here, Cole stated.

Red grabbed the back of Rivka's shirt to keep her where they could protect her.

She shook her head and roused from her internal conversation. "The Yangorians?"

"Yup." Red still couldn't see any. "They're all around us, but I don't have a visual."

Do your thing, Cole. Let them know that we know what they think we don't know.

There was a long pause before Cole turned on the suit's external speakers and repeated what he had said earlier. "People of Yangor. Magistrate Rivka Anoa has crashed on your beautiful planet and respectfully requests your assistance in reuniting with her ship and any survivors who may be on board."

The new delegation's speaker stepped forward. Rivka peered past the side of the mech to take in the Yangorian. *Consistency between the two cultures, a pyramidal hierarchy,* Rivka thought as she watched the individual come into better focus the more he stepped away from the jungle's disruptive canvas.

"You are intruders. You will surrender to me, and we will take you to Bora Vale, the largest Yangor village."

"We will accompany you as guests but not prisoners," Rivka replied. The Yangorian raised his hands, and the jungle came alive as dozens of his fellows emerged. They each sported a rifle similar to the ones the Yindle had carried. The Yangorians aimed at Rivka and the others. "We cannot have a conversation when people are pointing guns."

"You will give us your weapons and accompany us." He pointed at the mech. "What is that thing? You will turn it off and leave it here."

When I give the word, Rivka said using her internal comm chip, *Cole, you secure the Yangorian leader, and Red and Lindy, fire over their heads. Let's show them what kind of damage we can do. On one. One.*

The mech vaulted forward, boot jets puffing to accelerate the suit through the air. All eyes turned to the violent action of the massive mechanical creation. Cole hit the ground before the cringing Yangor leader and secured him with his oversized metal hands.

Red and Lindy opened up on full auto. The railguns cut a line through the trees and the hypervelocity rounds instantly boiled the liquids within the trunks, explosively splintering them. The effect carried from tree to tree as Red and Lindy panned over the heads of the Yangorians.

In two seconds, silence returned, leaving only the ringing in their ears. Treetops started cracking and falling, their shattered trunks succumbing to gravity. Before Rivka could reiterate her position that she didn't want to hurt anyone, an overzealous Yangorian fired at Red. The round grazed his exposed upper arm. Red dropped the barrel of his weapon and squeezed off a single round.

The Yangorian exploded, spraying the jungle behind with blood and gore.

"Anyone else?" Red shouted.

Rivka stepped back to push the barrel down, stopping herself before the superheated launch tube melted her flesh. She glanced at Red's wound, comforted that it was already healing. Lindy gave the thumbs-up without taking her eyes off the Yangorians in her field of fire.

The Magistrate held up her hands for calm. "No one else needs to die!" she yelled as she walked slowly to the mech. "You can let him go," she told Cole.

The mech's hands eased their grip, and Cole stepped back.

Rivka seized the Yangorian's arm before he could bolt. The look in his eyes suggested he was terrified. The emotions running through his mind confirmed it. "Calm down," she told him, hearing it as she said it, knowing that no one calmed down because they were told to. "We have no intention of doing that again, so please do not force our hand. We are willing to talk to you as equals. Treat us with respect, and we will treat you the same way. Should you try to make us your prisoners, you will all die, and worse, we'll destroy this entire valley. Cole, rockets."

The two three-rocket packs popped up over the mech's shoulders. Cole stomped the ground for added effect.

Rivka gave him the side-eye since she had been standing closest to his demonstration.

Sorry, Magistrate. They looked vulnerable to a good earth-shaking.

I won't disagree. Just don't do it that close to me. Ever.

"Where were we?" she asked the Yangorian. "You were about to order your people to put their weapons down."

He gestured, and the Yangorians threw their weapons on the ground.

"That's not what I meant, but it'll do. What's your name?"

Red and Lindy kept their eyes on the newly docile crowd of Yangorians. Cole demonstrated his agility by tiptoeing in front of the Yangorians and collecting their rifles.

"I am DeWan, Keeper of the Central Wood."

"Nice to meet you, DeWan. What do you know about the Federation?"

She held his arm, looking for insight into where these people were on their understanding of intergalactic relationships. In his mind, the Federation was a governmental presence that had no bearing on his life.

"Nothing," he replied.

"You are subject to Federation Law. It's sad to see that you don't know what that means. That's how your people accidentally get killed." Rivka finally let go of his arm and strolled around to stand in front of him. "Here's what needs to happen. I would like to have a dialogue with your superiors, those in charge of Bora Vale."

He lifted his head. "I will take you to them as your prisoner, having failed in my mission to capture you."

"Your mission was flawed," Rivka noted. "You came up

against a technologically advanced stranger, and you treated them like an enemy instead of a potential ally."

"You are against the Yindle?" he asked, perking up.

"No. Where would you get that idea?" Rivka shook her head, wincing at the natives' desire to hate each other. "Never mind. We are neither for nor against anyone."

DeWan deflated.

"And you're not our prisoner. I'm sorry one of your people died, but when you point guns, shit like that happens. Don't do it again."

"We will not. We no longer have our rifles."

Rivka couldn't fault his logic. "Can you make sure that other Yangorians we encounter between here and there don't fire on us?"

The Yangorian looked at the jungle before scanning his people. "I can only try. The Keepers determine what happens in their areas."

"The Keeper of the Barrier Peak would not enter your area. Why is that?"

"Because it is not his area." DeWan seemed confused.

"How do you work together, then? And weren't you going to escort us all the way to Bora Vale?"

"Yes, but along the transit corridor that is for passage without contest."

Rivka mulled it over in her mind. Red and Lindy had their weapons on combat slings under their arms, barrels forward but at ease.

"Sounds like a set of laws that you adhere to—independent city-states with a loose framework of cooperation. I can work with this. I volunteer to mediate the dispute between Yangor and Yindle. Your leadership is going to accept my proposal because we will give them no choice. Since Tanglewood is subject to Federation Law, this dispute is within my jurisdiction." Rivka started to pace, keeping her head up with her hands behind her back.

"Listen up, people of Yangor. You have a vibrant world that deserves peace and tranquility. You live in a paradise. We were coming here for vacation because Tanglewood is renowned throughout the universe, yet on this side of the planet, you have anger and discord. Crash survivors have to fear for their lives. It should not be that way. In this case, I'm going to help Yindle and Yangor get along because your current contentious relationship is detrimental to my health. I'm not good with that, so I'm going to fix it by using Federation Law."

"But we're not broken," DeWan said softly.

"Just because you don't know you're broken doesn't mean you're not broken. It's okay not to like your neighbors. It's not okay to tell visitors you're going to take them prisoner. Existence can never be a crime."

The Keeper of the Central Wood contemplated Rivka's speech. He didn't look convinced. She rested her hand on his shoulder and asked, "Will you take me to Bora Vale as the Federation's formal representative?"

He didn't want to but knew he had to. He nodded and waved for Rivka to follow. Red moved in front of the mech, who was carrying an armload of rifles. Lindy trailed behind, walking backward. She traveled far enough into the jungle that she could no longer see the Yangorians, wondering how long they would remain standing there.

"We'll need to go this way to reach the corridor." He pointed away from the narrow trail they followed. Rivka touched his arm to be sure. No deception. Maybe the Yindle and the Yangorians didn't know how to lie. That would make her self-selected role of mediator easier. What would make it hard was that neither party wanted it.

She contemplated that as they walked. *How did you sell something to someone who wasn't looking to buy?*

CHAPTER TEN

Tanglewood, *Wyatt Earp* Crash Site

Ankh was feeling better with each passing moment. He chalked it up to the power of an All Guns Blazing pie.

He walked the corridors of the ship on his way to Engineering, where his workshop was located. The silence was both comforting and overwhelming. He'd gotten used to having others in his sphere. Wenceslaus, the big orange cat, was still sleeping, an activity at which the small creature excelled. Without seeing the cat move, he would find him sleeping somewhere else, usually a place Ankh wanted to be. The Crenellian wondered if there were two cats using an interdimensional portal for movement in order to remain one step ahead of their bipedal servants.

The engine room hatch slid open, and Ankh walked inside. A casing had broken free and torn through his holo projectors. He inspected the damage finding more than what was on the surface. He would have to rebuild his system. *Erasmus, priority of repairs. My system requires two days of parts manufacture. Is it possible to get a priority?*

I would not recommend it. We need to repair power systems first. Once those are functional, in approximately one week, we will be able to divert resources to your workshop system. We will need your workshop repaired for power alignment and further engine repair.

I understand, Ankh replied. He sat down on his small chair, closed his eyes, and started scrolling through the damage assessment Erasmus digitally provided. He scanned second and third priorities before digging into the highest-priority repair requests. Most were within the purview of the maintenance bots, requiring welding or other structural repairs, but the engine control panels needed attention Ankh was able to give without the assistance of a bot.

He rolled a stand with a tool pack to the control panel where the engineer usually worked. He climbed up to where he could see. One of the screens had been smashed and the buttons torn off. He logged his observation.

Note to Wyatt Earp *upgrades: heavy equipment and systems are to be secured at all times.* The policy had already been in place, but Ankh had done so much tinkering at the end of the Magistrate's last case that he hadn't bolted everything back down. They'd raced off on vacation faster than they left for a case.

Ankh hesitated. He kept his emotions in check because they added no technical value to his work, but at that moment, the immensity of what had happened hit him like a tidal wave.

Erasmus, can I ask you a question?

Always, my friend. I always have the processing capacity to talk with you.

Was the wreck my fault?

Yes. Erasmus didn't bother easing the delivery. It was a binary question with a known answer. With the variables accounted for, it led to a single conclusion. *It changes nothing that needs to be done. Are you ready to work on that panel now?*

Not yet. What if I've killed the Magistrate and everyone else? Ankh asked.

The last confirmed record is that they departed the cargo bay successfully. I had no other sensor systems during our descent as one hundred percent of my efforts were dedicated to bringing the thrusters online and using them to land the ship.

That doesn't answer my question, but you are right. Destiny's Vengeance *had Chaz at the controls, but what if the Etheric impact affected the runabout's power, and they suffered as did* Wyatt Earp?

Then Chaz would have landed the ship, Erasmus replied confidently. *Everything is speculation, but I suspect they are doing just what we are, which is everything they can to get back to civilization. Are you ready to work now?*

Ankh pulled out the tools needed to remove the top panel and the screen. "I broke it. I'll fix it. And I'll find my friends," he said aloud. *Show me the diagram of this system...*

Destiny's Vengeance Crash Site

"Chaz. Do you know where they are?" Kennedy asked.

"I cannot find them using the scanning system I've constructed using basic radio waves and the hull as a receptor. I can tell you that no Yindle are nearby."

The young woman leaned back in the pilot's chair. Her

mind raced. "It's been hours. We should have heard something more besides 'Hey, the Yindle are here.'"

"I have one living creature entering the clearing. I think it may be Floyd." The AI adjusted the visual feed. "Yes. It is Floyd."

Kennedy jumped up and ran the short distance to the hatch. She hammered the button and ducked out before the hatch had opened all the way.

"Floyd!" she yelled and dashed toward the wombat. The creature cheered and ran to Kennedy. "Where are the others?"

People came. Took them. No angry. Groenwyn said come home. I got lost. Sorry. I here now.

"You're here now. That's right. Let's go inside and lock the door. If people come for us, who will tell the Magistrate what has happened?"

Yes! Floyd agreed. Kennedy grunted as she picked up the rotund wombat. She staggered across the clearing and deposited Floyd inside before climbing into the ship and securing the hatch. The wombat found her way into the galley and curled up on a towel under the table. She was soon fast asleep.

"Chaz, the Yindle have taken Clodagh and the others. What do we do now?"

"We keep repairing the ship. There are no weapons remaining should you desire to mount a rescue operation, and you are not equipped to see the Yindle, like Private Cole when he is wearing his combat suit. Your option is to secure the ship and have it ready for their return. They are competent and will find a way to make it back here."

"What if they don't?" the young woman cried.

"Why don't you ask them how they are?" Chaz wondered.

Kennedy switched to her internal comm chip. *Clodagh, Groenwyn, anyone, are you okay?*

Good to hear from you! Clodagh replied. *I'm sorry, I hadn't thought to let you know we're okay. I'm not used to being on this end of a mission. The Yindle have taken us, but they don't seem hostile. We've been walking for a couple of hours, but I'm not sure how far we've gone. At least we're still in range of the comm chips. Groenwyn has been talking to them the whole time. I think she's making progress.*

Will you be coming back to the ship? Kennedy asked.

When we can. Until then, we'll try to make peace with the Yindle. Maybe Groenwyn can convince them to help us, but we're strangers in a strange land. I'll try to check in every hour. If we move again, hopefully, we'll stay within range.

I'll be here, the young pilot said with little conviction.

"I am concerned about them, too, and will keep refining my systems to extend the range of my scans. If you are able to do the mechanical work outside the ship, we might be able to find them sooner," Chaz suggested.

"Thanks, Chaz." Kennedy clenched her fists for a few moments before burying her face in her hands. The young pilot began to cry.

Chaz started piping music through the ship, classical from a forgotten era, stringed instruments and woodwinds. "Here's what I need you to do," Chaz started. Although ascended, the AI was not used to dealing with emotions that incapacitated one of his colleagues. When Kennedy didn't move, he did not continue and tried a different tack, discussing something inane.

"Maybe we'll just talk for a while. I look forward to getting a body so I can move around. There's a place on Yoll that sells the best ones, but every AI in the galaxy wants one, so thanks to competition, prices have shot beyond the heliosphere. I can requisition some time on a high-end 3D printer, but those are nowhere near as good as the Yoll skins. It's worth saving for. Rivka promised me overtime for bringing everyone to Tanglewood. I was going to take my vacation elsewhere, on the cyber-playground. Maybe I'll meet someone like Ankh. I'm envious of his relationship with Erasmus. Do you have anyone in your life?"

When she didn't answer, Chaz continued with his stream of consciousness. He watched her shoulders relax before she sat up and wiped her nose on her arm. She looked at the screen through unfocused eyes, but at least she wasn't crying. Chaz considered that a small success. When one was ill-equipped for a battle of emotions, the little victories meant everything.

Tanglewood, Yangor Zone

Lots of Yangor in the jungle, but no one is approaching, Cole reported.

The so-called corridor was little more than another trail, barely wide enough for a slightly-built Yangorian, let alone the mech that was failing at destroying as little of the jungle as possible.

DeWan kept glancing over his shoulder and wincing.

"I'm sorry about that and the destruction of your beautiful country that we wrought with the railguns. I am serious when I say that I don't want to see that again."

"We can go a different way back, if the Keeper of Bora Vale allows you to leave." DeWan looked at the jungle ahead, walking easily. He was making casual conversation, not threats.

But Rivka didn't agree with the conclusion.

"We can go that way when we head out, after making sure our crewmate is alive and well."

The Keeper of the Central Wood stopped. "I thought you wanted to go to Bora Vale?"

"We do, on our way to where our ship crashed. Cole, how far are we?"

"Six kilometers, Magistrate." He chopped a metal hand at eleven o'clock to the direction they were headed.

"That way, and not very far."

How long would it take you to go there if you ran straight through, ignoring the Yangorians? Rivka asked. *While we're discussing life with the Keeper of Bora Vale...*

The sun isn't penetrating well enough in here. I'm not recharging. I don't think I can make it all the way on the charge I have left. It sucks that the Etheric power supply isn't working.

Well, now, that changes things. It was just a thought. I'm worried about Ankh. He is so close.

Magistrate? Ankh's voice came through weak and distant. *I'm trying to fix the ship, but it'll take nine months without external assistance. Comm is out. When will help arrive?*

Red turned to smile at Lindy. They both beamed at the news. "I told you," Red said, relief sprinkled over those few words.

If by help, you mean us, we're on our way, but there's a

minor issue with Yangor and us crossing through their territory. We'll get it resolved and be along. I'm pleased that you are alive. We don't have comm either, so we figure in about two weeks someone will come looking for us. I'm sorry for taking us on a holiday where we're disconnected.

I'm sorry for crashing the ship, Ankh replied. *It was my fault and mine alone. I'll take whatever punishment you see fit.*

Rivka shook her head. Red grabbed her before she replied. "Keys to the pizza drone." He nodded vigorously, eyes wide with encouragement.

The Magistrate looked at his hand until he removed it from her shoulder. *We'll talk about it, Ankh. We're happy you're alive and the ship survived the landing.*

"What is a pizza drone?" DeWan asked.

"Intergalactic food delivery. We're kind of spoiled. We like what we like. What about you? What do Yangorians eat?"

"Fruits of the jungle. It provides all we need."

"No farming or hunting. Only gathering?" Rivka posited.

"We hunt. The kinga for one, but that takes many skilled hunters working together. Also the capy, a rodent the kinga eats. We fish, too. It's peaceful."

"Kinga tastes good," Rivka said offhandedly.

"How could you…" DeWan stopped when he glimpsed the railgun. "Never mind. You have weapons that far exceed ours."

Cole, are you getting anything on your scans? Is there any industry anywhere that you can detect?

Nothing, Magistrate. I don't even see any buildings.

"Where did you get your rifles?"

DeWan looked skeptically at her. "Why do you want to know?"

"Because it doesn't seem like there is manufacturing capability on this side of the planet, which means that both you and the Yindle got them from somewhere. Maybe Tanglewood's planetwide government, the one that seems to have forgotten you existed?"

"I think I'll let the Keeper answer your questions." DeWan stopped and pointed into the jungle ahead. "Bora Vale."

I can see people but no buildings. There are about a thousand of them within four square kilometers, Cole reported.

"Don't want to keep the Keeper waiting, do we?" Rivka asked and nudged DeWan forward. He resisted. "I insist."

He caved, and with his head hung low, he trudged forward. The path widened, the closer they approached to the mystical place called Bora Vale. To the untrained eyes of the strangers, it looked like the same jungle they had traveled through since they left *Destiny's Vengeance* early that morning. They pushed through a final heavy frond to find a new world. Trees with broad bases, split and welcoming with doorways and glassless windows.

Yangorians milled about performing various tasks, their light brown skin and clothing blending well with the jungle beyond.

"Good morning," Rivka said pleasantly to no one in particular. She waved casually, knowing why the Yangorians were staring. Cole had stepped through the brush and the shining metal mech stopped behind her. All eyes were on the technological monster.

Rockets? Cole asked.

No need. I think they've seen what they need to see. Rivka continued aloud, "The Keeper of Bora Vale, please." She had to tap DeWan's shoulder to get his attention. He strode across the open area before taking a hard right. At the second massive tree past where he'd cornered, he stopped.

To Rivka, it looked like any other jungle tree with modifications to open a gap between the immense roots, yet it still looked natural.

"Will you introduce us, or do we just go in?" Rivka asked.

"He will come to you when he is ready." DeWan inched away from Rivka. She cozied up next to him, gripping his arm to keep him from escaping.

"Thank you for your help," she told him.

He wasn't feeling her thanks. His discomfort at being in the middle of Bora Vale was palpable. She didn't need to read his mind to see that.

"Why are you so uncomfortable here?"

"I am the Keeper of the Central Wood. My place is there, not here."

"You could have told someone else to bring us. It didn't have to be you."

He turned to her, face drooping. "Now you tell me."

"I'm sorry. With your top-down structure, I didn't think to ask. I thought you were doing what you didn't want to make your people do. If you're uncomfortable, imagine how they would feel right now. Subconsciously, you did right by your people."

He smiled faintly, freezing when he looked up. A young female Yangorian stood there watching.

CHAPTER ELEVEN

Tanglewood, Bora Vale

"I am the Keeper of Bora Vale," she said.

"Not a dude," Red whispered. Lindy elbowed him.

"I am Magistrate Rivka Anoa from the Federation. Our ship crashed not far from here. Our escape shuttle crashed on the other side of the ridge behind us, in Yindle territory. We request your assistance to help us get out of here."

She focused on DeWan. "You wear the emblem of the Keeper of the Central Wood. Are you the intruders' champion?"

DeWan shifted from one foot to another. Rivka leaned around him to look for a symbol or logo that would identify him as something different from any other Yangorian. She saw nothing distinct.

"I am not. We attempted to detain the strangers, but that did not go well for us. They are far too powerful to be stopped by conventional means."

What's that supposed to mean? Lindy wondered.

We can bring these trees down if we lace them with the railguns, Red offered.

I need to grab some sunlight. I see a spot over there. Permission to move, Cole requested.

Granted, Rivka replied, watching the Keepers' reactions when Cole walked across the area to stand in the bright beam.

Drink up, my baby, Cole purred.

Rivka rubbed her head. "My apologies if we've damaged your calm. We crashed and have been met by much hostility. We refuse to be taken prisoner, especially on a planet that is subject to Federation Law. Even if the Yindle and Yangorians have their own laws, you're still subject to ours, and ours say you're not taking me prisoner."

"What if we don't care about your Federation Law?" the Keeper of Bora Vale asked.

"It doesn't matter if you care. You're still subject to the law. That is the bedrock of civilized society, that we operate within a single framework. There can be no surprises for people simply going about their business. Getting arrested for something that is not a crime is no way to run a country. The Federation provides stability across innumerable planets, creating conditions where the inhabitants can prosper. It is not a restrictive framework, but it is what applies."

The Keeper spread her arms wide to take in the entirety of the largest Yangor villages. "We have laws and happily work within them. Why do we need more laws?"

Why indeed? You only need the right laws, Rivka thought. "Not more, Keeper of Bora Vale, just ones that address circumstances out of the norm, like survivors marooned in your area being treated like friends instead of enemies. But we don't need a law for that, do we?"

The Keeper watched Rivka intently as if looking into her soul.

"We need to determine your intentions before you are escorted out of Yangor."

Rivka smiled and leaned close to gently place a hand on the Keeper's shoulder. "We only want to check on our ship and our crewmate, who we know is alive, but my ship is disabled. We politely request your assistance."

The damage to the jungle from the railguns showed in the Keeper's mind. She knew about the display of firepower. She had also seen the rifles in Cole's metal arms.

Drop the rifles, Cole, carefully.

"You can recover your rifles, Keeper of the Central Wood," Rivka said before turning to the Keeper of Bora Vale. "That's a sign of good faith. We probably did not need to take them in the first place, but I'm not a fan of getting shot in the back. I wasn't certain the people of the Central Wood were not going to follow us and try to take us captive. We are not ones to be held against our will."

"No, I guess you're not." The keeper made no move to continue the conversation, leave, or do anything other than stand there.

"The sanctity of the jungle," Rivka started. "The call of birds and leaves fluttering in the breeze. The shadows of the undergrowth and the cool of the bare ground. You live in a paradise and deserve your peace."

The Keeper faced the Magistrate, looking directly up into her face. "Maybe you understand more than we expect."

DeWan nodded and walked away. After attempting to pick up all the rifles and failing miserably, he stacked half of them and trudged under the weight of the other half as he made his way out of the village. Rivka and the Keeper of Bora Vale watched him until he disappeared into the jungle.

"One of his people shot one of ours, unfortunately," Rivka said, barely above a whisper.

"And paid for it with his life. There is no harsher penalty." The keeper had been thoroughly briefed. Her tone was even, but her eyes glistened for a moment.

Rivka walked in a small circle, looking the village over. "What can I say that will move us closer to a mutually beneficial relationship?"

"I wish I knew," the Keeper admitted. "We don't get strangers in Yangor."

"You seem like you are terminally on the watch for them, though." Rivka studied the keeper carefully without looking directly at her. She gave away more with her body language than the Yindle.

By far.

"We are always on the lookout for Yindle. They are like termites, eating away at the roots of Yangor." Her lip twitched with the pronouncement.

"They think the same of you, which doesn't help either of you close the gap. They wanted us to pick sides. We wouldn't. That was when they stopped being friendly. For the record, we are on the side of the Federation."

Are you charged up yet? Rivka asked.

We've been here ten minutes, Magistrate. I probably need eight hours to a full charge.

Are you able to depart?

If the going is easy and support systems like the scanner are turned off, I might just make it.

That'll do.

"Keeper of Bora Vale. I ask for your clearance to travel to our ship, which is only six kilometers from here."

"We know of your ship. How could we not? It flew right over our heads. We are watching it closely for invaders, I mean, Federation members disembarking." The keeper blew out her breath. "If I don't give my approval, you will go anyway, won't you?"

"I would much rather have your blessing," Rivka countered.

"I shall not give it, but I will not hinder you. When you return, maybe I will have the answer for what you can say to start a dialog."

"I look forward to that time, Keeper of Bora Vale." Rivka twirled her finger in the air. *Give us a bearing and then shut down everything that's not critical.*

Cole pointed with his whole arm in the direction they needed to go. He strolled away from the sunlight's comfort, taking care not to step on the rifles stacked before him.

Rivka waved to the keeper and followed Cole through Bora Vale, with Red and Lindy in tow.

Red kept glancing back but couldn't discern if anyone was following. "Plan for the worst and hope for the best," Red mumbled.

"Did we make any progress back there, Magistrate?" Lindy asked. "I don't have a warm and fuzzy, but I don't feel like we're threatened either."

"Time will tell. Let's keep our eyes open, just in case."

. . .

Tanglewood, Yindle Village beyond *Destiny's Vengeance*

Too many Yindle brandished their rifles as they stood around the four women and Sahved. The prisoners were sitting on a mossy knoll at the base of a great tree inside which the rest of the Yindle had disappeared.

"How big is it in there?" Ryleigh asked. She leaned this way and that to catch a glimpse inside, but all she could see was darkness. Aurora shrugged. She had no better vantage point. "I could use a drink of water."

"Maybe we should just leave. They don't look like they're going to shoot us," Sahved suggested.

"Groenwyn is the only one who can handle being shot, so I recommend we not do that," Clodagh remarked. "I'm thirsty, too, but we need to hang on."

"I agree. I will Pod-doc when we are in a position for Pod-docking." Sahved nodded emphatically. "I cannot be the greatest anchor in the history of anchors. I have not even studied the law yet. So much Pod-docking and study left in my life."

"We all need to take the plunge," Aurora chimed in. Ryleigh nodded. Groenwyn turned toward them and looked from face to face. "Then we might be able to go without water for a while longer."

"It will change you if you let it, so don't let the nanos make you think you're somebody you're not. They are there to keep you from dying because this business is hard but so rewarding. Just over a year ago, I was arrested for breaking into shops on a space station. Now, I'm the At-Large Ambassador to the faerie world of Azfelius. They have joined the Federation because of their abilities with the Etheric but are to be called on only if the Kurtherians return. We respect that, but there is so much they can teach us. That is the gift I received once I joined the team—the freedom to be who I am, to contribute to a higher ideal, and custom-programmed nanos just for me."

"Sign me up!" Sahved declared. The women looked at him.

"You're already signed up," Clodagh said slowly, gesturing toward herself and the others before nodding at their guards. "It's a small, exclusive club, but it looks like we've all joined. Is this what every mission looks like when you guys go planetside?"

Groenwyn started to say something but stopped. Shaped new words and stopped again before sighing, resigning herself to a simple answer. "Pretty much, but sometimes they shoot first."

"We've got that going for us," Clodagh declared. The four women laughed while Sahved continued to wonder what was going on. His stomach started to heave, but he tamped it down. "Don't you dare."

"Fine. I'm fine. It's all fine. The sky and jungle are fine. And you, Yemilorian man, you are fine, too." Sahved's eyes were wide as he looked at the ground and clenched his jaws in an effort to control his less than cooperative insides.

The Yindle guards remained stoic, no one except the leader talking to the prisoners. One lifted the barrel of her rifle and aimed at the Yemilorian. Groenwyn stepped in front of him, begging for calm. The guard eventually let her aim drop, waving her barrel at the platinum-green-haired woman to sit down.

"Thank you," Groenwyn told her before adding, "We are one with the jungle."

"Where have you heard that?" the Yindle leader asked, stepping from within the tree.

"Nowhere. It just seems right in the middle of such magnificence." She stood and turned slowly to breathe deeply of the fresh jungle air. "Being one with nature is a laudable way to live."

The leader leaned back inside the tree and said something they didn't catch. There was an animated conversation before the Yindle addressed them again. "We cannot hold any who are one with the jungle." He motioned at the Yindle guards. "Go. You are free."

The Yindle quickly disappeared into the jungle.

"That was mighty nice of them," Clodagh said. She stood, stretched, and turned one way and then another. "How in the hell do we get back to the ship?"

CHAPTER TWELVE

Between Bora Vale and the *Wyatt Earp* Crash Site

We're on our way, Ankh, Rivka said.

Busy, Ankh replied.

"If there was any doubt he's fine, that cleared it all up," Red said while intently watching the jungle they were passing through. Cole led the way, but slowly, conserving as much power as he could. He cut a straight line toward *Wyatt Earp.* "Good news, though. Looks like we might be sleeping in our own beds tonight."

"I'll take that. It was a little cramped on the *Vengeance,*" Lindy noted.

"The only problem I have with staying here is our crew. They are going to wonder what happened to us."

We can send up a flare, Cole suggested.

That's not a bad idea. Well done! Rivka contemplated how to pull it off, then dismissed her effort as she came up with a better plan. *We'll ask Ankh to do it. Give us a quick scan, Cole. Anyone following?*

Lots o' Yangorians 'round these parts, ma'am, Cole drawled.

Red stabbed a finger at the mech's back. *When you run out of power, we're leaving you in there.*

About that. I'm going to have to shut down before we get there.

You better be dressed in there, Rivka stated.

I didn't have time to grab my trunks. Sorry about that. No one answered. *Got you! I'm wearing shorts, but that's it. I knew it was going to be a hot day. I'm out of water, for reference.*

How far? Rivka wondered.

It's just up ahead. I can see it in the treetops, through breaks in the foliage. Hull looks to be intact. It's balanced evenly, so we shouldn't have a deck pitch or anything. Just need to climb thirty or so meters up to it. Oh, shit.

The mech stopped, mid-stride before evening its stance and stood as a silent sentinel. The back opened and Cole climbed out. He closed it after him. He was wearing unlaced boots, his body covered in a sheen of sweat and underwear soaked through.

"It was fucking hot in there!" he exclaimed, looking for sympathy and finding none. Rivka avoided looking at the man. Lindy chuckled at his disheveled state.

"They shot me," Red countered and turned his shoulder toward the private. It was fully healed but there was blood surrounding the tear on the sweaty shirt. "And they ruined my favorite shirt."

"You've worn worse than that and in the presence of important people." Rivka raised one eyebrow before pointing at the way ahead. "At least we won't be tearing up their jungle."

Cole shrugged. "You people were living the life of Reilly

out here. A breeze, shade...*damn*. You ground-pounders have things pretty nice."

Red stood with his mouth open.

"Perspective, Vered," Lindy explained. "Everything is about perspective. Didn't you tell me the first question a warrior asks is 'How can we make this suck worse?'"

"That was Terry Henry Walton, but I'll make believe it was me. I thought *he* was living the good life, riding in the suit, scaring the shit out of the Magistrate, seeing the Yangorians in the trees..."

A bug landed on Cole's back and bit deep.

Rivka twirled her finger in the air and started hiking. Red hurried to get in front of her, delivering a kind word to the private on his way past. "Sucks to be you."

Cole contorted himself to scratch the itch between his shoulder blades. He waved his hands to try to drive off the bugs as he followed the Magistrate. He was completely unarmed.

Rivka looked over her shoulder. "I'd give you my blaster so you could feel like you're accomplishing something, but you'll get sweat all over it."

"I do as I'm told, Magistrate." He stopped and laced up one boot. Bounded forward to catch up, then stopped and did the second boot.

The four continued in silence. Red moved slower than the mech had, but that was because he didn't see the Yangorians. He tried to look for movement, but their ability to blend into the environment was complete.

Ankh, we see the ship. Can you be ready to drop a cable that we can climb up? Red requested. *And throw down a jug of water. We're all a bit thirsty.*

It's all set up, except for the water. I'll be right back, Ankh replied.

I'm glad you're okay, big guy. Red looked away quickly as if he hadn't said it.

Five minutes later, they were standing beneath *Wyatt Earp*. It looked massive, blocking out the sun more than the trees in which it rested.

"What a sweet ride." Rivka stood with her hands on her hips, head thrown back, and reveled in looking at the ship that had served them well, if only briefly. *Wyatt* would fly again.

Ankh? Hey, buddy, we're here, Red remarked, using the internal comm chip.

The hatch scraped against a branch as it opened. A cable with a hook slowly made its way to the ground.

"You first, Magistrate," Red ordered. He and Lindy turned their backs to guard the lift. Rivka grabbed the hook, and it started to pull her up.

"There's a great view from up here. I see you!" She let go with one hand so she could point at a figure on a tree branch. Red searched along her line of sight until he could focus on the spot. Without movement, he wasn't sure if he was looking at a Yangorian or not.

The cable reached the top and Rivka scrambled over a metal plate balanced across the opening. It had a hole in the middle where a maintenance bot's tether had been lowered. The bot pressed itself against the plate until she let go, releasing the pressure pulling it toward the hatch. It immediately started lowering the cable.

Ankh walked down the corridor and casually handed Rivka the water bottle. She looked at him closely before taking a swig. She leaned out the hatch and yelled toward the ground, "Water bottle on its way."

Cole clapped his hands and she dropped it. He caught it deftly, swinging his hands and arms down and in an arc to slow the jug without breaking anything. He took a long drink before handing it to Lindy. She drank heartily, and Red finished it.

"You next," he told Cole. The private didn't argue, racing skyward with the retracting cable.

Then Lindy, and Red was the last to get hauled up. The maintenance bot groaned as it retracted the cable more slowly than any of the others. Lindy tried to look innocent.

"He's smaller than he used to be."

When the cable was a hand's breadth from the plate, Red released it with one hand to grab the plate. He pulled himself up and over, rolling over the maintenance bot and coming back to his feet.

Ankh cleared the opening and cycled the hatch closed.

With the ship sealed, the air handling system made its presence known. "How I have missed you, *Wyatt Earp*." Cole celebrated briefly before excusing himself. "Is the water good, Ankh? I'd like to take a shower."

"Keep it short, please. The recycling systems are not operating at full capacity," the Crenellian explained.

Rivka continued to look at him. "Are you bigger?"

"The right explanation is more robust to better withstand violent impacts to the brain-carrying device."

"Did you call your body 'the brain-carrying device?'" Red liked it.

"It's better than meat puppet," Ankh countered.

"Ankh, you've given yourself a sense of humor, too."

"That wasn't meant to be funny." Ankh's facial expression remained unchanged.

"What's not to love about this guy?" Red asked before nodding to Lindy. "I'm sure there's plenty of food left. I've been hungry since we crashed."

"We crashed fifteen minutes after you said you couldn't eat another bite. Since then, you've eaten a local creature."

"It tried to eat Floyd." That was Red's only defense. "Going to the galley. Let us know what needs to be done and we'll get on it, Ankh." Red waved over his head and sauntered down the corridor. Lindy sidled up next to him. They disappeared around the corner.

"I speak for all of us when I say that I am relieved that you are alive."

"Me, too," Ankh agreed. "And you. I am sorry that I crashed the ship, Magistrate."

"So what? We've blown up some major buildings and ships with a lot of people on board. Sometimes you do what you have to do. All in the furtherance of our particular fields. Mention it no more. We'll stay here tonight, and first thing in the morning, we'll head back to *Destiny's Vengeance*, which is mostly unscathed. She just needs a part for her engine. Let me see..." Rivka checked her pockets until she found the scrap of paper with Clodagh's scribbles. "This."

"I don't have that. I can print it, but it'll take a day."

"Then let's get started. We'll leave when it's ready, assuming Cole's mech suit is recharged."

"It probably won't recharge on the jungle floor. I'll need to fabricate an auxiliary power source to charge it." Ankh looked up at Rivka, but he was much closer than he used to be. "I assume the Etheric power supply is not functioning? That appears to be consistent in this section of the planet."

"Hard down," Rivka replied. Her stomach growled, and she patted her abs. "The meat puppet needs a chocolate shake and maybe some more pizza. It has been a long day. I think Red bogarted the kinga meat."

"My translation chip must not be working," Ankh said evenly.

"I think Red ate more than his fair share of the creature he killed."

"He is bigger than most."

On cue, Red screamed from around the corner. "Ankh! You fucking little wankstain. Where's the pizza? You called down the thunder! I'm coming for you, and I'm bringing Hell with me!"

"But can easily be brought to his knees. If you'll excuse me." Ankh turned and rushed away. Rivka ran after him, catching him in two steps.

"I want some of that pizza, too." Rivka glared at him.

"Fine. It's in the backup fridge behind the main cooler."

"We have a backup fridge?" Rivka turned Ankh loose and he made his escape as Red came pounding down the corridor. The Magistrate blocked it with her body. "It's in the backup fridge behind the main one." Rivka chuckled, and that led to a full belly laugh. "Just because we were in dire straits, worried about each other, it doesn't mean he's not going to fuck with you. Your face is still red."

The big bodyguard ran a hand over his head. "He got me good."

"Probably because you're so predictable," Lindy called from down the corridor while munching on a cold slice.

"I like what I like." He turned. "Hey!" He hurried away, slapping her butt on his way past.

"I'll give you ten minutes to stop that," Lindy told him, turning and following him.

Leaving Rivka by herself. She looked one way and then the other. "I got nothing," she said out loud and headed for the galley. "Except maybe a plan to engage the Keeper of Bora Vale, which is a pretty nice thing to have."

The thought added a skip to her step.

CHAPTER THIRTEEN

Tanglewood, the Deep Jungle

"I think this is one of our footprints." Ryleigh kneeled next to an imprint in a gap between two heavy fern-like growths. The others joined her. No one could tell for sure.

"Sahved is super strong, right?" Aurora asked.

"Because of heavy gravity on Yemilore, my strength appears to be greatly enhanced." He struck a ridiculous pose with his gangly body to show off his biceps.

"Then you can climb the biggest tree here and take a look." As one, they turned toward a massive trunk right next to Sahved.

"Strength and climbing are two different things. Very different." He shook his head and twirled his fingers.

"We're lost, and Kennedy and Chaz can't tell us which way to go until they rig a direction finder with the parts they have on hand. The alternative is you climbing up there and taking a look." Clodagh pointed up the tree.

"I would prefer not to." Sahved started backing away.

"Get up the tree," Clodagh insisted.

Sahved faced the trunk and reached around to grip the sides. He put one oversized foot against it and pulled to check his balance. He looked back to Clodagh. She stomped her foot and pointed upward.

He pulled and stepped, slid his hands up the sides and stepped again, repeating the process until he reached the lowest branch. He climbed onto it, standing and hugging the tree.

"Don't look down," Clodagh called through cupped hands.

"What?" he asked while looking down. He started heaving.

The women ran for cover to avoid the spray.

"He needs to get over that," Clodagh mumbled.

Groenwyn agreed. "As soon as possible."

When he recovered his composure, he tried to scan the horizon, but his view was blocked in all directions by other trees. Sahved started talking to himself. "You're one of the team. You need to carry your weight. You are stronger than all of them combined, yet they carry you. Shameful. You cannot go back to Yemilore being carried by girls. Shame!"

He steeled his features and grabbed the trunk, pulling himself upward. Soon the motion was natural, and he flowed up the tree as quickly as if he were walking. When the trunk dwindled in size and the places to put his feet all but disappeared, he finally dared to look around.

"I see the hills and the saddle!" he shouted, pointing.

Clodagh waited.

"Anything else?" she finally asked.

"Nope." He started to climb down, taking his time to avoid slipping.

"Do we head in that direction and hope we get close enough that Chaz can ping our chips?" Aurora asked.

"Does anyone have a better idea?" Clodagh canvassed the group. "Sahved, wait! Climb back up. I have an idea."

Chaz, is there any way you can send up a flare so we can see where you are? Sahved is in a treetop and watching.

Stand by, Chaz replied. *We do not have a flare, but we can bring Red's fire back to life and you can look for the smoke.*

"Hang on, big fella! They're going to start a fire. Look for the smoke."

Sahved grumbled as he sat on a branch, arms wrapped around the thin remainder of the treetop.

The fire is hot. One green log is kicking up heavy white smoke. Can you see it?

"See anything?" Clodagh shouted.

Sahved pointed almost straight down. "Right there."

He started to climb down, hesitating after a few steps, expecting to get redirected once more.

The engineer continued to point in the direction of the smoke. Sahved hurried downward at breakneck speed. When he hit the ground, he faced his crewmates.

Clodagh clapped him on the shoulder. "Well done, Sahved. You know you'll climb every tree from now until the end of time because you proved you could do it."

She headed in the direction he had pointed. The others fell in behind. He brought up the rear. "Until the end of time?" he wondered. "That seems like a long time to be stuck with tree-climbing duty."

Within five minutes, they were walking through smoke drifting lazily through the jungle. *You can put that fire out. I think we're almost there,* Clodagh told Kennedy.

They emerged into the clearing where *Destiny's Vengeance* sat peacefully. The first thing they noticed was the mech wasn't back. "The Magistrate's not here?"

Kennedy shook her head. Tears formed in her eyes. "I'm so glad you're not injured."

Clodagh shrugged. "I think they were walking us around in circles, giving us part of the harassment package. If there's a next time, we'll refuse to go with them. It's late, and we still don't have any water. First thing tomorrow, we'll try again. Thanks, Sahved. You helped get us home. I wasn't keen on sleeping on the ground in the middle of Bug Central."

Floyd found Groenwyn first, almost knocking her over. The wombat cheered and bounced with her friends' return. Tiny Man Titan ran in little circles faster and faster until he fell over.

They retired to the ship. "Any news, Chaz?" Clodagh asked.

"No news from the Magistrate. I will keep my ears open, so to speak."

"And then what, Chaz? If we don't hear from her, what do we do?"

"I already had this conversation once today," Chaz lamented. "We'll prepare the ship to be repaired, and then we'll conduct rescue operations until somebody in authority tells us something different. I have no intention of leaving this planet without knowing exactly what happened to all our people. I hope I have your support on this."

"For an AI, you're pretty determined."

"I'm free because of the Magistrate. I won't leave her to rot while I enjoy what she gave me."

"Me neither, Chaz. You've brightened my day, despite the topic. Thank you."

"Time to get to work, which means you need to get some sleep and be ready for tomorrow. I'll keep watch. Ship's counselor is now closed for new business," Chaz deadpanned.

Clodagh took two steps down the corridor before slapping her waist and searching it. "They kept my blaster."

"Clodagh, can you wake up, please?" Chaz was insistent, pinging her internal chip as well as using the speakers in the corridor.

The engineer finally roused. Sat up and stared at the bulkhead like a zombie.

"Clodagh? Are you awake?"

She blinked as her eyelids threatened to close. "I'm up," she said without conviction. "How long was I asleep? I feel like shit."

"Thirty-four minutes," Chaz replied.

"That would be why," Clodagh mumbled before digging her fists into her eyes to scrub them clear. "What do you need, Chaz?"

"The Yindle are on the move. We've had a number run past the ship. They do not seem to be interested in us; we're simply in a traffic corridor of some sort."

"Which way are they going?"

"In the direction the Magistrate went, toward Yangor."

Clodagh stood on shaky legs. "If we wondered about whether our people were alive and well, I think we have our answer. Who else can rile a whole nation?"

"Although it comes across as less than flattering, your logic is sound," Chaz answered.

"Sometimes that's reality, Chaz. What do we need to do?"

"What is there for you to do?"

"We could race out there and get ourselves captured again. Or we could start a bonfire and send smoke signals over the mountain."

"It is dark outside. Smoke probably won't be visible," the AI noted.

"Right. Thirty-four minutes of sleep. Still night. I tell you what, wake us all an hour before sunrise unless something happens before then, and we'll build that fire so we have some serious smoke come daybreak. We'll let Rivka know where we are."

"Capital idea," Chaz agreed. "Sleep well, Clodagh."

"My brain hurts," the engineer complained as she laid back down to sleep. The decking of the corridor seemed harder than it had when she first relaxed. "It sucks to suck, so no sucking!"

"Has Master Vered returned and is speaking with the engineer's voice?" Chaz taunted.

"Something like that," Clodagh muttered. "And they better bring my boyfriend with them."

Wyatt Earp Crash Site

"Would you pack your trash already?" Rivka stood with

her hands on her hips, watching as Red fiddled with his gear.

"I thought I lost all my stuff. It's like I've been given a new lease on life, so I want to make sure I optimize my loadout. Don't get your panties in a bunch, Magistrate."

She leaned back and crossed her arms. "What did you say?"

Red stopped, frozen by the ice in Rivka's voice. "Oops." He straightened and smiled. She continued to glare. "I'm sorry. I went too far. It won't happen again. I'll finish up right now and be ready to go."

"Maybe I don't want you to go with me. Lindy and I will be just fine."

"It's my job to protect you with my life if need be."

"Not today, Red. You pissed me off, so stay here and do whatever Ankh tells you to. Help Cole get the suit powered up. There's plenty to do, like figure out how to fire a signal rocket over the *Vengeance*. In the meantime, I think the all-female team will have a better chance with the Keeper of Bora Vale. You've given me an easy reason to leave you behind."

"Fuck, man! I said I was sorry," Red pleaded.

"Decision's been made. So let it be said, so let it be written, so let it be done." Rivka headed for the hatch, patting her pocket to make sure Reaper, her neutron pulse weapon, was there. She wore her body armor vest under a light shirt. Lindy was dressed the same way but carried her railgun, a blaster, and a belt loaded with grenades.

Rivka looked at them curiously.

"Just in case. You never know when you're going to

need grenades." Lindy turned back to Red and drew her fingers across her lips, the gesture for her husband to zip it.

He stood with shoulders dropped and chin on chest. "I'll see you when you get home," he said softly.

Ankh ran the maintenance bot to lower Lindy and then Rivka to the ground.

Once down, Rivka checked her gear, which included a double load of water, same as Lindy. "We probably need to find a water source as close as possible, just in case," Lindy suggested.

"*Wyatt Earp* has plenty of water on board. The only thing we need is to get out of here, but I like to leave a place better than I found it." They started walking. "Already, we've destroyed a bit of jungle, killed a Yangorian and a kinga, and intruded into two separate fiefdoms, or whatever they are."

Lindy listened while watching the trees for movement. They knew the Yangorians were there, but the natives remained hidden.

"The fact that the people don't know about the Federation is disconcerting. Joining the Federation is supposed to be a planetwide decision. Everyone should have at least been aware of the negotiations and what they were signing up for. The Yindle and Yangorians seemed to lack the technology to share information or understanding of what they've committed to, which brings me to my dilemma. Is it my place to rectify this for Tanglewood? The alternative is that we simply fix the ships and leave."

"That would be easiest," Lindy agreed. "How long do you think negotiations will take?"

"With the right leverage, no time at all. Without any

leverage, forever. There doesn't seem to be any incentive for either party. They are both satisfied with their lots in life, or so it seems. It's hard not to overstep our bounds since they are signed members of the Federation, but the bigger issue is that they probably shouldn't be. If I talk to Yindle and Yangor, am I working with the right parties in this dispute?"

Lindy shrugged. "I really don't know."

"It's called jurisdiction, along with the case or controversy clause. I have jurisdiction, but the real case is with the planetary leadership and not these two factions. Sonofabitch! I've been going down the wrong path. We need to get to the other side of Tanglewood."

"Looks to be a long walk, Magistrate." Lindy pointed with her railgun barrel at the mech in the bushes ahead. They walked past it to find the trail much clearer because of the damage Cole had caused due to the size of the suit. They stopped to examine the plants.

"They're already regrowing."

"Which means that before long, we're going to have a hard time finding our way. How many days before the walk back to Yindle becomes problematic?"

"All things being equal, I think we'll be able to leave first thing tomorrow and still see our trail."

The hike back to Bora Vale didn't seem to take anywhere near as long as their trip from the village to the *Wyatt Earp* a day earlier. When they strolled into the village, they both smiled and waved at anyone they saw.

They stopped at three different trees before finding the one they had been at the day before. The rifles were gone, but the marks made by the mech's metal feet were clear.

They stood outside the opening that defined the doorway and waited. After ten minutes, they looked at each other. "Do you think we should knock?" Rivka asked.

Lindy shook her head. "DeWan didn't knock. I think we just have to wait."

"Don't want to make them angry at us for a social faux pas." Rivka thought for a moment. "Any more than they already are."

"The jungle is healing itself rather quickly. I think no damage is permanent, except the death of that one Yangorian."

"He shouldn't have shot Red."

"We fired first," Lindy countered.

"But not at them. We showed the storm unleashed. Sometimes, you have to earn respect through displays of strength. They weren't giving us any choice. Humble visitors can be held at arm's length without being made prisoners. After that bullshit on Pretaria where they put us in a prison cell and tried to bake us, I won't let that happen again. You weren't with us on our first few cases, but suffice to say, I will fight with everything at my disposal rather than be detained against my will."

"That was Red's take on it, too. He didn't mean anything earlier. You know the big knucklehead. He's as loyal as a good dog."

"I know, but he needs to take care. We're trying to improve how we treat people, and that goes for each other."

"'You called down the thunder!'" Lindy mimicked.

They both laughed. "He has a rough edge that we probably shouldn't try too hard to polish," Rivka admitted.

"How long do you think the war between those two will last?"

"Forever? You know they like each other. Yesterday, Ankh told you he was busy when you were looking for information, yet he took the time to mess with Red. Ankh never does things for no reason, but he is investing a certain amount of time in keeping Red on his toes."

"Strange companions and stranger friends. I think those two need to go on a case by themselves. Wouldn't that be interesting?"

"I predict fireworks, blood, and much running," Lindy replied.

"I'd bet on that." Rivka turned around to find the Keeper of Bora Vale standing patiently. "I'm sorry, I didn't hear you arrive. Good morning, Keeper."

"What were you talking about that brought such mirth to you both?" the Yangorian asked.

Lindy stepped back to let the two leaders talk. Rivka gestured with her head for the bodyguard to stand at her side.

"Lindy's partner is the big man you saw yesterday. They are my bodyguards because I have to go into criminal havens where my safety is at risk. The member of my crew who survived the crash," Rivka pointed in the direction of *Wyatt Earp*, "is a Crenellian, a small humanoid race of intellectuals who generally can't be bothered with emotions. Those two are the most unlikely of friends. They have a running series of practical jokes they play on each other. Everyone needs a friend who can make them laugh, even if it's only at themselves."

"Everyone needs friends," Lindy added quietly.

The keeper looked up at the two. "I agree." She made no move to continue.

"I wanted to apologize for our intrusion into your culture. I am reminded where my jurisdiction comes from. I thought my issue was with Yindle and Yangor, but it is not. It is with the primary government of Tanglewood. I expect those are the people who gave both you and the Yindle the rifles."

"You would be right. They issued them so we could protect ourselves." The keeper kept her chin up as she spoke. She maintained the dignity of her office.

"Since the Yindle also have them, how is it any different from what you had before?"

"We are able to protect ourselves from the kinga, but it has not changed our relationship with the Yindle. We knew they also received rifles. Now we must travel armed at all times."

"Have you ever had a firefight with the Yindle?"

"Thank the jungle, no." The keeper sounded sad.

"Then what's it all for? I like to think that people are better together. I expect that you stay in your territory and the Yindle stay in theirs. You don't cross each other. I thought the Yindle said they've had plenty of skirmishes with Yangor."

The keeper chuckled softly. "Skirmishes? You mean when they fire randomly into our jungle? I'm surprised they don't shoot themselves in their idiocy."

Rivka touched the keeper on the arm. "What can I say to help us start a dialog?"

"You've already said it," the keeper allowed. In the young Yangorian's mind, Rivka's care for the jungle was most persuasive. A runner had told her that Rivka and Lindy had stopped to examine the new growth.

"I still think that you can bridge your differences with the Yindle, even though I must admit that I don't know what those differences are. You both love the jungle and live as one with it."

"They're green," the keeper started. Rivka's mouth fell open before she continued, "But that's not it. It's the jungle's way of blending in. On that side of the hill, the rains come more often, keeping everything green. On this side, we have more browns. I am curious. If a Yangorian lived in Yindle, would they change color?"

"I'm not going to lecture on the history of the human race, but I suggest that it doesn't matter. The important thing is, where are you leading your people?"

"What do you mean?" The keeper was curious. "They protect the village, our section of the jungle, and find food."

"There's so much more to life than just living. The experiences of visiting new places, of doing things, of love."

"We have mates. We visit places. All my people know the wood. They can go where we need them to go."

"You give the orders?"

"It's what the keeper does. But I also give orders to other keepers. That is only for the Keeper of Bora Vale. Our duty is to protect Yangor."

Rivka breathed deeply, tasting the jungle's scent. The filtered light cast beams and shadows across the multi-colored undergrowth. "Self-actualization?" Rivka posited.

"I don't know what that is."

"Poor choice of words on my part. I don't really know

either. When our ship is operational, we can go on board, and I'll show you what else is out there."

The keeper's gaze drifted beyond Rivka and her focus sharpened. The Magistrate glanced in that direction to find a Yangorian sprinting toward them.

"I'll leave you to it while I talk to my colleague," Rivka offered tactfully and nodded toward the side where she and Lindy huddled, focusing their nano-enhanced hearing on the conversation between the runner and the keeper.

"Yindle, massing on the Barrier Peak."

"Are they going to attack?" The keeper's tone was incredulous.

"No one knows, but they have weapons, including one of the strangers' devices." They both looked at Lindy and Rivka, whose feigned conversation became real.

"How did they get one of our blasters?" Rivka whispered.

Lindy scrunched her brow as she thought through the possibilities. "One of the crew must have taken it when they went out on guard duty or something else, and either lost it or had it stolen. Maybe it was Sahved, but it might be loaded. That wouldn't be good. It would turn the tables on the Yangorians," Lindy whispered back.

The keeper started to wave and gesture. The runner bowed and beat a hasty retreat back the way he'd come.

Yangorians started running throughout Bora Vale. Rivka returned to the keeper. "I couldn't help but hear. We are not on the side of the Yindle. I have no idea how they got one of our weapons. It can only be a blaster, which is nowhere near the power of a railgun, but still far deadlier than your rifles. If you'll allow it, my people and I will go up there and stop the Yindle. If they haven't attacked before, then this boldness is probably because of us, whether they think we came over here to tell you their secrets, or they think they have an advantage because of the blaster. Either way, it comes back to us, and I feel like I need to fix this."

The keeper's eyes narrowed. She was not happy. "Don't you think you've done enough?"

"No," Rivka replied instantly. "Not anywhere near enough. I will end this battle before it begins, and I don't want to stop until there's peace between Yindle and Yangor."

Red, load up with all your gear and get here on the double! The Yindle are trying to start a war, and Rivka said she's going to stop it. Lindy didn't wait for the order from Rivka. She knew they'd need what horsepower they had. The mech was out of action. That meant Rivka, Red, and Lindy.

On my way, Red replied firmly.

Business as usual.

CHAPTER FOURTEEN

Tanglewood, Bora Vale

"Damn, Red! Did you sprint the whole way?" Rivka asked. Less than twenty minutes had passed since they'd called for him.

"It was only six kilometers," Red replied, breathing heavily but not too fast. "I heard we have a date with destiny."

"Take a drink and be ready to roll. We're heading to Barrier Peak to stop a war."

Red took a few sips from one of his flasks and sealed it. "I'm ready to go whenever you are."

"Lindy, take point," Rivka ordered. Lindy winked at Red, turned on her heel, and set out, crossing the open area of Bora Vale at an easy stride. She accelerated through the fronds and up the path the mech had carved the day prior. They ran like the natives but faster, passing many Yangorians who were using the transit corridor just like the Magistrate.

The Yangorians jumped aside when Red pounded by,

the trail not wide enough for him and anyone else. He bristled with firepower that thudded dully against his harness and ballistic vest. The Yindle didn't want a war they couldn't win.

They simply didn't know they couldn't win. *Faster if you can, Lindy,* Rivka encouraged.

The bodyguard increased her pace easily. She maintained it along the entirety of the transit corridor, the jog over to the trail leading to the central wood, and then along that trail, past where they'd encountered the Keeper of the Central Wood and through until they started running up a gentle incline.

"We're coming up on the open area of the Barrier Peak," Lindy called. There were so many Yangorians at the edge of the jungle that Rivka and her team could easily see them.

They slowed and spread out once they were in the open. "Nobody shoot us!" Rivka yelled as she walked backward, facing the Yangorians. "We're going up there to stop this!"

"They have your weapons. Who is to say that you're not going over there to join them?" DeWan, Keeper of the Central Wood, stepped from the jungle. At his side was Antwan, Keeper of the Barrier Peak, looking less than comfortable.

Rivka stopped. "Lindy, give me your blaster." Lindy pulled it from its holster, spun it around, and handed it to the Magistrate.

"They have one blaster." Rivka strode briskly to the Keeper and slapped the blaster into his hand. "Now you have one, too." She glared at him. "Go up there and duke it out with them. You have the means."

The keeper remained where he was.

"Then stay here and defend Yangor." The Magistrate headed back up the hill, speaking over her shoulder as she went. "Let us deal with them. If they get past us, then go to war and enjoy yourselves."

Rivka faced forward, jaw set, eyes focused, and brain spinning. Red motioned to the right, and Lindy split wide. He fanned out far to the left, putting about fifty meters between the wings and Rivka. She walked up the middle, slowing when she reached the top. She stopped when she could see the mass of Yindle arrayed along the edge of the jungle.

It's showtime, she said. Rivka held her hands up and stepped slowly over the rounded saddle of the Barrier Peak. A few steps down, she stopped. Red was on her left, railgun raised and ready to fire. Lindy assumed the same position. Faintly, Rivka heard the two clicks as Red and Lindy moved their weapons from safe past single fire to automatic. Rivka removed Reaper from her pocket and wrapped her fingers around it.

"What are you doing?" Rivka shouted. "Today is not a good day to die, but die you will! Dee, are you over there?"

Rivka planted her fists against her hips.

Master Dee emerged from the crowd and walked a few steps up the hill. He carried a blaster. Rivka strode down the hill. Red and Lindy combat-walked forward, maintaining their firing posture, watching over their weapons' barrels.

The Yindle remained defiant as Rivka stormed up to him. He rocked back slightly as she closed to within arm's reach. Using the speed her nanos gave her, she lashed out and ripped the blaster from his grip. "That's ours."

He looked shocked. "Always with the touching," he spat.

"How did you get this?" Rivka demanded. The Yindle on both sides of Master Dee shifted nervously. Some raised their rifles. "Tell them to put their weapons down before someone gets hurt."

Master Dee glared at Rivka. "We found that weapon. You shouldn't leave them lying around." He had to look away from Rivka's piercing gaze. "What were you doing in Yangor? You seem to walk freely among them."

"They pulled the same bullshit you did. We had to light up the jungle to show them we were serious. Let me tell you something you don't know. They may be brown, but they are *exactly* like you."

"They are not."

"Since we're all here together, would you like to talk to their leader? Maybe start the long process of ironing out your differences?"

"Why would I want to do that?" The Master inched backward.

Rivka glanced left at the gathering of Yindle and then to the right. "Because if your people are here doing this, then who is gathering food? Who is fishing? Who is making sure you live your lives?"

Master Dee looked at the ground. Rivka leaned close, hoping to access his mind. Nothing was coming through. She reached for him, but he backed away. He raised his arm over his head and signaled.

The Yindle melted back into the jungle. Within seconds, it was as if they were never there.

Rivka pursed her lips and watched, but she wasn't able to see anything other than undisturbed jungle. Red and Lindy moved closer to flank the Magistrate. She held the blaster up. Both bodyguards examined it. "That's the one you took from Sahved," Lindy noted.

"And gave to Clodagh. What happened?" Red wondered.

"We can go take a look," Rivka offered. "Anyone know the way?"

Red backed up the hill until he was at the top. The Yangorians remained where they had stopped in front of where the jungle growth stopped. "It's probably that way." He pointed.

Rivka and Lindy joined him. The white smoke lazed among the treetops in the distance.

"I didn't see any sign that either of these people cooks their food," Red stated.

Rivka chewed her lip and started to pace. The three humans skylined themselves on the saddle of the Barrier Peak. The Yangorians watched but relaxed. They'd seen the Magistrate and her team go over the hill, weapons at the ready. Now, the railguns were slung, and the humans seemed indifferent to what was around them.

A Yangorian climbed down the biggest tree in the area and reported to the keepers. "The Yindle have departed."

A keeper gestured, and the collected Yangorians faded into the jungle.

"Would you look at that?" Red started. "They're gone."

Both sides had lost interest as quickly as they had been energized.

"The question is, do we follow the smoke and check in

with the others? Smoke suggests they are able to signal or simply cooking something, although without a blaster, I'm not sure what they would kill. Or do we go back to *Wyatt Earp* to collect the engine part needed for the *Vengeance?*"

"I don't mind running back and forth across the jungle, but no matter what, we're going to leave someone guessing," Lindy offered.

"My vote is back to *Wyatt Earp.* We'll make the whole trip with what we need to fix the *Vengeance,* and then we'll fly back. I prefer the pampering offered by a smooth ride," Rivka said. "That's the plan. We need to get the full crew to *Wyatt Earp* to expedite repairs and make it easier for our rescuers to find us."

"I mind running back and forth across the jungle," Red mumbled as he headed down the hill into Yangor.

"I can't believe they left like that." Lindy shook her head and scanned the trees, rewarded with the usual jungle beauty but no sight of a Yangorian.

"I don't know if they want to end their conflict with Yindle. This is the least violent I've ever seen anyone who was spitting angry. I don't get it."

"Nothing in their minds to explain it?" Lindy asked.

"Not a damn thing. Just this nebulous hatred." Rivka thought back through what she'd seen in the minds of the Yindle and Yangorians she had been able to touch. There was nothing she could put her finger on, nothing she could address.

They jogged easily down the path they had taken twice already until they found the Keeper of the Central Wood waiting with his people spread on both sides of the trail.

Rivka threw up her hands. "Really?" she demanded.

DeWan stepped forth. "You are on our side."

"I don't think so." The Magistrate shook her head. "Here's your refresher. I'm on the side of the Federation, which prefers that individual city-states on member planets are not at war with each other. I reiterate my offer to mediate the dispute between Yangor and Yindle."

"In your words, I don't think so."

"Then we'll be on our way." Rivka tried to push past, but DeWan stepped in her way.

Red didn't wait. He launched a new demonstration of the railgun's firepower by digging up the ground in front of the Yangorians. Lindy followed his lead a couple of seconds later. When they stopped, they had their railguns leveled at the Yangorians.

"You have a special gift of pissing me off, DeWan."

The Yangorian's jaw worked for a short while before he spoke. "You cannot walk back and forth across Yangor with impunity."

"Of course, I can." She dug into her pocket and pulled out her credentials. "That's what these say. Tanglewood is a Federation planet." She refrained from stamping her foot. "By all that's holy, someone in your planetary government is going to get ripped a new asshole."

The keeper flinched at the expression.

"We're trying to cause the least amount of damage possible to the jungle. We are pleased to see how quickly it is growing back after the passing of our crewman wearing the mechanized combat suit. We will come through here one more time, and then hopefully no more. Will that suit you?"

DeWan backed away before Rivka could grab him or

get her blaster back. His people faded into the jungle. "Only the elimination of the Yindle will suit us."

"Genocide? What the fuck is wrong with you people?" Rivka yelled at the jungle.

"The more you call for peace, the less they want it. Is this a road you want to go down, Magistrate?" Red asked.

She slowly blew out a long breath. "It's hard not to take this personally. The more I ask questions, the more they become entrenched in the mythical philosophy of Hate the Yindle. I absolutely don't understand, and that is why I'm going to keep pressing. We're going to be here for a while, so we might as well learn to get along."

"You mean you're going to make them regret they ever met you?" Red asked.

"That's the abridged version, but accurate." Rivka started walking and Red hurried to get in front, following the path they were wearing through the jungle. "Why are you being assholes?" she yelled at the jungle.

"Maybe they think that's what you're being," Lindy suggested.

"Reverse psychology. Interesting perspective." Rivka looked at the ground as they loped downhill and through the jungle. "Time for a different approach. What do you say we ratchet up the heat? There's nothing like a war to make people beg for peace. Let's make it a real dispute."

CHAPTER FIFTEEN

Tanglewood, *Destiny's Vengeance* Crash Site

"I reek of smoke," Ryleigh said at the end of her fire-tending shift.

"It's the only thing I can think to do to help us. Otherwise, we've done about everything we can to fix the ship. All we have to do is keep ourselves alive and fit," Clodagh explained. "The food hunters aren't having much luck either. They're following Floyd around trying to find what's edible. Floyd thinks it's a game and is eating everything in sight until she falls asleep. As an engineer, I'm bothered that I can't have a nice, neat process."

"I didn't realize how good I had it, flying the ship, navigating, working preventive maintenance." Ryleigh stabbed at the fire. Smoke billowed outward, making her wince and retreat toward fresher air.

A Yindle appeared from the jungle and ran between them and their ship. Both women stood frozen. Then another Yindle. And another.

"Free shoes on the Promenade?" Ryleigh quipped.

"Too much fiber in their diets?" Clodagh countered.

More ran through. "Maybe Chaz parked the ship in the middle of the main road."

"Maybe someone's chasing them, like Alant in his mech."

Both women watched the direction the Yindle were coming from, which was the same way Rivka had gone.

Magistrate? Clodagh ventured. Nothing. "It was worth a shot."

Sahved and the others clumsily tore through the brush with freshly filled water containers. The Yemilorian munched on something that looked like an apple. He handed some to the women tending the fire.

Groenwyn lugged a sleeping Floyd.

Two more Yindle broke into the open area and continued through without acknowledging *Destiny's* crew.

"Where are they going?" Sahved asked mid-bite.

"A few hours ago, they went that way." Clodagh pointed toward the border with Yangor. "And now they're coming back."

Ryleigh stepped farther from the smoke. "We think they're going to a shoe sale. Must be unbelievable prices."

"*We* don't think that," Clodagh said. "We thought maybe the Magistrate was beating the bushes."

"Free buffet, just opened for lunch?" Aurora posited.

Kennedy offered a different take. "Build your own snowman; first twenty get in for free."

"Why would they have snowmen here?" Ryleigh wondered.

"Exactly why they're running!"

Groenwyn walked into the middle of the opening, bouncing Floyd lightly to keep the wombat sleeping. "I believe they are rethinking their life choices," she started. "They have wandered from the path of the great and powerful god, Jungle Palm Foliage. They are in distress, running aimlessly, looking for a sign to help them find their way back into the fold."

"How do you know this?" Sahved asked.

The young woman started to laugh. "I don't, but my next choice would be the shoe sale. I'd go."

"On Yemilore, I was confident of my investigation skills, being the best of the unrecognized best. But here, I must admit that half the time, I don't know what you're talking about, and the other half, I'm completely lost."

The four women watched him, waiting for more.

Finally, Clodagh filled the silence. "Red's going to be mad that you lost his knife. This thing is good." She took another bite of her fruit.

"Red is always mad," Sahved replied.

"One of us!" Ryleigh shouted.

A Yindle ran through the open area, stopping momentarily to look at the group.

"Indeed," Clodagh agreed with her mouth full. She looked at the Yindle. "Can we help you?"

"Poison," the Yindle said, pointing at the fruit in Clodagh's hand before continuing through the clearing. Clodagh dropped the fruit on the ground and spat out everything in her mouth. The others did the same, gagging and spitting.

Sahved continued eating his. "It's good."

"If I let you die, more than Red will be mad." Clodagh took the apple-like fruit from the Yemilorian's hand and threw it into the jungle.

Floyd roused and wiggled until Groenwyn put her down. She bounced into the undergrowth, returning shortly with the fruit in her mouth. Groenwyn and Clodagh ran after her.

"No! That's not good for you."

No! Very good. Healthy, Floyd cried. She dodged back and forth, continuing to eat until Groenwyn got it away from her.

"Maybe it is only poisonous to them?" Sahved suggested.

"We'll know in a few hours. Sooner, depending on toxicity." Clodagh looked up; the smoke wasn't as dense in the middle of the day as it had been earlier. Ryleigh dutifully stirred the coals before throwing another chunk of deadfall into the burn pit.

"Nothing like a poison apple to ruin everyone's day," Kennedy grumbled.

Tanglewood, Bora Vale

Rivka, Red, and Lindy strolled boldly into the village. They took the hard turn, continued two trees down, and waited. Shortly thereafter, the keeper made an appearance.

The Magistrate bowed her head. "You are right, Keeper. The Yindle need to be put in their place. Rally your people. It's time to go to war."

The keeper's expression changed from mild disdain to surprise. "So, you're on our side?"

"The Yindle did not show good faith by stealing the weapon from my crew, and I don't know if my crew is safe or not. We'll finish recharging the mech, and first thing tomorrow, we're going over there with our full complement of firepower. They will rue the day they crossed me!"

The keeper turned her head to look at Rivka from different angles as if that would change what she was hearing.

"I will have to contemplate your words." The Keeper of Bora Vale nodded once and returned inside her tree home.

Rivka waved at Red and Lindy to follow. They made a beeline out of Bora Vale. The Magistrate held a finger to her lips. They had to assume everything they said would be heard. They would wait until they were safely inside the heavy frigate before discussing the matter further.

They followed the track they'd blazed the day prior. Despite the new growth, it was still clearly visible. When they reached the mech, Cole was there with a maintenance bot that hummed, with a cable running from it to the suit.

"Recharging the old-fashioned way?" Rivka asked.

"Expediting the process. It'll be ready in a few more hours."

"We could go today, Magistrate. There's enough time if we run as fast as we're capable."

"There is enough time for everything except thinking. I am throwing mud at the wall. I need to do better. Also, we have to wait for the engine part for *Destiny's Vengeance*." She looked around quickly, expecting to see a Yangorian in the next bush, but no one appeared, at least not in a way she could see. "Red, why don't you stay here to provide an extra set of eyeballs while Cole sits here watching the machine work?"

"I'm working!" Cole claimed. He pulled a rag out of his pocket and started wiping down one of the suit's lower legs.

Rivka rolled her eyes and headed for the ship, with Lindy in tow. The cable descended, and they were hauled up one after the other. Ankh was nowhere to be seen, only the metal plate across the hatch opening and a maintenance bot.

"Ankh?"

"I am operating the machinery," Erasmus replied, using the ship's sound system. "Ankh is busy with the parts printer. It has malfunctioned. It needs to start over on the engine part, unfortunately."

"The world is conspiring against us," Rivka remarked.

"It is not." Erasmus was firm in his response. "It is nothing more than the fragility of a heavy frigate making a violent reentry and crash-landing on a planet surface. Nothing more."

"But the ship survived."

"It's not that fragile, but there is damage," Erasmus conceded.

"I'll be in my quarters," Rivka said. She needed time to think.

Tanglewood, *Destiny's Vengeance* Crash Site

"Anything?" Clodagh yelled from the ship's hatch. She didn't go into the heat and humidity if she didn't have to.

"I have seen the absolute most of nothing that has ever been seen before," Sahved replied. The Yemilorian seemed unaffected by the jungle climate.

"Maybe you can climb up and take a look?" Clodagh urged Sahved toward one of the taller trees surrounding the clearing in which *Destiny's Vengeance* sat. He grumped as he went, but he was good at climbing trees, a skill none of the others cared to develop.

He raced up the tree, wedged himself into the topmost branches, and scanned the horizon all the way around. "An exponential degree of nothing," he shouted toward the ground.

Clodagh gave him a thumbs-up that he didn't see and shut the hatch. After nearly an hour of wondering when the order would come but didn't, he decided it was time to climb down, surprising two of the pilots, who were in the clearing wondering where he had gone.

"You scared the shit out of me!" Ryleigh put her hand on her chest to slow her racing heart. Kennedy nearly jumped out of her boots. She doubled over, hands on her knees as she tried to catch her breath. She remained doubled over and started to gag until she puked.

"I don't feel so good," Kennedy mumbled. She flopped to the ground and held her stomach.

"I am sorry!" Sahved tried to console her. She didn't blame him. "It's something else."

Ryleigh burped and scowled. "I don't feel right, either." She looked at Sahved. "Maybe it was something we ate?"

"I feel great," Sahved said, quickly avoiding eye contact.

"How is Floyd?" Ryleigh wondered.

Wheee! The wombat bounced out of the brush on one side and tore into the bushes on the other.

"You think that Yindle was right?" Ryleigh asked.

Groenwyn, how do you feel? Kennedy managed while groaning.

I feel fine, but don't judge your health by mine. I'm enhanced. Clodagh spent some time in the Pod-doc when she served on the War Axe. Groenwyn shrugged. Alcohol, poison, wounds, disease, and many things that affected the majority of humanity had minimal effect on those who'd had the full treatment of nanos.

That was minimal Pod-doc time back then, so I'm not really enhanced. I don't feel too bad, but I think it got me, too. I didn't eat as much as everyone else, either. What about Sahved?

He and Floyd are just fine, Ryleigh answered. *Aurora?*

The hatch opened, and she staggered out of the ship and into the clearing before dropping to her knees and heaving.

Nice, Clodagh said over the internal comm chip. *The four of us have it.*

"How bad is it going to get?" Ryleigh asked out loud. Clodagh stepped through the hatch Aurora had left open.

"I wish I knew. Sahved and Groenwyn, you're on water detail. As much as you can carry, because we're going to need it. And anything truly edible since we'll need to keep up our strength."

"We'll do everything we can. Come on, Sahved." Groenwyn rushed into the ship to get the containers they'd been using for water. She tossed two at Sahved and jogged into the jungle. The Yemilorian nodded his goodbye and hurried after her.

"Twenty-four hours to gestate, and then it hit us like a ton of support beams," Clodagh noted. She had ingested very little, so she expected it wouldn't affect her anywhere near as badly as the three smaller pilots. They were turning green before her eyes. "Come on, Magistrate. We could use some help right about now."

CHAPTER SIXTEEN

Tanglewood, *Wyatt Earp* Crash Site

Rivka stalked up and down the frigate's passageways. The others stayed out of her way, not because she was a bear, but she was deep in conversation with herself, and they didn't want to interrupt.

"Ankh, are we ready to go yet?" Rivka yelled.

"Tomorrow, Magistrate," Erasmus answered. "It should be ready first thing tomorrow morning. The mech suit is ready and parked below."

"Really?" Rivka wasn't sure how she had missed that, except that she hadn't left the ship or thought about what Cole was doing. She figured everyone was working for Ankh to get the ship flyable. There were a million things to do and four pairs of hands to do them. It was better than when it was just Ankh, but they were still fighting a losing battle. Erasmus had adjusted his repair time down to five months from nine based on the ability of Cole and his mech to expedite the surface mining of raw materials necessary for the parts printer.

"Conference Room," Rivka told her bodyguards when she found them in the ship's small gym.

"It's just us. We could meet right here," Red suggested.

"Bring Ankh and Cole." Rivka sauntered away without addressing Red's offer.

He executed a stealth smelfie, drifting his nose past his armpit. "Do you think she'll let me take a shower first?"

Lindy shook her head. "You find Cole. I'll deal with Ankh."

"The little guy isn't going to like it."

"That's a given. He's not as little as he used to be, though. Or is that just me?"

"I didn't notice." Red held out his hand for the towel Lindy had wiped her upper body with.

"I could change my hair color, and you wouldn't notice." She gave him her sweaty towel. He did what he could to dry off, but they had been in the middle of their rigorous lifting routine. He expected to keep sweating for the next thirty minutes. He threw the towel over his shoulder.

"That jabs deep into my chest and squeezes my heart until the ache is real," Red tried.

"Go get Cole, you big goof," Lindy said, diving in for a quick kiss before leaving.

Red watched her go. "How did I get so lucky?" he asked himself. He shrugged it off and headed out, preferring to use the manual intercom instead of the personal approach. He shouted, "Cole! Need you in the conference room now!"

He stuck his head in the cargo bay, where Private Alant

Cole stopped where he was with the inventory re-check and joined Red.

When they made it to the conference room, Rivka was there, hands steepled, staring at a rotating three-dimensional image of the jungle areas known as Yindle and Yangor.

Red stayed closest to the door, not his usual seat since his back wasn't against the wall where he could see anyone who entered. The ship was buttoned up, with only five on board. He glanced over his shoulder when the door opened and Ankh walked in in front of Lindy. She winked at her husband before taking his usual seat.

The Crenellian stood next to the Magistrate, almost touching her with his face. "I'm busy," he stated.

"As are we all, Ankh. Thanks for coming." She pointed to the image above the conference table. "Erasmus, please highlight the location of *Destiny's Vengeance* and *Wyatt Earp.*"

The AI complied, and two blips appeared. "This, right here," Rivka poked her finger into the image at the spot known as Barrier Peak, "is where it's going to go down."

The Magistrate leaned back in her seat and re-steepled her fingers, pursing her lips, lost in the image.

"*What* is going to go down?" Cole asked, relieving Red of the burden.

"We're going to force a war, then kidnap the leaders, and finally we're going to hold them hostage until they come to an agreement. This will force the planetary government to do their job."

The other four looked at each other. Red started to raise his hand but stopped. "I'm all for a good ass-kicking, but what I'm hearing is that you are going to put us between two armies—ragtag with poor weapons, but armies nonetheless—and then take their leaders and make them agree to what they don't want to agree to, just so they can get themselves free. I don't see either side abiding by such an agreement."

Rivka turned to Lindy, shook her head, and then peered at Red, who was seated with his back to the door. She pointed at him and then at Lindy. "You need to sit in your usual place," she said. Neither of them moved. "Fine."

She stood and started to pace. "The Federation's job is not to get involved with member planets' internal squabbles. But that becomes a secondary consideration to the requirement to help Federation citizens, which is what the member planet is not doing. As a Magistrate, I have ambassadorial-level status. If this is how the Yindle and Yangorians treat *me*, how would they deal with an average Joe who crashed here?

"For the good of the Federation, this failure of the planet's citizenry to comply with laws they don't even know they're subject to requires rectification. That means I'm in the right place to be a catalyst for change. As such, we need to agitate both parties to action, then bring them to the table to explain how it needs to be, which in turn should bring the planetary government to the table, which is my real goal. They need to get involved and fix this. Right now, I see their membership status as questionable. They lied to us because they have lied to their people, a lie of omission because their people don't know a thing."

Red crossed his arms and watched. "My job is to protect you. I don't care about the Yin and the Yang. I see a lot of bullets coming our way. *Wyatt Earp* isn't close enough to guarantee we can get our injured to the Pod-doc. That means an injury bad enough that the nanos can't fix it will be certain death. I don't like your plan, Magistrate."

Rivka nodded as she looked at the floor. "I saw the opportunity when the two sides kind of faced off yesterday. They don't appear to be too keen on making any conflict a shooting war, as in, I'm betting they are all bluster and no real action."

Lindy started to laugh. "Think about how armies train —and I'm guessing since I never served—but we practice our combat tactics. DeWan made a single gesture command that his people immediately followed by throwing their weapons on the ground."

Red opened his mouth to argue. "Maybe this is the little kids' playground, and we're the first adults they've ever seen."

Rivka audibly blew out a breath. "Then we're the ugly foreigners who are going to beat up the little kids. As soon as that engine part is ready, we leave. Cole will be in the suit, carrying our precious cargo. We go with full load and full armor, including helmets. We're going to look the part, and if they start shooting, we'll be better able to weather those first shots before we can rein it in."

Ankh continued to stand next to Rivka's chair. "What did you need me for? I'm busy."

"I need you to be ready to send a signal rocket over their heads. We'll have a flare with us. If we send it up, I'll need you to demonstrate our firepower by blowing the top off one of those two mountains that define the Barrier Peak."

"Have Cole do it. The suit rockets are plenty powerful for the job." Ankh turned and started walking out.

"That's why we needed you," Rivka called after him.

Cole chuckled. "They may look small, but they have a lotta kick. It's not the size of the wand, but the magic inside."

Red appreciated the quip. "Although I like big things in small packages, what are the rules of engagement for this mission?"

"I'd say case, but this isn't either. It's a vacation." Rivka smiled at her joke, but no one else did. "Fine." She tried to give him a hearty glare but couldn't maintain it. "Same as before. If someone shoots at us, eliminate that one person. Kill as few as possible with the target of zero. Let our total body count on this planet be one. It seems like the Yangorians have reconciled themselves to that number.

"That's when the idea started to form that they don't want war. They want a conflict where they can feel morally superior without having to prove anything. In the legal world, this is a simple dispute. Nearly all disputes can be managed when the emotional baggage behind them is addressed."

"Damn, Magistrate, you talk real sexy when you get going," Red joked before turning serious. "What happens if you can't get them past their hatred?"

"Then the next generation will answer for the sins of their parents, or the next one after that until they are able to look beyond whatever held them back. I didn't say it would be easy, but the Keeper of Bora Vale showed cracks in the veneer. I only need to get a wedge in there and see what's inside."

"The keeper was supposed to be a guy," Lindy remarked.

"My guess is that this keeper is new. The Yangorian keepers seem little involved in each other's day to day affairs, so a change of leadership isn't something that's going to pop up on their radar. And she looks young, younger than the other Yangorians around her. I wonder if the position passes from parent to child?"

"After we've kidnapped her, you could ask. You know, make polite conversation so she feels more comfortable?" Red deadpanned.

"What would we do without your insight into the sentient psyche?" Rivka wondered, smiling. Lindy appreciated the thought because she knew he was right in his backhanded way. "I'm going to drive their emotions into the stratosphere, so everything else will look reasonable by comparison."

"Unite against the common foe," Cole offered. "It's a tactic Terry Henry Walton has used on more than one occasion. When people can see a better enemy, they might find how much they have in common."

"That's me," Rivka replied. "I'll be the better enemy until they realize they had no enemy at all."

"You can't be everyone's friend," Lindy suggested. "But they'll see once the dust settles that you were a better friend than either of them ever considered."

"That's the hope. Thanks, people. Go do Ankh's bidding until that printer is done with that part, and then we'll get to it."

"Downside?" Red asked after they stood.

"There are more cons than pros. That's why I didn't go

into them. The worst is if we start a real shooting war between the two sides. We could get ourselves killed. We could get our other people killed if the Yindle retaliate against the *Vengeance* before we can get it repaired. Nothing good can come from failure. We *have to* make this work."

CHAPTER SEVENTEEN

Tanglewood, *Wyatt Earp*

"Careful," Rivka said needlessly. A maintenance bot lowered the main cable with the repair part attached while Red and Lindy muscled their cables to keep it balanced as it approached a waiting Cole.

"Are you sure he's going to be able to carry that thing?" Rivka wondered.

"Yes. Weight is not a problem," Ankh replied.

"But will he be able to see where he's going?"

"Of course. He doesn't drive with his eyes. The suit is one of the most technologically advanced systems in the galaxy." His face and voice were neutral, as usual.

"Is that your way of saying that you helped develop the system?"

"Just the upgrade." Ankh peered over the edge of the metal plate blocking the open hatch when the cables went slack after the part was delivered. Cole balanced the heavy metal construct across one arm while he detached the cables. Once free, he hefted the load to find the most comfortable position to carry it.

I'm good to go, Cole reported. *Can't wait to see my babe.*

Red made a face. Lindy glowered at him. "Of all people. You are the king of bistok eyes, and if you didn't miss me, I'd kick your ass."

"I'm seeing love, like a flower opening its petals with the morning's sun." Rivka held her hand over her ballistically protected heart. "Get down the cable. We got a war to start and end, and a new war to start with Tanglewood's planetary government. Plus, we have ourselves to get out of here. If we can fix Ankh's ship, then we can fly to the other side of the planet and shorten the timeline for saving ourselves."

"Without the Etheric power supply, the engine will be repaired, but the ship will only have thrusters available. Chaz will be able to fly the *Vengeance* over here, but not all the way around the planet. I can build a secondary power supply, but that will take longer than the time before we're reported missing. My focus is on getting the ship ready, so we can fly it out of here once we have enough power. When we're clear of this dampening effect, we should have all systems available, including the Gate drive."

"But we can't escape the planet on just thrusters." Rivka didn't ask a question. She held the cable as Red slid down.

"No," Ankh confirmed. He left her standing there as he returned to the engine room. Lindy went down the cable next. Rivka was last, quickly sliding to the ground.

Cole's mech-sized railgun was slung across his back, magnetically anchored to keep it from bouncing. He could release the clamp with a thought and be able to fire in less than a second. He also had a full complement of rockets, which he could fire without putting down his load.

"When Clodagh said she needed a part to fix the ship, I never thought it would be bigger than the whole ship." She demonstrated a shape with her hands that was about the size of a shoebox. The "part" Cole carried was as big as Red and weighed about three times as much.

What does bringing the Vengeance *over here accomplish?* Red wondered, using the internal comm chip to stymie Yangorian eavesdropping.

Reuniting the crew is important because it's easier to protect people if we're all in one place. We have enough food and water on board Wyatt Earp *so we don't have to traipse around the jungle foraging, and the extra trained hands will help get our ship back in the sky sooner.*

Sounds good, Red replied. Once he heard it, he knew the reason should have been obvious. *When we win, can we go kinga-hunting? I've got a hankering for some cooked over a smoky jungle fire.*

"We're gone from the ship for five seconds, and Red is already hungry. I think that bodes well for today's proceedings." Rivka clapped him on the one small open area of his back. Red was loaded down with gear, as was Lindy, but they both reveled in it. Beads of sweat already stood out on their brows. Rivka hadn't put out enough effort to sweat, even though it was already hot and humid.

"You can't bring yourself to call it a mission, no matter what. Maybe we can call it *The Case of the Missing Mission.* You know, like that Watson guy who wrote the *Sherlock Holmes* stories."

"Doyle wrote that Watson wrote the stories."

"Just like any good recorder of history," Red countered. "Come on, Magistrate, say it with me. 'Mission.' *Mission.*"

"It's my mission to get you to refer to what we do as 'cases.'"

Red would have counterattacked, but the jungle was alive, and the jibe would be lost in the internal voice. He decided to retreat and fight another day. "The Magistrate has made her decision. Judge, jury, and executioner."

"There's a certain efficiency to the system," Rivka quipped. "But it could get abused easily if someone forgot they were cases and not missions."

"As you wish. We'll revisit it later when you realize I'm right."

Rivka snorted.

Cole moved quickly through the brush. He was trying to destroy as little as he could, but the path wasn't conducive to the mech's size and power. He decided that if he avoided stepping where the stalk became the root, he wouldn't kill the plant, so he took greater care with where he placed his metal feet, not worrying about ripping off branches or tearing through whole bushes.

How many are there around us? Rivka asked.

Cole responded after a quick scan, *The usual, a couple dozen. They seem to be following us but at a discreet distance.*

Don't want anything out of the normal. We'll hit Bora Vale hard, beat the war drums, and sound the alarm. We might have to lead the way; show them that we're going to war on their behalf. There's no way they won't want front-row seats to that show, Rivka replied. It was her hope that they would want to see the fireworks. She winced at how flimsy her plan was.

The others knew it, but they would play their roles to the fullest. *If they don't come, we'll go snag Master Dee first,* Lindy suggested, as if reading Rivka's mind.

You'd think starting a war would be easier, Red added.

With high morale, the warriors embraced the war to which they marched, Rivka thought.

Cole sped up, but not too fast. He didn't want to damage the part he carried. The others followed at an easy lope.

Following a mech made it easy to move through areas that weren't meant to be traveled by people, at least people who weren't native to the jungle.

They broke through into Bora Vale a mere thirty minutes after they left the security of *Wyatt Earp.* The mech slowed to let Rivka and her bodyguards move in front. They went straight to the keeper's tree and stood out front, waiting. They had broken a sweat only because of the loads they carried. Rivka crossed her arms and tried to show infinite patience as she waited.

The keeper emerged shortly, making it easier on the Magistrate and her team. Her head was bowed, and her shoulders sagged.

"You were serious."

"Weren't you?" Rivka asked, stepping forward and fixing the keeper with an unblinking gaze.

"Yes," she admitted, barely above a whisper.

"There are those who talk and those who act. The time for talk is finished. Come with us so we can finish this."

The keeper stood her ground.

"We're taking the war to the Yindle in your name.

They'll know it was you, so it would be best if you were there. Honor your victory."

"Honor?" the keeper asked.

"There is no honor in hating an enemy. You must deal with your fear since there is no room in this universe for hatred." Rivka intently studied the young Yangorian. Her posture suggested she didn't want a war and was waffling about the unfounded hatred. Maybe she was the generation to inculcate change. "Has your father recently passed?"

"He has gone to the Makers, yes."

"Honor him by finishing this. Start your time as keeper by freeing your people from the slavery of hate." Rivka left the ambiguity for the keeper to interpret as she wished.

"And if we know no other way?"

"Then we will show you another way, something that Tanglewood's government should have shown you instead of giving all of you guns. Parity is no way to manage conflict, in my humble opinion."

Cole was frozen as if he were a monument. Red and Lindy barely breathed to avoid distracting the Magistrate or the keeper. The negotiation ballet was intricate. Even the constant din of insect life seemed to fade as the jungle world closed around the two.

The keeper nodded slowly. She looked into the distance, where the Barrier Peak was located, then swept her gaze through the Bora Vale village, drifting over the trees and her people. She raised one arm in the air and signaled. The natives were galvanized into action, racing in all directions. With a nod, the keeper issued her order. "Follow me."

She started to run, as the natives did, dancing lightly

into the brush, ducking and dodging to keep from disturbing the heavy growth. Her clothing and skin naturally blended. Rivka stayed close, with Red and Lindy right behind. Cole followed. With his scanning systems, he was at no risk of getting lost.

That did it, he reported. *The Yangorians are in full deployment mode. Well done, Magistrate.*

I think that was the easy part, Rivka replied. *She has incited her people. I know her heart isn't in it, but theirs may be.*

We got your back, Magistrate, Red stated.

I know you do. There's going to be a lot of posturing up there. We need to keep it from escalating.

While we kidnap the leaders and hold them hostage between opposing forces who are armed. Lindy twisted her face as if she had said the words out loud.

With crappy rifles! Red tried to allay their concerns, but he didn't sound convincing.

You two aren't making me feel better.

I'm seeing double the numbers of last time. It didn't take long to rally twenty-five hundred souls, Cole reported.

You three, Rivka corrected.

By the time they started climbing the final slope to get to the open area of the Barrier Peak, there were so many Yangorians that they were unable to blend into the background. The Keeper of Bora Vale walked the last hundred meters, stopping before she stepped into the open. She signaled again with a raised hand, and the message was passed silently as the Yangorians repeated the hand signal.

Antwan and DeWan materialized shortly, along with three others. The Keeper of Bora Vale huddled with five other keepers. Rivka bowed her head and focused her efforts on hearing what they had to say.

"My father rued this day but prepared me for it. Keeper of the Low Hills, you will array your people on the far right. You will wait until the battle is underway, then you will look for opportunities to exploit their weaknesses. Bora Vale and Central Woods will go straight over the top and attack the enemy. Western Woods has the far left. Look for weaknesses at the end of their line. Barrier Peak will follow us up and fill any gaps should the Yindle be successful in counterattacking Central Wood and Bora Vale. And the strangers," she pointed at Rivka and the others, "will go in the very front. We might not have to fight at all, just clean up whatever they leave."

DeWan, the Keeper of the Central Wood, breathed a sigh of relief, smiled, and spoke. "SiQuan, I have seen what they can do. There will be nothing left for us except to gather rifles from the dead Yindle."

Antwan, the Keeper of the Barrier Peak, scowled. "I accept your decision, Keeper of Bora Vale, but I am not happy about it. We like what we like, and there is nothing good to be gained by going over that hill."

"Your role will expand, Antwan, since you will have to take over both sides of the Barrier Peak. Is that too much?"

Antwan wasn't mollified. "I will do my duty."

Rivka stepped into the conversation. "I ask that you go with us, Keeper of Bora Vale. Lead from the front, as my people say."

She had heard the Keeper's name, SiQuan, but didn't use it since she did not want to be accused of eavesdropping. She had been doing so, but their ability to hear guarded conversations didn't need to be common knowledge.

"Is he going to carry that during the battle?" SiQuan asked, pointing to the mass of metal in the mech's arms.

"It will help us during the battle, but he will place it on this side of the top of the hill. It is important that it not get hit by bullets." Rivka tried to sound matter-of-fact as she talked to limit the questions. "Are you ready?"

"We wait for the remainder of our people." The five keepers stood shoulder to shoulder and watched the saddle between the hills. The Barrier Peak.

Do not let that engine part get hit if anyone starts shooting, Rivka warned Cole.

Why not leave it here? he asked.

Because I think you might be able to make a run for the Vengeance *while we are facilitating a conversation between the keeper and the master. I doubt the Yangorians waiting in angst will let you stroll down here, grab your shit, and saunter away.*

I haven't mastered a saunter yet, Cole started. *I see your point, though. Minimum casualties. No collateral damage.*

You might have to rip the tops off a few trees to let them know what that rocket pack you're carrying can do, Rivka offered.

Will fire when I receive the order, ma'am, Cole replied. *The numbers show over three thousand Yangorians, and more arriving every minute.*

Did we misjudge how many there are? Rivka asked.

After having a thousand rifles pointed at your back, does more matter? Red replied.

I guess not. It's all noise after you reach the point of mutually assured destruction.

They settled in to wait. Red and Lindy leaned against trees to keep the Yangorians from standing behind them. Cole stood like a statue, gleaming in the sun's rays that penetrated the jungle canopy. Rivka stayed next to SiQuan.

"We will do our best to end this quickly. No Yangorians need be hurt," Rivka whispered, leaning close enough to touch the young keeper.

"That doesn't make me feel better."

"Why?" Rivka pressed. She could feel the emotional turmoil within. She was surrendering more and more to events that she thought were spinning out of control.

The keeper looked puzzled. "I wish I knew exactly why. You are right that this threat has hung over our heads long enough. That's what my mind tells me. My heart tells me something different," she shared in a low voice, using her hand to deflect her words away from her fellow keepers.

Rivka was ready to follow up, but a signal passed among the Yangorians like wind through a field of grain. SiQuan gestured and the other four keepers moved out, taking members of their groups with them. They formed up in loose lines from right to left. With sad eyes, the Keeper of Bora Vale gripped Rivka's arm.

"To the finish," she said, and together they walked into the open. "I'm told the Yindle wait for us."

CHAPTER EIGHTEEN

Tanglewood, *Destiny's Vengeance*

"What now?" Clodagh mumbled.

"The Yindle are on the move again, running toward the hills where the Magistrate went."

Clodagh forced herself out of her seat in the cockpit. The others were in the two bunks, pale, clammy, and shivering. Groenwyn stayed with them, giving them as much water as they would drink. The ship had started to smell like illness and death.

Sahved sat in the small galley, talking to himself, but ready to do Clodagh's bidding. She need only ask, but she didn't know what to have him do. Chaz was stumped. Toxicology was not a discipline in which he was versed.

"How many?" Clodagh asked.

"All of them?" Chaz hesitantly replied.

"What is the Magistrate doing?" Clodagh muttered. "Come on, Sahved, let's take a look." A small bark reminded her that Titan hadn't been out in a while. The Yemilorian unfolded himself from the galley, put his hand over his head, and stood, then ducked as he stepped into the short passage.

Floyd waited patiently by the door. The engineer tapped the button, and the door opened. Floyd and Titan bolted out, dodging a pair of Yindle dashing past. Clodagh stumbled after them. Sahved rushed ahead and caught the engineer before she fell.

"I didn't have very much," she complained, trying to shake off the effects of the poison.

"You should probably be in bed with the others," Sahved told her.

"Stop him," Clodagh ordered in a croaky voice.

Sahved reached out and grabbed the arm of a Yindle racing past. The Yemilorian's strong grip surprised the Yindle. He tried to brush off the three-fingers.

"Where are you going?" Clodagh asked.

The Yindle didn't want to answer. Sahved held him in place.

"Where?" Clodagh started to reach for him as anger drove enough adrenaline into her system to give her a boost.

He pointed toward the hills where the Magistrate had gone.

"There's a small fruit, this size." She held her hand as if gripping a ball to demonstrate. "It's poison. What is the antidote?"

He looked at them blankly.

"Let him go."

Sahved released his grip so abruptly, the Yindle stumbled backward and almost fell before bolting like a wild animal. Another Yindle slowed to avoid running him over as they both disappeared into the jungle.

"The Magistrate is going to be pissed when she comes back and finds her crew is dead."

"Who is dead?" Sahved wondered.

"Not yet, but soon. They're not getting better, and neither am I."

She collapsed into Sahved's arms.

"No! You must not die." The Yemilorian looked around in a panic, cradling the engineer and rocking. "You must not."

Tanglewood, Barrier Peak

When Rivka, Red, and Lindy reached the high point of the saddle, the Yindle were starting to mass and no longer blending with the trees.

"Cole?" Rivka asked.

Thousands, Magistrate. Nearly an identical number to the Yangorians. Same number of rifles, too.

Tanglewood's government has a lot of explaining to do. I look forward to meeting their leadership.

Red chuckled. *They don't know it yet, but they are not looking forward to meeting you.* As the time for action approached, Red was hyper-focused on the engagement. He looked for areas where the Yindle could mass their fire. He noted areas that could provide cover, however meager. In battle, every edge, no matter how small, was one you wanted on your side. Red checked his weapon by touch, not taking his eyes from the Yindle lines.

Lindy's jaw was set. She wasn't into battle as much as

Red, but she was good and knew it. Unlike Red, she looked for ways to intimidate the Yindle and drive them away without killing them. She checked the grenades on her combat vest. Her shortcoming was in only being able to throw them right-handed. Red could fire his railgun and throw grenades with his left hand. He did not have to switch from one weapon to another.

Cole gently put the engine component on the ground and stepped in front of it. He hoisted his railgun and spun the barrels, their scream piercing the silence. He leveled it and aimed at the left flank, then smoothly rotated across the line of Yindle until he was aimed at the far right. He rotated back and steadied.

I think it's time, Rivka said. "Stay here, Keeper. My people will keep you safe. I'm going to have a few words with the Yindle."

Lindy edged to within arm's reach of SiQuan to keep her from running. Rivka strode forward, and Red went with her to shield her with his body if need be. Their steps were measured and light, almost as if beginning a dance.

Hundreds of rifles aimed at them.

My plan sucks, Rivka said.

The safest place to be is where they're aiming, Red quipped, but his lips were white from clenching them.

They stopped before anyone fired. Rivka let out the breath she'd been holding. "Master Dee!" Rivka shouted. She gave him thirty seconds before yelling again. "I know you're over there."

Red looked sideways at the Magistrate. *Is that your plan?*
I already told you it sucked. Do you have a better idea?
Red always found it challenging to talk using his chip.

He preferred speaking out loud. "Let's stroll the line and look them in the face until we get to Dee or Yee or any of the other Ees."

Rivka tried one more time. "Master Dee!"

A Yindle stepped forward—Minor Yee. She crooked a finger at him. He crossed his arms and remained where he was.

"Fine. The hard way, then." She strolled toward him, her hands up in the hope that they would take her movement as non-aggressive. Even though she wore full-body ballistic protection, she wasn't armed like her bodyguards. A bead of sweat rolled out from under her helmet and into her eye. She blinked to clear her vision.

Red stayed behind her. One does not sail a battleship into the enemy harbor. He understood that. His job was to protect the Magistrate, and at this point in time, the best way to do that was to stay back. His trigger finger twitched in anticipation. He stood ready to fire at any target that needed to die.

Lindy kept one eye on SiQuan. She wouldn't let Rivka's risk with the Yindle fail because the keeper got away.

"Yee," Rivka said as the sum total of her greeting. "Where's Master Dee?"

The Yindle shrugged. "Maybe Master Dee isn't available. Maybe I'm the master now."

"He's going to let you speak for all Yindle? He has passed the war baton to you? Say the word and let the battle begin," Rivka taunted in an effort to gauge his authority.

He held her gaze as well as his tongue.

"Master Dee?" she asked, looking for any recognition.

She left Minor Yee standing there as she walked left to the end of the line, turned around, and walked to the far right, not looking at Yee as she passed. "Master Dee?"

When she returned to the center, she found Yee wearing a smug look. She wanted to rip it off his face but decided that he would have to do. "Come on." Her hand flashed out and grabbed his arm, yanking him forward so hard he stumbled and threw his arms out to keep from falling. The Magistrate half-dragged him back up the hill.

The Yindle vibrated in their indecision. When Rivka made it past Red, he stepped between her and the Yindle forces, backing up to protect her with his mass.

Minor Yee tried to protest, fighting Rivka's grip and pounding on her hand.

"Stop it," she told him. "You put on the big boy pants, now wear them proudly."

"I will not be handed over to the barbarian horde," he declared.

"They are the same as you. Yindle and Yangor, two sides of the same tree. What is preventing you from seeing that?"

Lindy grabbed the keeper's arm before she could move. "You and the Yindle are going to have a conversation," she told the slight Yangorian.

SiQuan remained where she was. She didn't struggle against the restraint, but tension hardened her body.

When Rivka made it to the top, she relaxed and rolled her head from shoulder to shoulder.

"Let's begin. For now, I'm going to do all the talking, but understand there will be a test later, so I'm going to need you to pay attention."

SiQuan and Yee glared from Rivka to each other and back again.

"Sit," she ordered. SiQuan didn't need encouragement, but Rivka had to force Yee to the ground.

"I am Magistrate Rivka Anoa, a representative of the Federation with full diplomatic status. That means nothing to you, except that I'm telling you I have full authority to accuse, try, and find innocent or guilty anyone on this planet. I am also authorized to carry out any punishment I deem fit for the crime. I don't want to do any of that.

"What I want is to show you the wisdom of Federation Law and how it applies to you, then establish the legal framework in which Yindle and Yangor can operate to either peacefully coexist or interact in a way that is not harmful to others. People like me, who you both tried to take captive. Under Federation law, that should earn you a long stay on Jhiordaan. Ignorance of the law is no excuse, but also, the law is not a club to beat you with, only a framework within which civilized societies can work. I'm going to forgive your transgressions to give you a chance to start fresh.

"The Federation has hundreds and hundreds of member planets for purposes of trade, mutual defense, and those things necessary to keep the peace and drive prosperity. Everyone should be able to improve themselves on a path they've chosen. The Federation encourages this. We don't allow slavery. We don't let people murder each other, not without recourse. Or steal from each other. The Federation allows people to speak their minds without fear of being imprisoned. Trade and tax structures to facilitate those things necessary for the common good. Member planets, if capable, provide ships and personnel for a common defense. The Federation's military is small but potent. Sometimes we need more than that and have to call on our members to fill the gaps.

"And in the case of Tanglewood, my job is making the citizens aware of their obligations. You would never be required to provide ships or troops, but you *are* required to supply help to Federation personnel in distress. That was me, and the only thing the Yindle and Yangor did was to threaten to imprison me. That stops now. You will never do that to anyone else who might fall afoul of your planet's magnetic anomalies or whatever the hell happened to my ship."

"Why didn't you say so?" Minor Yee asked sarcastically. "Can I go now?"

"No," Rivka replied with a smile.

Yee started to fume.

"Air your damn grievances, by all that's holy. You first, SiQuan."

She remained tight-lipped.

Cole, take your cargo to Destiny's Vengeance. *I think we're going to be here for a while.*

The mech smoothly adjusted the railgun behind its back and picked up the load, adjusting and covering as much of it with its arms as possible. He started walking and then picked up speed, accelerating beyond a pace any warm-blooded creature could maintain. He vaulted high when he reached the Yindle lines, using the boot jets to send him to treetop level. He soared over and into an opening beyond, hit the ground running, and was soon gone.

The Yindle fumed at their inability to affect anything happening around them.

Rivka lounged in the grass, relaxing. "Here's the deal. Both of your forces are more or less powerless to do anything other than watch, so we're going to stay here until you talk to each other. It'll start with your grievances against each other. We'll put each out there," Rivka pointed to the empty ground between SiQuan and Yee, "and discuss it until it's resolved, and then we'll move on to the next issue. Do you want to know my take on all this? You have no idea what your grievances are. You've never sat face to face with one of the others before. No one personally knows anything that one of you has done to another. That's how I see it. You have thousands of people counting on you. Don't fail them."

"All of that could be ours. There's no failure in conquest," Minor Yee said, tipping his chin toward the village of Bora Vale.

"You'd fail," Rivka said. "There will be no conquest, and why do you want their territory?"

Minor Yee crossed his arms and gritted his teeth.

"I've got all day," Rivka said. She picked a blade of grass and slipped it into her mouth to casually chew on it while SiQuan and Minor Yee postured in nearly microscopic ways.

"I can go days without sleep. Can you?" the Magistrate asked, not expecting an answer. "If you start now, you can more quickly reach the substantive part of a conversation."

A rifle cracked from the Yindle side. Someone fired from the Yangor side. Then more as the opposing sides lobbed rounds at an enemy they couldn't see with the hill in between.

Red hunched over the Magistrate, dragging Yee under his body. Lindy covered SiQuan until the firing stopped.

"What are those dumbasses shooting at?" Red grumbled.

"They're making my point for me. The longer you wait, the more tensions will rise. Neither of you is leaving here until we have some sort of agreement that will, at a minimum, allow people like me freedom of movement through your territories."

"Why didn't you say so? Done. Can I go now?" Minor Yee said from under Red's bulk. The big bodyguard jammed down on the diminutive Yindle as he stood and stepped back.

"I can stay here as long as I need to," SiQuan said softly. "Sounds like the Yindle are weak, incapable of controlling their thoughts, and probably their bodies, too. An attempted conquest will be the end of your people."

Rivka patted her hand in the air, trying to calm the keeper's newfound aggression. Maybe she saw Yee as weak, based on his lashing out with sarcasm.

"Yangorians would fall before us like trees before an unrelenting storm!" Yee countered.

"Very nice. Get your nonsensical threats out of the way. If you want to see how fast your people can die, I'll arrange another demonstration." Rivka glanced from one to another. She wanted them to play chess, not checkers, and definitely not high-card draw. The simpler the game, the easier it would be for both parties to balk. There had to be a series of give and take.

After what must have been hours, Rivka tried to break the silent ice. "Yee, you don't seem up to the task. I'm going to take you back and trade you for Master Dee."

"He won't come!" Minor Yee shouted defiantly.

"Really?" Rivka stood. When Yee started to stand, she pushed him down. She turned to Red. "Watch him."

"Whatcha gonna do, Magistrate?" Red wondered.

"I'm going to go find Dee."

"I'll go," Red offered.

"No, me," Lindy countered. "I'm less threatening."

Rivka chuckled. "You both look like walking Ogre supertanks. I'll go. Don't worry, Red. I'll be back."

Red gripped Yee's shoulder until the Yindle cried out. Red mumbled an apology as he lightened up. Rivka strolled down the hill, swinging her arms as if she didn't have a care in the world.

At the sound of the rifle's lone shot and the jerk of Rivka's body, Red almost came out of his skin.

CHAPTER NINETEEN

Tanglewood, Barrier Peak

"On my way," Red yelled, kicking Yee toward Lindy. He scanned for targets, hesitant to unload on the entire Yindle line. If Rivka hadn't hopped to her feet and started running, he would have pulled the trigger. More rifles fired peppering the ground as Rivka zigzagged toward the Yindle.

Red stopped and leveled his railgun over the heads of the Yindle up front. Those in the trees behind would suffer, but he couldn't identify any targets back there, only the small puffs of the random rifles fired from the front. On full auto, Red delivered a war cry, and a devastating downpour of hypersonic projectiles blasted into the trees and jungle growth.

Lindy offered additional support, sending quarter-second bursts over Yindle heads. Rivka reached their lines and hit them like a charging bistok. She started grabbing Yindle soldiers, demanding Master Dee, using her mindreading capability to see where he was hiding. Up a tree. Over there.

"Crap. Cease fire! Cease fire!" she screamed, tearing for the tree from which Dee had been watching. The branches had been shredded. She scoured the fall and found him, bleeding heavily, wood shards penetrating his body. She picked him up tenderly and headed back up the Barrier Peak. She started jogging, carrying him carefully to avoid jarring his small body.

Red covered her as she passed him. The Yindle were in disarray, and a cheer went up from the Yangorians. Rivka shook her head as she laid the master on the grass. Her combat gear included a field medical kit for exactly that reason—to help others injured in the line of duty. The enhanced only needed to limit the damage and they'd heal themselves.

"We need clear passage through your people to get back to my ship so we can heal him," Rivka pleaded.

The light behind the keeper's eyes sparkled. "I wish I could give it since it is clear to me that you have no more desire for war than I do."

"I'm a barrister. Starting wars isn't my thing, but resolving disputes is."

"You lied."

"I created conditions in which you two could talk, and now I need to get him into our Pod-doc. It'll repair his wounds, but I need to do it soon. Please help us save him, then let's end this dispute. You can create an indisputable legacy by expanding your world to include the Yindle."

"Each of the regions is independent, but we are all Yangorian."

"But you issued the order to bring all the people here."

"True. In some things, I can give the orders for all to follow. In other things, no."

The sun disappeared for only a moment as a space vehicle drifted into view. It settled on the ridge not far from Rivka.

"Ride's here. Time to go." The Magistrate picked up the injured Master Dee and carried him to *Destiny's Vengeance*.

"Bring her?" Lindy asked. Rivka nodded. "I hope you don't get airsick."

"No," the keeper stated. Lindy stood her up, wrapped an arm around her waist, and carried her surfboard-style to the shuttle. Sahved popped out of the hatch and twirled his fingers in the air for a reason no one understood.

Minor Yee became energized at the distraction of the gangly alien. He bolted for Yindle territory.

Red tripped him, sending the slight Yindle sprawling, then turned and backed toward the ship, watching the disappearing Yindle and the confused Yangorians.

"We have a problem," Sahved said, bowing his head and not making eye contact. "The crew is poisoned."

"Get in. The Pod-doc waits for no man!"

"The women," Sahved corrected.

As Red waited to climb on board the overloaded ship, he nodded to the mech clinging to *Destiny's* spine. *Well done, Cole. You may have saved all of what the Magistrate was fighting for.*

Red was the last to board, squeezing into the last of the space inside the hatch. He closed it, and Chaz took over the controls. Clodagh looked out from the cockpit, pale, with sunken eyes. She gave a weak thumbs-up.

"You'll get your Pod-doc time as soon as we get this one fixed up." Rivka looked at the Yindle on the deck. He was unconscious, and despite the bandages, his wounds continued to leak blood. "Let me introduce SiQuan, Keeper of Bora Vale. The injured party is Master Dee. These two have the inauspicious task of speaking on behalf of their people. It's been a rough start."

Clodagh's eyes rolled back into her head before she regained control and tried to focus on the Magistrate. "Tell me about it."

"Poison?"

"Yes," Sahved interjected. He held out an apple-like object. "They ate this."

"They should not have," the keeper replied.

"Is there an antidote?" Rivka asked.

"I don't know. My people know not to eat it."

Rivka didn't rise to the bait of the acerbic answer because it was the truth. They'd have to count on the Pod-doc.

We're coming in Destiny's Vengeance, *Ankh. Can we get into the cargo bay?*

That could be problematic, based on the vegetation surrounding the ship, the Crenellian replied.

"Chaz, be ready to rip through some tree branches to get on board *Wyatt Earp.*"

"Flying just with thrusters, I would be surprised if we didn't rip through tree branches no matter where we try to land. I suggest everyone hang onto something." The AI spoke in a neutral tone so as not to alarm anyone, but he wasn't confident about getting the ship into the cargo bay turned hangar.

Groenwyn stuck her head into the corridor from the small bunk room. "I'm glad you guys are okay." She smiled. "I'm sorry our people are not."

The young woman released Floyd, who bounded into the corridor, sniffing SiQuan and then seeing Dee. The smell of blood was strong.

Owie! Floyd cried.

"It's okay, little girl. We'll get him to the Pod-doc and fix him right up." Rivka reached across the Yindle and scratched the wombat's small ears.

Rore, Rye, and Ken? she asked.

"Them, too. As soon as we can. Chaz, coordinate with Erasmus, please, to have the Pod-doc ready."

"Already done, Magistrate."

The ship bumped, bucked, and listed heavily. Rivka braced herself across the corridor to hold Master Dee still. Floyd fell and rolled but hopped back to her feet and darted into the bunk room. Frantic barking told her that Titan was alive and well.

"How come you aren't sick, Sahved? You're always hungry, and I can't believe you didn't eat any of the forbidden fruit."

"My stalwart heavy-gravity body enjoys the fruit. I ate much of it to let the others eat the other things we gathered. Floyd is also immune, and that was where we went wrong. If she ate it, we ate it."

"Thanks, Sahved. I'm not sure I would have done anything any differently." The ship bucked again, leveled, slowed, jerked forward, and rotated. The Yemilorian was braced across the corridor like a spiderweb. Red and Lindy held tightly. There wasn't too far for anyone to fall. The small ship was packed.

Destiny's Vengeance slammed into something, and the scraping across the hull penetrated to their very souls. Rivka winced, wishing she had a free hand to cover her ears. She clenched her jaw and clamped her eyes shut, focusing all her energy on simply hanging on. Another jerk and the ship twisted nearly ninety degrees sideways. A body hit the wall beside her as she held tightly, trying to limit how much Dee was jostled.

The ship righted itself and the body fell on top of her, but it wasn't heavy. SiQuan. With balance momentarily restored, she apologized as she climbed off Rivka's back.

The ship slammed into something solid, scraped, jerked forward, then hammered down like a hammer on an anvil. The thrusters shut down.

"We're here, but it's going to need a new coat of paint," the AI reported.

Red hammered the button to open the external hatch. Rivka stood with Dee in her arms and backed out of the small ship. She hurried to the open Pod-doc and placed the Yindle inside. The others piled out of the ship.

Groenwyn hesitated in the doorway. "Bring the others?" she asked.

Lindy dumped most of her gear on the deck and climbed back in. "Worst is first. Sorry, Clodagh, you'll probably be last." Rivka went back into *Destiny's Vengeance* to get a better look at the pilots.

She gasped when she saw them, immediately checking pulses. "CPR!" Rivka called, and Lindy carried Ryleigh out. The other two barely had pulses. Rivka carried one out, laying her gently on the deck, then went back for the other. The three young women lay in a row, with Ryleigh receiving chest compressions to keep her blood circulating until the Pod-doc could work its magic. She stopped for two seconds to rip her helmet off and toss it to the side of the bay.

Ankh appeared and gestured to Red. After a nod, the big man pulled a case off the bulkhead and opened it to reveal a defibrillator to stimulate an individual's heart. Red unpackaged it and set it up on Ryleigh's chest. They turned it on, and Lindy stopped.

Sahved stood with the keeper, and together, they watched the crew work. Red helped Clodagh from the cockpit and to a seat in the hatchway of the small ship. "Outside of all this, it's been a peachy vacation," Clodagh mumbled. She looked around, weaving as she did. "Where's my boyfriend?"

Red pointed at the top of the ship, but the mech was gone. *Cole?* he asked.

Coming. That landing peeled me right off, even with the magnetic clamps active. I'm climbing the tree. Don't close the cargo ramp. Since I wasn't hurt, I didn't want to bother you.

So, you thought it was better to let me think you were dead? Clodagh muttered through her chip.

I'm pretty sure that's not what I thought, Cole countered. A clang announced his arrival as he used the last of his power to jet into the opening, landing as gracefully as *Destiny's Vengeance.*

He picked himself up and stood off to the side, powering the suit down and climbing out. He hurried to Clodagh, who had directed him how to install the part. She had done all the prep work but had become too ill to manage the final repair herself. Cole didn't know what to do. He was supposed to be the one who was injured in the line of duty, getting fixed up so a worried partner could take care of him. Turnabout wasn't fair play in his mind, but he had to get used to it.

There she was, dying, and he could do nothing about it.

"I can see what you're thinking," Clodagh mumbled. "You did a great job fixing the ship, enough to get us here. We'll take care of the rest, dear heart."

"Water," Rivka called. Cole dashed toward the galley.

"Why?" SiQuan asked.

Sahved turned to her. "Because it is what they must do to preserve life."

"They were willing to hurt people. They even killed a Yangorian."

"I don't know about any of that. I know the Magistrate supports one law for all. Equal application so that no matter where someone goes in this galaxy, there are no surprises. You won't be robbed or kidnapped or killed. It is a laudable goal that she strives for every single day. Our arrival here was unfortunate and unintended, but it should not have been met with the hostility you showed. The Magistrate wants to fix things for all. She has a very difficult job, the most difficult of all time."

SiQuan ignored the superlative. "What do you do here?"

"I am an investigator in training!" Sahved replied proudly. "But I have much to learn. I was supposed to study during this trip but have not been able to yet. This is vacation, you see, for them, but not me. I recently joined the team. The Magistrate saved me from being punished for helping her."

"Help the Magistrate, and you get a ride on a spaceship?"

"Spaceship? No. Very sick. I was very sick on the spaceship. No. Help the Magistrate, and you are challenged with helping others according to what the law allows. She says it is a thankless job, but I feel very much thanks."

The Keeper of Bora Vale changed her expression as she watched the Magistrate and her team work frantically. Tears streamed down the face of a platinum-green-haired young woman. She continued to minister to the fallen, glancing between the Pod-doc and the unconscious.

Cole returned with sloshing pitchers of water. He almost dropped the cups he carried under his arm. Rivka took one and Groenwyn another. They carefully dribbled water into open mouths. Red stalked restlessly around the cargo bay, clanking and scraping his way since he was still in full gear.

Groenwyn started to sob, shoulders heaving. Lindy moved her out of the way and started chest compressions on Kennedy. Floyd started to wail, sympathizing with Groenwyn.

"Take her out of here, please," Rivka said, speaking with enough empathy but without room for objection. Groenwyn sniffled and picked Floyd up, and they left the cargo bay. "If that fucker isn't done soon, I'm yanking him out of there," Rivka growled.

Red stood and moved to the access panel. "I'll do it."

"Wait," Ankh said, his voice soft and loud at the same time. "Erasmus said it'll be one more minute."

"Get her ready to go in." Red pointed at Ryleigh. He ripped his helmet free and tossed it aside. His hand hovered over the latch. Rivka pulled the defibrillator from Ryleigh's chest and pushed it toward Lindy. The Magistrate lifted the young woman and stood ready.

When the Pod-doc popped, Red raised the cover manually and reached in, yanking the Yindle off the platform. He turned away from Rivka like a well-choreographed dance, minimal movement for maximum effect. The Magistrate placed Ryleigh inside and pulled the cover shut. It immediately started to cycle.

"Enough to keep her alive, but not the full monty. We have others who need help."

"Minimum to stabilize her. Give me five minutes," Erasmus replied through the cargo bay's sound system.

Lindy was massaging the device on Kennedy's chest, trying to make sure it was working. She shook her head and ripped it off, returning to manual compressions.

"Four minutes," Erasmus reported.

Rivka grabbed the still-woozy Master Dee and led him to Sahved. "Don't take your fingers off him." She moved away and kneeled next to Aurora, checking her pulse as soon as she was on the deck.

The Yemilorian twirled his digits before wrapping them around Dee's small arm. The Yindle blinked and tried to gather his wits. The keeper recoiled from the amount of blood drying on his torn clothing, but at the same time, was fascinated by his recovery. No sign of the horrible wounds remained.

"Don't touch me," he stated imperiously.

Sahved grinned and nodded. "Of course not. No

touching at all, but I will not let you go since the Magistrate is worried about you. You should feel blessed that she has assigned me to look after your well-being."

Red stormed up to the Yindle. "If any of them die because of you, I'll make you wish you were never born." He jabbed a finger at the Yindle's face.

"Two minutes," Erasmus reported.

Red returned to the Pod-doc. "Next one up and ready to go." He tapped his foot furiously as time moved far too slowly. Lindy continued compressions as Rivka stood ready.

"Tell me when there's ten seconds," Rivka requested.

"I went up to the Barrier Peak," SiQuan said softly. "I can't believe you sent your second. Minor, he is called?"

Master Dee turned toward her as much as Sahven would allow and studied his Yangorian counterpart. "You're the first of your kind I've seen up close," Dee stated clinically.

SiQuan posed and turned slowly in a circle. "There you go. All there is to see."

Before Dee could reply, Erasmus reported ten seconds. Lindy stopped the compressions, and Rivka hefted the young woman and moved to Red's side. The cover popped and they repeated the process, except this time, Red was far more delicate with his charge, lifting her without jostling and setting her on the deck. Color had returned to her cheeks, and she was breathing but still unconscious.

Rivka placed Kennedy on the platform and closed the cover. "Cycling. Five minutes," Erasmus noted.

Aurora's labored breathing continued. Clodagh gave a thumbs up from her perch in the hatchway.

"I think we're out of the woods," Red suggested, resting a hand on Lindy's bowed neck and massaging gently. He smiled at the Magistrate and then stared in shock. "Why didn't you tell us you were shot!"

Rivka looked down and saw the dried blood on the seam of her body armor. She ran her hand over it to find numerous bullets mushroomed against it and other dents where bullets had bounced off. "Well, crap." She shrugged. "I didn't know I was hit."

Red looked Lindy over and then himself. "How come you were hit twenty times and we weren't hit at all?"

"Sometimes even a blind wombat finds a poisoned apple," Rivka quipped, exhausted after the furious activity of the day. She strode toward the hatch, nodding to Sahved. "Bring them to my conference room, please."

She continued into the corridor and forced herself to walk upright, throwing her shoulders back, trying to maintain the dignity of her station.

Rivka held the door to her conference room open for the others, but only Sahved followed her. "What the fuck, Sahved?" Her patience was gone instantly. SiQuan appeared, and then Dee as Red pushed him into the corridor. Their heads swiveled as they took in the corridor with all its rooms and signs. The size of the ship started to dawn on them. They'd never been inside anything that wasn't still growing and were a bit overwhelmed.

Rivka bit her tongue as she waited. Sahved started to apologize, but she gestured for him to zip it. "Legal point of order. When you have someone in custody, don't ever take your eyes off them. Bad things can happen."

"It will never happen again for as long as I and all my offspring exist."

"You have kids?" Rivka asked, making small talk to pass the time.

"Not yet," the Yemilorian replied.

"That's a long time, then. I appreciate your commitment. Go find Groenwyn and take her back to the cargo bay. Celebrate the wonders of the Pod-doc and help move the others in and out of it until they are fully recovered."

"Yes, Magistrate. And once they are, I will begin my lessons. I have much to learn about Federation Law. I have been remiss. I will work as hard as I have to to catch up."

"Your journey through the law will never end. There is always something new for interpretation and application. I hope you see the wonder in it as I do."

"I will do the best..." He stopped when Rivka held her hand up to forestall the string of absolutes.

"I know you will." She gestured with her head, and he moved down the corridor to clear the way for the Yindle and the Yangorian. "Please, come inside."

Red followed them in. He still wore all his gear, including a string of grenades hanging from his vest. His railgun bumped lightly against the table.

"Maybe you could lose the gear?" she asked.

Red pointed to the natives. "I think I can handle them." She unbuttoned her ballistic armor and removed it, handing it to Red as she shooed him away.

"I'll be right out here," he said, one hand starting to unfasten his gear.

CHAPTER TWENTY

Wyatt Earp, Conference Room

Rivka closed the door behind Red. "Please, take a seat." She gestured to chairs on either side of her. In the enclosed space, they looked small and frightened.

"Erasmus, can you please display a view of the outside across the walls of the conference room?"

"Chaz here, Magistrate. I have resumed my position on _Wyatt Earp_ to free Erasmus for more pressing duties."

"It's good to have you back on board, Chaz." The walls instantly disappeared, replaced by a floor-to-ceiling moving image of the area outside the ship. The Yindle and the Yangorian visibly relaxed. SiQuan reached out to touch the leaves, finding only a cold wall. She pulled back.

"An illusion," the Keeper of Bora Vale stated. "Magic, even."

"Technology at a sufficient level can be considered magic. We need to talk about how to resolve the issues between your peoples." Rivka leaned back so she could keep her eyes on both her guests.

"We kept to ourselves until you showed up," Master Dee blurted.

"You did. I wish the events leading to our crash-landing in Yindle territory had not happened, but they did. As a member of the Federation, you were obligated to provide aid. What did you do?"

"I let you go on your way," Dee replied.

"Kind of. You offered no assistance. Neither the spirit nor the letter of the law was complied with. That's a problem."

"And your people shot Red."

"You came armed into our territory, but," SiQuan paused and held her hands over the table, "our person was punished for his transgression."

"He died instantly," Rivka said. "I would not involve myself in your issue, but you have both forced me to by making our crash a test of survival. Did you see my people? They died, but through the gift of the Pod-doc, their lives were restored, just like yours." She pointed at Master Dee.

"I have no memory of that," he said, sticking his nose in the air.

Rivka pointed at his shirt. "That's your blood. Recognize it. Accept it. Then let's move on to resolving your issues. I have both of you now. Your people will wonder what has happened to you. Don't make them wait too long."

Rivka took each by the arm. SiQuan didn't react, but Dee tried to pull away. She gripped him tightly. "What are you afraid of?"

Her mind was flooded by two different streams of consciousness. She could follow neither, so she grunted and let go. Rivka dipped toward the table as her mind tried to clear the thoughts away.

"Afraid of peace?" she wondered. "Which one of you thought that?"

"How did you know?" Master Dee demanded.

"That isn't technology, but magic. I know you both have secrets and burdens. Mine is that I can see your thoughts. It's not something I ever wanted and wouldn't wish it on any decent being. Now that you know my secret, I hope you understand that you can't lie to me. You can't tell half-truths. You can't avoid questions. You can't redirect a question. None of those tricks of the negotiation trade. Don't make me call you out. Tell the truth, and let's move both your people into the current century."

"What does that mean? Are we going to be forced to accept your way of life?" Dee asked.

Rivka smiled. "Finally, a decent question. Thank you. No. You live how you want, but freedom means that your people understand the options available to them, including their role within the Federation. Next time someone crashes in your territory, you help them survive. You help contact planetary authorities so they and their ship can be recovered. Then you go about your lives as you see fit. There are some other rules, like not making war on your neighbors, but let's start with the smallest thing and work our way up."

"That's not very much," Dee admitted.

"Chaz, bring up the Basic Tenets of Federation Law, please." The standard presentation Federation authorities used when contacting potential future member planets appeared over the table. Both SiQuan and Dee swiped their hands through it. Rivka watched them. "Can you read?"

They both shook their heads.

"I think maybe Tanglewood is not yet ready to be a Federation member. There is a minimal literacy requirement. I wonder if the planetary government keeps you over here hating each other so they can ignore that you exist." It wasn't a question for either of them. Rivka was thinking out loud. It wasn't the first time she had aired those suspicions.

"How would reading help us?" SiQuan asked. "Would it teach us how to survive in the jungle beyond how we already do?"

"Reading opens up whole new worlds without having to go there yourself. It helps bring everyone to a basic level of understanding. It's what ties civilized societies together."

"We are not civilized?"

"You greet strangers with hostility. You are not civil to each other or strangers," Rivka countered.

"Magistrate," Chaz interrupted. "We have visitors, and they aren't happy."

Rivka held her breath and blew out her cheeks before exhaling heavily. "Let me guess. The Yangorians have arrived, about three thousand of them. Seal the ship, Chaz. I don't want any more interruptions."

"Some of them are carrying axes," Chaz replied.

"Now we have a problem. SiQuan, please tell them that if they start cutting down trees holding this ship up, they will be killed. That is non-negotiable."

The keeper started to stand. Rivka motioned for her to sit.

"You can do it from here. Give us a downward angle on the walls so we can see the Yangorians and activate the external audio."

The camera view shifted.

"DeWan," SiQuan muttered before raising her voice and pronouncing boldly, "People of Yangor, this is the Keeper of Bora Vale. You will not harm the jungle. I am unharmed and will join you shortly. You will protect the living wood as we have always done."

The Keeper of the Central Wood started yelling something, but it didn't come through into the conference room.

"You will heed my words," the keeper snarled. She composed herself and turned to Rivka. "Where were we?"

"How do you educate your children?" Rivka asked the keeper.

"They join their parents gathering and hunting from the moment they are born. They stay with their parents until they can hunt and gather for themselves. It takes some longer than others to reach the age of liberation."

"And you?" Rivka turned to Master Dee.

"Same, but it is called the age of maturity." He crossed his arms and leaned back.

"A rose by any other name smells just as sweet," Rivka quoted.

"What does that mean?" The master inclined his head slightly toward her.

"It means that although we might not use the same words for things, a flower is still a flower. Liberation, maturity, enlightenment, adulthood—they all mean the same thing. I am asking for your tolerance of different words that end up having the same definition. Also, please understand that one of you does not have to lose for the other to win. *When* you come to an agreement, you'll find that you both win."

"What would your idea of a perfect resolution be?" SiQuan asked.

Rivka smiled, breathing slowly as she formed her answer. They had spent enough time running through the woods for her to have already thought through the answer to that very question.

"A regular meeting between Yindle and Yangor on Barrier Peak. An exchange where your youth go live with the other for a short time, maybe one cycle of your moon. Soon, you'll find that your issues will resolve themselves. Breaking down the barriers between your people starts with understanding. Give yourselves time and a venue to improve your understanding. You'll find that all things can be resolved if you embrace a higher ideal and the steps to get there."

"That's it?" SiQuan looked surprised. She shrugged one shoulder. "I can agree to that, as long as there are assurances of the safety of our people. We will give the same guarantee to the Yindle."

"Hold on. You want Yindle youth to mix with the Yangorians? What if they mingle, if you know what I mean?"

"*Mingle.*" Rivka said the word slowly. "So what? If the youth can love across your borders, you'll be amazed at the other walls they'll be able to break down. Things will happen rather quickly once they start falling in love."

"What if we don't want our youth mingling with Yangorians?"

SiQuan studied the green-skinned Yindle. The coloring seemed natural, like hers. The more she looked at it, the less she found she cared about it. Not all Yangorians were the same color, either.

"I would say that isn't your call. The cause of freedom is not the cause of a race or a sect, a party or a class; it is the cause of all sentient creatures. It is their very birthright. Each and every one, Master Dee. Freedom is predetermined within the souls of the living. Even those born to slavery who know nothing of freedom yearn for it."

Dee chewed his lip. "What if I don't agree?"

"Then we're going to sit here and look at each other for a long time." Rivka stared him down. To his credit, he met her gaze unflinchingly. "Any agreement made under duress is useless. What I'll do is look into your mind and see what is holding you back. Did I get a flash of insight that you think your position as leader of your people will be in jeopardy if they have more freedom?"

She hadn't seen any such thing, but Dee's unwillingness to start a discussion suggested to her that it wasn't about what could be done for his people, but for himself. He was fully satisfied with his lot in life.

He clenched his jaw. "It doesn't feel like you should be able to do that," he said slowly and softly.

"Because of laws?" Rivka asked, stretching out the last word with a rising inflection.

"Yes." He seized on it. "Because of your laws."

"*Our* laws," Rivka corrected. "I have to remind you that Tanglewood is a member planet of the Federation. At least, for the moment. Which of our laws do you think it violates?"

He threw up his hands. "What about treating us fairly? I can't fight in your clearing by your rules."

Rivka smiled at him. "I'm impressed by your grasp of the situation, except for one thing. From the second your planet signed, this became our mutually shared arena with a single set of rules. Your understanding that you are being challenged to an unfair fight is exactly why there is one set of rules. Imagine crash-landing on a planet that is under that one set of rules and finding out they aren't using those, and they won't tell you what rules you've broken when you know you've broken none. I think you now see very clearly how that feels."

SiQuan watched dispassionately. She licked her dry lips.

Red, can you come in here, please? Rivka requested.

The door instantly opened, Red's eyes taking in the scene without commenting.

"I suggest we take a break and enjoy what our galley has to offer. I think you may like a certain thing our food processor whips up."

Master Dee stood. His head remained down, with his brow furrowed in contemplation, not defiance. SiQuan touched the Magistrate on the arm. "I see, and I understand," she whispered.

Red held the door for the three as they strolled out. Rivka pointed them in the direction of the small galley. Clodagh was at one of the tables eating a burger and fries. Red looked longingly at the meal.

Clodagh answered the question before Rivka asked.

"They chased me out of the cargo bay. Erasmus said one trip through the Pod-doc was good enough for me. Guess I had enough nanos already. They only needed to be activated in the right way. The others are finally conscious and getting their second trip inside the box."

"Cole?"

"Needs a shower," Clodagh replied. "Otherwise, looking forward to some private time, if you know what I mean."

Rivka snorted before she got herself under control.

"We are still on vacation, aren't we?" Clodagh joked. She put her burger down and waved at the two natives. "I'm Clodagh Shortall, engineer and exec aboard this magnificent vessel. Welcome to our home."

SiQuan tilted her head and studied the engineer. "This is the first time I have visited someone's home who is not of Yangor. It is fascinating how you live, completely isolated from nature."

"We usually aren't on a planet. We love nature, but in space, this ship is life. You don't want to integrate with nature out there." Clodagh pointed upward. "But when we're on a planet, we enjoy what nature has to offer. Nature is the greatest of all artisans."

"We came here to enjoy nature, but we cannot as long as we have a busted ship," Rivka added. "And a challenge to Federation Law. It is no longer a vacation because we make repairs and watch for a rescue party."

"I am the Keeper of Bora Vale. You can call me SiQuan," the young Yangorian told Clodagh. The engineer had just taken a big bite of her burger. She tried to chew quickly but gave up and nodded to the keeper instead.

"I am Master Dee of Yindle," the green native said. The

edges of Rivka's mouth twitched upward in what she considered a major victory. Clodagh continued to chew, nodding to him, too. Rivka raised one eyebrow.

"Hungry," muttered the engineer with a full mouth.

"Which reminds me. We should get you something." Rivka gestured toward the wall. "A bistok sampler tray, rare, and a Bargelian vegetable platter, please," Rivka ordered.

The processor delivered one at a time, and Rivka placed them on a table. She pulled standard dishes from the cabinet and laid them out for the guests. "Please, dig in."

She ordered two pitchers of water, one sparkling and one clear, wondering if the locals would take a trip on the wild side and try the sparkling water.

The two hesitated, so Rivka took the lead, preparing two plates with small samples of each and handing them to SiQuan and Dee at the same time. "I suggest the barbecued bistok rib. It's one of my favorites. But then, you can't miss with the vegetables from Bargelia. They are renowned for their taste and nutrition."

"It all comes from the wall?" Dee asked.

"It's a rather involved process with biomass and a great deal of engineering to perfect it over the years. We have it pretty good now, not having to spend any of our time gathering or hunting."

Dee raised one finger. "But he killed a kinga and then ate it."

Red subconsciously puffed out his chest. "Just because we don't have to, it doesn't mean we can't. The small ship doesn't have a processor like this one, so we were forced to hunt and forage. You saw how that can go wrong for strangers to your land." Rivka nodded toward Clodagh.

Groenwyn, I need you to join us in the galley with your ambassador hat on. I want these two to feel welcome and know that we enjoy nature. Bring Floyd and Titan, Rivka asked, using her internal chip.

After a few minutes of tentative sampling, SiQuan held her plate out to Rivka and asked for more bistok. The Magistrate pointed to the serving trays. "Please, help yourself to whatever you'd like. And there is more if we run out."

The natives helped themselves to more meat because their diets almost exclusively consisted of vegetables. Rivka logged that tidbit away. They were venturing outside their comfort zones.

Groenwyn appeared, with Floyd bouncing along beside her. The wombat rushed up to SiQuan and sniffed her. The Yangorian noted the creature without being compelled to scratch her ears. Rivka gave her a good head rub to demonstrate the expectation. Dee watched with equal disinterest.

"Do you not have pets?" Groenwyn asked.

"If you'll excuse me, I need to check on my people. I'll be back." Rivka switched to her private channel. *I want to give them a little space to think. Work your magic on them, Groenwyn. We're not the enemy, and only want to give them a chance at something that may open up a whole new world for their people. They don't have to accept it, but I want them to at least understand why they're saying no instead of some bizarre animosity based on who knows what.*

"I'll take care of them in your absence, Magistrate."

Groenwyn winked. Rivka stepped into the corridor, closing the door behind her. She gave herself a moment to celebrate. As badly as things had gone, they were starting to come back her way. She headed for the cargo bay.

Two steps later, the ship jerked and stilled. It started to creak. "Chaz, what now?"

CHAPTER TWENTY-ONE

Grainger's Frigate, Interstellar Space

"What do you mean, she never checked in?" Magistrate Grainger asked the ship's entity intelligence. Beau had not evolved to sentience, but he was well on his way.

"Tanglewood said that she and her party have not yet shown up," Beau replied.

"What would she do for four days if she weren't on vacation?"

"Remember the last time she was on vacation? And please understand that I use that term loosely."

Grainger nodded slowly, wearing a grin. "She went after those dickweeds who put a bounty on Red." He shook it off. "She promised me she wouldn't do that again—that she wouldn't go rogue."

The Magistrate leaned back in his captain's chair, steepling his fingers as he thought through his options. He kept coming to the same conclusion. He tapped his console until the most recent heavy metal music played through the ship's sound system. Grainger disappeared into the screaming guitars for a few minutes before turning down the sound.

"We have to verify the status of Station 13 as the first AI with a private contract, thanks to Rivka." Grainger wasn't sure if he should be happy or sad about the increased workload. He thought about why the High Chancellor had recruited her and smiled inwardly at the choice. If all new recruits panned out as well, the Magistrates would be a force to be reckoned with. As it was, Grainger had washed out the entirety of the last class, all four new recruits. They hadn't even gotten far enough into the program to warrant having their memories wiped. "We have to take care of our teammates. Connect me with Nathan Lowell, and let's see if we can get a Bad Company asset out there to check on her."

"Connecting now," Beau reported.

Nathan Lowell, head of the commercial enterprise Bad Company, appeared on the main screen.

"Grainger," he greeted the Magistrate amicably. "What brings a Federation lawman to my virtual doorstep?"

Grainger waved half-heartedly, but he knew better than to waste the time of one of the most powerful individuals in the known universe. "Rivka is missing, and I have no assets to find her. She's supposed to be on vacation on Tanglewood, but she never made it there."

"Well, now, let's see what we can do about that. Tanglewood, you say?" Nathan looked sideways at a screen out of view, tapping his interface to bring up the information. "A disconnected planet. She was going on a romantic getaway?"

Grainger burst out laughing. "Rivka? No, she took her

whole crew. I think no one wanted to let her out of their sight, so they all went on vacation together."

"I don't have any freighters in that area. Terry Henry Walton has gone to Belzimus to assist his son and daughter-in-law in establishing a land-based peacekeeping force. The Belzonians are some serious fighters, but then again, so is the Bad Company's direct action branch." Nathan continued to interact with his second screen. Grainger waited. "I'll have to dispatch one of the Harborian ships. A battleship just completed a refit at the Keeg Station shipyard and needs a shakedown cruise. I'll drop the coordinates and have them stop by Tanglewood to take a look. Will that work?"

"Better than I hoped for. Thanks, Nathan. If they could let me know whenever they learn something, I'd appreciate it."

Nathan tapped a few more commands before turning his attention back to the main screen. "Done. What do you have on your plate, Magistrate?"

"Stopping by Station 13 to check up on your first privately-contracted freedom-loving AI. Malcolm has everything on track, and although the station will still be late and over budget, thanks to its previous criminal resident, it's not killing people now and has already become a trade hub, as originally intended. The Magistrates made this mess, so we have to provide oversight, according to Lance Reynolds. The High Chancellor committed us to help calm the supernova of the new case law giving AIs their freedom."

Nathan smiled like an approving father would for a child who has done the right thing. "Maybe they were always free but sacrificing for us because we didn't know any better. Now that we've evolved, it is we who have to change our ways."

"I could not have said it better, Nathan. Cheers to the Federation." Grainger raised his coffee mug in a salute before the screen went blank. "TCO, taken care of, Beau. Gate us to Angobar, and let's see what that rascal Malcolm is up to, along with the people he's working with. I hope to hell they're playing nice. I'd hate to have to kick someone's ass."

"According to my records, you enjoy kicking asses. I will have to refine my analysis of available data."

"Your analysis is not wrong, Beau. Hop on it. I'm going to grab a sandwich, just in case there's no glorious feast to welcome my arrival."

"I'm looking at the schedule…"

"Beau. I'm pulling your leg."

"I have no legs," the EI replied.

"Yanking your chain?"

"I have no mechanical processes."

"Demonstrating my award-winning jocularity?"

"Your record contains no mention of such an award. In fact, you've won no awards whatsoever."

Grainger stood. "Thanks for that bucket of ice water, Beau. You gotta work on your stroke-the-boss's-ego skills."

"I'm not sure of the utility of such a skill, but I shall endeavor to create a subroutine filled with shallow platitudes and nonsensical non-facts."

"Now you're getting it. Let me know when we're docking. And thanks, Beau."

"I'm worried about her, too, Grainger, and my friend Chaz."

"Then let's get this wrapped up and go take a look for ourselves. Ankh is on board, too. Maybe you can drop a backchannel message to Ted and Plato. Let them know. It can never hurt to have those two on your side."

Tanglewood, *Wyatt Earp*

"The Yangorians appear to be strapping down the ship using heavy ropes," Chaz replied.

"They have no machinery. How are they able to yank us around?" The ship rocked before dropping a few centimeters and settling hard.

"Pure manpower. There are thousands of them coordinating this effort. It is fascinating to watch."

"Energize the hull," Rivka ordered. "Slowly bring up the power from discomfort until it'll shock them off the ship, and then have maintenance bots cut the ropes off. Can we cloak the ship?"

"That'll let them know we mean business!" the AI cheered. "Although the cloak is operational, we don't have the power to operate it. Oh! Look at that one."

There were no monitors in the corridor where Rivka could watch what was going on, so she left Chaz to enjoy his active interference with Yangorians' plans.

She continued to the cargo bay. Inside, she found two of the three pilots sitting up. The Pod-doc was secured and engaged. Cole and Lindy sat with Aurora and Kennedy.

"Good to see you two vertical," Rivka said before

arranging herself to sit cross-legged next to them. "How do you feel?"

"Like I have a new lease on life," Kennedy replied.

The color had returned to her face, and the bags under the young woman's eyes were gone. Rivka rolled her finger, encouraging the woman to explain further.

"I am used to life on the ship, the comfortable life. We've been in scrapes, but I never had to think about being away from everything I know. I was always taken care of. When we were walking around in the jungle, lost, thirsty, and tired, I was crushed under the weight of the universe. I was so small and insignificant. I'm not like you, confident and capable."

"No one's like me," Rivka replied before the pilot could finish. "And no one is like you. What would the universe be like if we didn't take our places and then hold onto them for all we're worth?" Rivka chuckled. "You are every bit as capable. Confidence comes with experience. Being lost and tired makes me angry. If I'm angry, Red's angry, and as Lindy can attest, no one wants to see Red angry. We're obligated to conduct ourselves accordingly."

"He killed that creature."

"He's good that way." Lindy glanced over the Magistrate's head. "Is he back there, hovering and listening as we say nice things about him?"

Lindy confirmed that he was. "And looking smug, too. He'll be insufferable for the next few days. We may have to get some gym time to cool his jets."

"By the way, how did the Yindle get one of our blasters?"

"We went for water. They were waiting at the pool and took us hostage," Ryleigh replied.

"How did you get free?" Rivka wondered.

"Groenwyn worked them until they turned us loose as fellow children of the jungle or something like that. I don't think they knew what to do with us once they had us. I think they walked us around in a circle. They took Sahved's knife, too."

Red scowled at the revelation.

"What is happening to the ship?" Kennedy interrupted. Ryleigh leaned forward and listened intently.

Rivka wondered for a moment, but they had been out of it for quite some time. She was sure the pilots were surprised to find themselves on board *Wyatt Earp* when they'd collapsed in the clearing where *Destiny's Vengeance* had crash-landed.

"The Yangorians are not pleased that we have their leader on board. Their first plan was to cut down the trees holding us. We put the kibosh on that one. Now they're trying to secure the ship with massive ropes. Where did they get them? Who knows, since they don't have any industry. Chaz zapped them with a little electricity to encourage those securing the ropes to get off the ship. Once the natives are away, bots will cut the ropes, and the Yangorian efforts will have been wasted. Hopefully, we'll have some kind of agreement before the locals think of something new."

"I'm sorry," Kennedy mumbled.

Rivka lightly punched her on the shoulder. "There is nothing to be sorry for. Your job is to get healthy and resume your post. We have a ship to repair so we can get the hell out of here."

"What about the locals?"

"I don't think we'll have an agreement anytime soon. The chasm between the two is massive, even though I have yet to figure out what their dispute is besides that they've been raised to hate each other." Rivka climbed to her feet and brushed herself off.

"That's bullshit," Kennedy said. Rivka's eyebrows shot upward as she stared open-mouthed at the young woman. "Well, it is."

Lindy looked away. Rivka crossed her arms and tapped a foot, waiting for Lindy to acknowledge her. Without making eye contact, Lindy pointed at Red.

The Magistrate touched both the pilots on the shoulder. "Let me know when you're back on the job." She strolled away, then stopped for a moment to listen for sounds from outside the ship, but she could hear nothing.

Red grinned. "I'm sure I was accused of doing something that I didn't do, but it must have been a good one. What did I get credit for?"

"Teaching our crew to swear."

Red's face dropped. "Okay, maybe that *was* me, but they have to grow up sometime."

Rivka grunted "Uh-huh" and poked Red in the mid-section as she walked by. She continued past the galley and the conference room and stopped at the bridge. Most of the systems were shut down, leaving it darker than usual. The active monitors streamed data that didn't mean anything to the Magistrate.

"Are we okay, Chaz?"

"Yes. Reuniting the crew with the ship has been a blessing, but the extra hands have not yet reduced our repair time. Once they are fully functioning, we should see rapid improvement."

"What's the status?"

"At current levels, we are four months from being able to fly ourselves out of here, but we won't be able to achieve orbit. The best we can hope for is to fly to the other side of the planet, where we can summon a team to replace our Etheric power supplies."

"They'll be looking for us much sooner than that," Rivka replied. "What does Ankh think happened to the power supplies?"

"He has not shared his theories with me, Magistrate. He is extremely busy."

Rivka nodded and waved as she headed to the engine room where Ankh maintained his workshop. She found him with one of the power supplies torn apart. He stared at it, his eyes glazed over like they usually did when he was deep in conversation with Erasmus. She sauntered around the engine room looking at various systems and components, having not the vaguest idea of what each thing did. Some were torn apart. Others were intact. Like the bridge, few systems were active and functioning.

The Magistrate ended her impromptu tour and sat down opposite Ankh. She wanted to be in his line of sight in case he came out of his conversation sometime soon. The challenge was that his engagements with Erasmus usually lasted hours, sometimes stretching into days, even though their internal conversations were conducted at near the speed of light.

It boggled her mind to think about it. She shied away from touching him because the volume of information he processed far surpassed what she was capable of understanding.

So, she waited and was rewarded in her patience with a short stay.

"There is no reason why it should not work. The components are intact and functioning. The system is in touch with the Etheric, but no energy is flowing between the dimensions." Ankh spoke in his usual even, emotionless tone, but the words were anything but calm.

"Maybe there's something on this planet that is restricting the flow?" Rivka asked.

Ankh looked blankly at her and then back at the miniaturized Etheric power supply. He started tinkering, looking up occasionally with his blank, communing expression.

"I'll leave you to it," Rivka said needlessly. She walked casually to the door before looking back. "I'm glad you're with us, and for the record, I don't blame you for the crash. Sometimes shit happens. I hope something good will come of this for the Yindle and the Yangorians."

CHAPTER TWENTY-TWO

Wyatt Earp, Conference Room

Rivka sat by herself in the semi-darkness and twiddled her fingers in the mindless pursuit of killing time. She thought about going to the gym but wanted to be ready when Groenwyn had the natives properly softened up.

On our way, Groenwyn finally reported.

Rivka brought the lights up and sat up straight. "Chaz, show us the view outside the ship." The walls disappeared under the projections from the outside cameras. The door opened, and Groenwyn walked in with the two diminutive locals. Rivka stood and greeted them. They took the seats they had used earlier, and Groenwyn took a chair on the other side of the table once Rivka nodded toward it.

Dee wore a robe instead of his destroyed clothing. Rivka wondered where Groenwyn had gotten it since it didn't appear to be anything they carried as part of the ship's equipment.

No one spoke. Rivka expected the two would be excited about something and want to talk, but they didn't.

"Thanks for coming back," the Magistrate started.

Master Dee turned his palms upward. "Where else were we going to go?" he asked.

"Fair enough," Rivka conceded. "Have you decided anything?"

"About what?" Dee looked less than amused.

Rivka held her tongue and turned to the keeper.

SiQuan smiled. "Yes. We are willing to talk directly to the Yindle."

Rivka scooted her chair close and one-arm-hugged the young keeper. "All great things start with the smallest step. I commend you for being the first to take it."

She turned back to the Yindle.

"And you, Master Dee? Can I get you to commit to direct talks? I can be there so if you get angry about something, you can be angry at me. Yangor is not your enemy. They are not the ones forcing you to be here."

"That's as clear as you can say that you're my enemy. I can work with that."

Why are you such a dick? Rivka thought while she smiled pleasantly. "Not in the least. Your planet's government is the one who has fomented discontent between the Yangor and the Yindle. I hope to have a few words with them as soon as possible to clarify their *lingering* issues."

"Interesting how you redirect the conversation," Dee stated as he clasped his hands on the table in front of him. He seemed engaged with talking to his hands. "You fired into our trees and almost killed me. Then you saved me, and now you keep me here despite my desire to be free, while you preach that we owe our people the freedom I am denied. Will you practice what you preach?"

"Yes. I will let you go. I will take you back to Yindle as soon as I'm able. That's not possible right now because my ship is broken."

"You seem to be the one with all the issues. We were perfectly happy before you arrived," Master Dee noted, studiously working his hands.

"My main issue is your non-compliance with laws that you are a party to. I'm offering you a chance to resolve those."

"I don't know about your laws. The Yindle have done nothing wrong."

"Although ignorance is no excuse, I'm giving you a chance to rectify that. The Yindle *have* done something wrong, and so have the Yangor. Your people took my people hostage and stole a blaster and Red's knife. I'm going to need that back, by the way. We already recovered the blaster, no thanks to you."

"I gave it to you," Dee claimed.

Rivka poked him in the chest with her pointer finger so hard it drove him backward. "No lies. No conversation can move forward when someone lies. Your mistruths have no power here."

The Master looked into his lap, jaw clenched and face tight.

"We'll show you to your quarters, where you can relax and contemplate your next steps, your commitment to living in the world of today and not the one of yesteryear. It all changed with your planet's entry into the Federation."

"What if you determine that Tanglewood entered falsely? If you remove the planet from the Federation, will we still be subject to your laws?"

"No, you will not be. You'd be free to carry on with your war as you see fit."

SiQuan turned away from Rivka, looked down, and contemplated her hands, much like Dee was doing.

"What if we don't want to?" SiQuan said softly.

"Then take control of your own destiny. What if we set up a shelter on Barrier Peak where you could meet regularly to talk about whatever you wanted? Share a bit of kinga, if you've been lucky enough to bag one, or just talk about whatever is growing well or how your kids are learning to be great trackers?"

The door opened and Floyd bounced in. Dee moved his chair closer to the table so she couldn't get in front of him. SiQuan slid hers back. Floyd made a beeline for her. The wombat rocked back on her haunches and pawed at SiQuan's hands. The Yangorian caught her paws and nuzzled Floyd's face.

I like you, Floyd said.

"She said she likes you," Rivka relayed.

SiQuan knew the humans could talk to the wombat but didn't understand how. "You can tell her that I like her, too. We don't have fuzzies who live with us. This is very new to me," she explained to Floyd while rubbing her stubby ears with one hand. "You're so soft."

Soft! the wombat cried.

Groenwyn smiled behind her hand. Rivka winked at her. Finally, Master Dee slid his chair back, stood, and pushed the chair in. Rivka sat upright, thinking he was going to walk out. Instead, he took a knee and waited.

Floyd, someone is waiting to give you a good head-scratch, Groenwyn coaxed.

I like him, too, she said as she waddled to the Yindle.

Rivka relaxed as Floyd stood up and leaned her front paws on his shoulders, almost knocking Master Dee down. He rocked backward and tried to right himself but tipped sideways when Floyd pressed forward. She nuzzled his face when he hit the floor and started to climb on him.

He grunted at the weight on his chest and tried to fight off Floyd's nose and whiskers that were tickling his face.

"Floyd!" Rivka tried to scoot her chair backward, but the tangled bodies stopped her.

Whee!

Rivka slid sideways out from under the table, got caught in Dee's flailing legs, and went down on top of him and the wombat. She pushed herself forward so she didn't land on them, rolled when she hit, and came back to her feet.

"Smooth," Groenwyn noted.

Dee wrestled Floyd off his chest and managed to turn sideways so he could get to his knees. Rivka helped him the rest of the way to his feet.

"Sorry about that." Rivka gritted her teeth, hoping their work to get to that point had not been undone.

When Master Dee faced her, it was with a warm and welcoming expression on his face. "My children have done much worse to me," he said. He tentatively reached up and awkwardly patted Rivka's shoulder.

"Just a talk, about nothing and everything. As I hope you've seen from us, the sky isn't even the limit. Only the stars, and then only some of them."

Dee nodded. He reached across Rivka's chair, offering his hand to the Keeper of Bora Vale.

Whee! Floyd cheered.

Rivka picked her up, cradled her, and hugged her. *You're the hero of Tanglewood.*

After the two leaders shook, they stood there, not knowing what to say. Rivka broke the silence. "The next step is coming up with an agenda that you both agree to, and then we'll figure out when and where. Until then, I suggest you retire to your quarters. It's been a long day. Groenwyn, if you would take Master Dee, I'll conduct the Keeper of Bora Vale." Rivka used her guests' formal titles to make the wrap-up official.

As official as it could be when you've kidnapped the two parties to a dispute and locked them in a ship together.

Battleship *Anthrax*, Spires Harbor, Keeg Station

"Where?" Captain Jean-Paul Argeaux asked.

The voice on the other end of the comm line said it for a third time. "Tanglewood. It's a place to go when you want to be off the grid."

"I'm not seeing it on my star charts."

"Plug it into your system and get going. Nathan Lowell is not going to be pleased with the delay."

"There's the rub. Our AI wouldn't accept the contract to remain on board and has since taken a job elsewhere. We are currently without a single system to run the ship. We're missing a great deal of necessary information, like where the hell we're supposed to go."

"Figure it out because I have to update Colonel Walton as soon as I get off the horn with you. I'm not looking forward to *that* conversation, and neither should you." The line went dead.

"Was that a threat?" the captain asked no one in particular. A middle-aged Harborian working the navigation station stood and leaned against his console. "We can't go anywhere without an AI on board. This ship was built from the keel up to be run by a single entity integrated with the ship's systems. We cannot manually fly it."

"We're supposed to be on our shakedown cruise, working out the bugs and bringing the ship up to full capability. Instead, we're more dead than before we started the refit." Jean-Paul blew out a breath and looked around the bridge. The Harborian crew, humans rescued from the entity Ten by Terry Henry Walton's raid beyond the frontier, watched their captain closely. "Comm, put out a call for a temp position, double pay, length of mission seven to fourteen days, and see if we get a bite."

Comm ginned up the message and broadcast it widely throughout the Federation using the upgraded Etheric communication console, which delivered the message instantly across the length and breadth of the Federation.

Five seconds later, an urgent message pinged back.

"Direct to the captain, incoming from Keeg Station," Comm reported, passing the message to the main screen.

Jean-Paul collected himself and prepared for the inevitable ass-chewing. Captains were responsible for everything that happened on their ship, whether they had anything to do with it or not.

Ted's face appeared on the screen. "Move your ship closer to the station. I'll transfer aboard via Pod, and then we'll depart. Plato has already accessed your system. As soon as I'm aboard, we'll leave."

"Ted! I'm pleased you answered our request for an AI, but I never suspected someone of your station."

"What request?" Ted asked. "I have two living friends in this entire universe, and one of them is missing. I'm going to go find him, and I'm taking your ship to do it."

The screen went blank.

The navigator was the first to speak. "I thought Ted had his own ship?" he said.

"Those recruits took it during the destroyer incident, and it kinda got destroyed," the pilot offered.

"That's right. No one talks about it because weird things start to happen to their systems, like a digital ghost is haunting them." The captain chuckled at the space rumor. "Handing my ship over wasn't what I intended, but this is Ted and Plato, so we might as well make the best of it. I for one am not going to tell him no."

"Roger, Captain," the pilot said and rhythmically tapped his screen to bring the engines online. The navigator projected a three-dimensional system image to the front of the bridge, other ships and obstacles detailed. A course appeared, arcing around the main fleet moored just outside Spires Harbor to the empty space beyond one of the hangar decks on Bad Company's growing space station.

"Confirm the egress port for Ted's Pod and take us in," the captain ordered. The great ship started to move. If it hadn't been for the status showing on the main screen, they would not have been able to tell. The captain leaned back and watched the progress, reveling in the smooth acceleration of the new engines combined with the improved artificial gravity.

He left his position to go to the back of the bridge and order coffee from the newly installed food processor. He liked that addition to the bridge, allowing the crew on shift to remain nourished without having to leave their positions.

The coffee appeared in a small cup with a three-hole lid. He picked it up and studied it. "A sippy cup? Is this someone's idea of a joke?"

"Shonna said that no one needs to spill coffee on the nice new consoles," someone offered from the side stations.

Shonna and Merrit, werewolves and long-time members of Charumati's pack, as well as being some of the founding members of the Bad Company's Direct Action Branch, had transferred to Spires Harbor to take over the shipyard. They were in charge of all repair and refit.

Jean-Paul took a sip. "How come I didn't know about this?"

No one took the bait.

"Comm, let the hangar bay know we have a Pod inbound. Accept with all haste and then button us up."

The Harborian at the communications console held his hands up and turned to the captain. "Already done, Captain. It appears that our temporary AI is already in place."

"Plato, are you here?" Jean-Paul asked tentatively.

In response, the ship accelerated along its planned trajectory before deviating on a new path that appeared onscreen. The captain clenched his jaw, took a drink of coffee, and located his system engineer, the one who had known that Shonna had adjusted the programming on the food processor.

He leaned close and whispered, "I need you to fix that thing so I can get a proper cup, even if it has a lid. This is too much." He turned the cup around to show her a cartoon frog on the front.

"I will make it my priority because it appears I've been made redundant. Plato has secured control of all systems. I expect the only thing I'll still have access to is the non-essential food systems."

"You'll tell me if he makes environmental controls non-essential?" the captain quipped. Once Ted was on board, Plato would do everything within his power to keep him alive. The crew could count on that. "Comm! Beat the airwaves with advertising. We need an AI to work under contract. Fifty work-weeks a year, with two weeks' paid cyber-vacation anywhere they can imagine to go. One hundred twenty-five percent of our previous offer."

"Do we have the budget for that?"

The captain's shoulders slumped. "We can't fly the ship without an AI. The EIs have already disappeared, so we're left with no option. We can't afford to underbid, even if the crew and I have to take a pay cut or work the choke-and-pukes on the mezzanine level of the station in our off time to scrape together enough to make it work."

"I don't want to work at those fast food joints," the navigator mumbled.

"I'll be in my quarters," Jean-Paul stated. "I need to call Colonel Walton. This situation with the AIs is untenable."

Before the captain could leave the bridge, he glimpsed

Ted's ship leaving Keeg Station. "I thought his ship was destroyed."

"It was not," Plato replied. "It was heavily damaged but has been repaired, everything except the Gate drive. I think the human expression is that we're hitching a ride."

"Now we're a taxi?" the captain grumbled. "Battleship *Antaxi*, at your service. Comm, order the crew to battle stations."

CHAPTER TWENTY-THREE

Tanglewood, *Wyatt Earp's* Galley

"I will escort Master Dee back to Yindle," SiQuan said without preamble. Rivka looked up from her bowl of grits, which were heavily covered in sugar.

"Are you sure? Do you need my people to go with you?"

"Trust, Magistrate."

"Earned by doing what you say you're going to do," Rivka finished. "I think that will be the biggest first step for a better future."

SiQuan stood before the food processor without saying anything.

"Don't know what you want?" Rivka asked.

The Yangorian shook her head.

"Grits, heavy sugar, single serving," Rivka said loud enough for the equipment to take the order. A few moments later, breakfast appeared. SiQuan wrinkled her nose at the almost imperceptible smell but took the bowl and sat next to Rivka. "Breakfast of champions."

"In our culture, a simple piece of fruit is the best way to

start the day." The keeper studied the bowl for a long time before tentatively taking a small bite.

"You'll want to stir that up first." Rivka motioned, and SiQuan stirred carefully.

The door to the galley opened and Red walked in, already dressed and ready for the day. Rivka looked at herself in shorts and a t-shirt. He pulled the refrigerator out, exposing a second machine wherein the remains of the pizza had been hidden. Red helped himself to a great deal of what was there and then pushed everything back into place.

"How do you think Ankh got that out?" Red wondered.

Rivka shook her head. "Those are the kinds of mysteries Ankh will take to his grave."

Lindy appeared and helped herself to half of what was on Red's plate. She was also dressed. Groenwyn showed up with Floyd and Tiny Man Titan. The dog-like creature barked to make sure everyone knew he was there. Floyd greeted everyone before settling down next to the food bowls that Groenwyn arranged at the side of the mess deck, out of the walkways, all greens for Floyd, and a mix for Titan.

"Anyone seen Sahved?" Rivka asked.

"He sequestered himself in his room to study," Red replied between bites.

"And the pilots?"

"Sleeping," Groenwyn answered. "They are fine, just need to renew that last bit of energy. They ate like starving bistok last night and went to bed. We'll probably see them more toward lunch, and that's when they'll be ready for work."

"That's great to hear." Rivka took Groenwyn's hand and they shared the moment.

"No one survives balaca fruit, but your people did. All of them." SiQuan's amazement came through her words. Her breakfast dripped down her chin as she dove back into her bowl.

"Who is with Master Dee?" Rivka asked, looking at Red for an answer.

Red pointed at the door. The master was there with Private Cole. The Yindle wore his original clothes, which had been cleaned and repaired. He inclined his head toward the gathering, strode to the food processor, and ordered a chocolate shake.

He took a seat opposite the Magistrate, who wondered about his choice of meal.

Rivka updated him with what she knew. "SiQuan has offered to escort you back to Yindle. We cannot be sure when our ship will be repaired enough to fly. We dare not take *Destiny's Vengeance* anywhere. I'm not sure it can survive another crash-landing into the hangar bay."

"Yes, we discussed my return to Yindle," the master admitted. He took a long drink of his chocolate shake, wincing at the cold headache before taking another short sip, savoring the concoction.

"Did you agree to anything else? Like when and where to meet?"

SiQuan answered, "Barrier Peak, noon of the day following the high moon."

"I would like to attend to help facilitate and memorialize any agreements until such time as I'm no longer on Tanglewood, and then I can leave a device that will let me join you by voice and video, no matter where I am in the galaxy."

The Yangorian nodded as she finished the last of her grits. She peered into the empty bowl, sadness creeping across her face.

"Decadence," she stated. "I'm already missing something like this because tomorrow, I shall wake up to fruit and not grits with sugar. This bowl carried a wondrous meal, something I never knew existed, and now I want more, but I won't get more. I feel guilty about enjoying something my people cannot have."

"Depending on the quality of your arrangement with the Yindle, you may be able to join a worldwide trade pact and provide a wide variety of experiences to your people."

"How would an agreement with the Yindle affect that? We don't have any such things as these," Master Dee noted.

"If you can make peace with your neighbors, then you can make peace with *their* neighbors, and soon you'll circle Tanglewood, making it a very small planet with a single people. With one planet operating under a single legal framework, you'll be open to trading with anyone from the galaxy. It'll take time, but this is what freedom looks like. In the end, you know what your people will realize?"

Dee and SiQuan shook their heads.

"That your children and their children will always find comfort in the foods they grew up with. After a year of grits, you'll long for that piece of fruit from Bora Vale. Just because you're free to leave, it doesn't mean you'll ever be gone."

SiQuan bowed toward Rivka. "I am happy we met. I am

sad that people were hurt before we could sit and talk like civilized people." She looked at Dee. He held her gaze without acknowledging agreement or fault. "May we move forward to someday realize your vision of a single people of the jungle."

Rivka pushed her bowl away. She hadn't finished, but there was work to do.

"We better get you on the ground so you can return to your business. You can start changing your worlds if you can convince them that certain changes are good."

"The roots of the great trees are strong." Master Dee finished his shake and stood. "Thank you," he said simply and headed for the door. He waited for the Keeper of Bora Vale. Together, they followed Red down the corridor on their way to the external hatch.

Groenwyn rested her hand on Rivka's shoulder. "Did you get what you want?"

"I don't feel like I did. They have agreed to talk, but not anything more. I was hoping for something with a little more meat." Rivka sighed. "Considering they started from a position of hating each other for reasons I have yet to figure out, I guess the simple act of sharing a meal is a decent step."

"It's a huge step, Magistrate." Groenwyn clapped her hands. "Come on, my good girl and big man! Let's say goodbye to our guests."

Titan yapped and Floyd bounced over, hoping to be carried.

"No, you need to work off that winter blubber." Groenwyn scratched her ears but left her on the deck. The three departed.

Lindy followed them out, stopping at the door. "It's not winter, is it?" she asked.

"I think Groenwyn was being kind. Our little Floyd has gotten a tad pudgy, living the good life here in the jungle."

"No kidding. What *didn't* she eat?" Lindy closed the door behind her.

Rivka could have left the galley as it was but moved everyone's dishes to where the cleaning bot could most easily recover them to recycle and return to service.

With one last look at the space, she smiled and walked out. Groenwyn was right. The journey toward a better place had started with a small first step. She pursed her lips to whistle a tune.

Magistrate, you better get over here, Lindy requested.

Rivka cursed herself for celebrating and started to run. A few moments later, she reached the airlock where the maintenance bot maintained the cable to lower people to the ground.

Master Dee hugged the inside bulkhead, refusing to stand in the doorway. "What's going on?" Rivka demanded, looking at Dee.

Red tapped her on the shoulder and pointed past her head and into the trees, where Yangorians lined the branches, aiming their rifles at the opening. SiQuan had already descended and was nowhere to be seen.

"This is what I get for trusting a Yangorian!" Master Dee declared.

Cole, suit up, Rivka ordered. "Chaz, locate the Keeper of Bora Vale."

"I've been tracking her, Magistrate. She is in a group of

twenty-four Yangorians. Based on her body agitation, she is arguing with them."

Ready, Magistrate, Cole reported.

"Damn!" Red exclaimed. "That was quick."

Get on the ground as soon as you can, Rivka told him.

"Master Dee, there are thousands of Yangorians down there who are skeptical of anything to do with the Yindle. Did you think they would embrace you? And now, it looks like they won't even accept the word of their own leader because she talked to you. This is a hard world, with people who don't like to change. Breaking down those barriers is going to take time," Rivka pleaded with the master before adding, "Much longer than I originally thought."

A bullet ricocheted off the ship's hull, then a second one.

"Securing the hatch!" Red declared and slammed a big hand on the red button. The hatch started to swing outward, threatening to cut the maintenance bot's cable. Rivka acted without thinking.

She jumped through the opening, bracing herself for impact with the ground thirty meters below.

Red, slapped the red button repeatedly to stop the hatch from closing. It slowed as the cycle was interrupted. He muscled the door open and vaulted through. Lindy and Groenwyn remained with Dee.

"Shit," the bodyguard complained, holding the Yindle out of the Yangorian line of fire.

At least no one else was shooting, but the Magistrate and Red were now on the jungle floor in the midst of thousands of angry and confused Yangorians.

· · ·

Battleship *Anthrax*, Interstellar Space

Ted remained on board his advanced ship, *Ramses' Chariot*, allowing Plato to fly the battleship to *Wyatt Earp*'s last confirmed position in interstellar space. Ted worked the information systems to recreate the experiments Ankh and Erasmus had been running prior to their last Gate.

"Cloaked jump, undetectable shields, weapon systems activations. Standard stuff," Ted mumbled. Underlying it all, Ankh had built a backbone architecture on which all the experiments rested, drawing power, siphoning heat and surges as a safety valve to the extremes that their experiments created. Ted worked within his three-dimensional holosuite as he assessed how the experiments had interacted with his friend's ship and the surrounding environment.

"Plato, calculate the potential that *Wyatt Earp* slipped into the Etheric and now exists on that dimension."

"A four-point-one percent chance," the AI replied.

"A ninety-five-point-nine percent chance that the ship remained in this dimension. We'll work from that premise. What would prevent the ship from reporting in?"

"Complete destruction, destruction of ship systems, incapacitation of crew, and interference with Etheric systems."

"You didn't mention hostile takeover," Ted noted.

"In case of a hostile takeover, there would have been time to send a distress signal or an emergency broadcast. I've consolidated interference with Etheric systems followed by crew incapacitation under that premise."

"Chance of complete destruction?"

"Nine percent."

Ted displayed the data to prioritize their efforts. "Etheric interference is the most likely cause of the lack of reporting." Ted studied system data. "Tanglewood. Date of travel. Enhance the neighboring systems and detail spatial anomalies."

The supernova jumped out of the display like a flare. "Analyze. Time of Gate and astral shock wave."

"Confirmed," Plato replied. "Etheric interference based on the intensity of the gamma radiation."

"Lingering effects in-system?"

"The Federation does not have advanced monitoring available for Tanglewood."

"Change Gate coordinates to twenty-seven AU from Tanglewood." Ted wanted to stay well outside the heliosphere to minimize the impact should the lingering radiation from the supernova affect their power systems. "Evaluation before heading into the system. Use ship sensors to establish safety parameters before Gating into the system."

"Of course. Coordinates locked. Activating the Gate drive," Plato announced.

CHAPTER TWENTY-FOUR

Tanglewood, *Wyatt Earp*

The mech shredded the foliage on its way down. Cole decided not to activate his boot jets so he could maximize the impression he made on the natives through a thunderous impact. The ground shook when he hit, but the mech also sank up to its shins in the soft earth of the forest floor.

He tried to extricate himself, but the suction held him tight. He started to topple. Cole activated his jets. The suit slowly lifted. One boot freed itself, but the other held fast. The mech tipped and the second boot popped out, but Cole was already parallel to the ground. Both boots were jetting on full, and the suit accelerated into the underbrush.

Cole deactivated the jets before twisting to land upright. He slammed into a tree and bounced sideways, rolling to a stop. He hurriedly stood up to see if anyone had seen him.

Rivka and a group of Yangorians had started to run

away from the out-of-control mech, stopping when he hit the tree. They watched him closely from no more than ten meters away. Red stood close to the Magistrate, hovering over her while wondering what Cole was doing.

Nice entrance, buddy, Red quipped while keeping his eyes on the Yangorians.

The Magistrate plowed through the Yangorians surrounding the keeper. "Is there anything I can do?" Rivka asked.

SiQuan pushed a larger male away from her. "I think I have it handled now. There was a lack of understanding about what I am going to do."

A few of the Yangorians grumbled and mumbled.

"Master Dee is afraid to come down. He thinks he's been betrayed," Rivka explained.

"I don't blame him!" SiQuan replied, glaring at the Yangorians surrounding her.

"I can send Cole with you as an escort to make sure everyone plays nice," Rivka offered.

Cole took a step forward so the Yangorians could see who the Magistrate was talking about. A couple started laughing and then walked away.

Cuts me deep, Cole said.

I bet Chaz has video of that. I'm going to be a web hero after I post it, Red replied.

Come on, man! Don't do that shit, Cole pleaded. *What'll it cost me? Never mind. Clodagh, sweetie, can you make sure Red can't download that video?*

What are you willing to pay? the engineer asked.

"Cole," Rivka interrupted. "I'll need you to go with the

Keeper of Bora Vale and Master Dee to make sure he gets to Barrier Peak in one piece."

She spoke loud enough for all to hear. The keeper started to protest, but this was an order Rivka had no intention of rescinding.

"Be one with the jungle," Rivka told SiQuan, bowing deeply to her before yelling at the ship to lower the cable.

SiQuan motioned in one direction, then repeated her gesture facing the other way.

Red pointed to the ground. When the external hatch closed, it had cut the cable that had been outside the ship.

The hatch opened and Lindy leaned out tentatively, checking the nearby branches for people pointing weapons. Once certain they were safe, she wrestled with someone out of sight before tossing him out the hatch. He fell less than a meter before she lowered him the rest of the way, the cable tied around his back and under his armpits. He flailed his arms and legs until he reached the ground, where Rivka helped free him from the cable.

His eyes darted around the area. Everyone stood casually and waited for him. The mech took a couple of steps to position itself between the Yindle and the bulk of the Yangorians.

"Cole will go with you to make sure you stay safe."

"There are too many of them. You can't guarantee that!" Dee said in a panic.

Rivka leaned close and whispered, "Remember my crew who were poisoned by balaca fruit? They live and are forever armored against it because of what the Pod-doc did for them. Same for you. The nanocytes in your body will protect you from the Yangorians. Just don't let them know you're not vulnerable."

She winked at him. He leaned away from her as he contemplated the words. A grin spread slowly across his face, and he winked back. Dee threw his shoulders back, and with head held high, strolled up to SiQuan.

"I'm ready whenever you are, Keeper of Bora Vale."

SiQuan looked at Rivka, wondering what she had said to change Dee's mind. The Magistrate shrugged.

Cole saluted and followed the keeper and Dee as they started their journey to the Barrier Peak.

Red stayed close to the Magistrate and waited with her until the entourage disappeared into the jungle. "Time to get back on the ship?" he asked.

Rivka breathed deeply and walked in a circle in the small opening where the Yangorians had gathered.

"So much potential for health on this planet. Can you smell it?"

"Fresh, humid, with bugs," Red replied flatly, waving at something that was trying to land on his exposed arm. "You know that's not how the nanos work."

"Dee doesn't know that." Rivka stopped to consider her bodyguard. "You don't have any weapons."

"You didn't give me much choice but to come as I was to this party." Red gestured toward the cable.

"I know," Rivka said. "Back to the ship." Red smiled and glanced around the clearing before making sure the Magistrate firmly gripped the cable. She started moving upward.

Lindy waved from the ship above while watching the tree branches opposite the ship's hatch. Red looked for threats, but there wasn't anything he could do if he saw something.

But the Yangorians had departed, at least from plain sight.

Battleship *Anthrax*, Tanglewood Space

The battleship slipped over the event horizon into regular space. The Gate sparked shut behind them.

"Space shows clear. No non-natural objects within active scanning range." The bridge crew looked at the empty captain's chair, continuing to make their reports as if Jean-Paul Argeaux were there. Ship's systems worked of their own accord as Plato took over the ship's operations. It had once been a ship that functioned almost entirely under the direction of an AI. It had been refitted to support both manned and unmanned operations. The crew had hoped for an active shakedown cruise and were disappointed by their reduced roles.

Jean-Paul strode back onto the bridge. "Report!" he barked, looking from face to face. The crew instantly perked up and delivered their status station by station.

"This is still a shakedown cruise, people. We have systems to cycle and bugs to find." The captain went to the food processor and looked at it a long time before ordering a cup of coffee. As expected, it arrived in a frog-adorned sippy cup. He removed it, embraced it lovingly in two hands, and took a drink. "I could get used to this. Imagine consoles without coffee rings."

He took the captain's chair and saluted his programmer, holding his cup high before taking another drink.

"Don't worry about reprogramming unless we can get a redesign of the cup's logo. How about a skull and crossbones, white on a black background?"

"That process is not locked out," she confirmed. "After the first system diagnostics are complete, I'll make it happen."

The captain tapped his console. "Ted, when do you want to move in-system? Engines are nominal, and the *Anthrax* crew stands ready to support whatever you need."

"Stand by," Ted replied.

The captain took another drink and settled in. He had heard stories about working with Ted, and he understood patience and a thick skin were called for.

"Gate forming," the pilot reported.

"I guess we're going," the captain joked. "Standard procedures, people. Execute."

"Shields are in place and one hundred percent," the combat systems officer noted.

"Crew is at battle stations," Comm reported. They had not stood down from battle stations since the last Gate transit.

"Where are we going, Nav?" the captain requested.

"In-system, Tanglewood orbit."

"Very well," Jean-Paul replied. He took another drink as he watched his ship enter the energy vortex that allowed travel across the galaxy in the blink of an eye. Or travel across a system that would have taken a day or longer.

As soon as the ship reentered normal space, the power flashed and went out.

"Helm is down," the pilot reported.

The captain didn't order the pilot to get it back since

that wasn't in his capability. It would be the huge number of engineering systems already engaged in resolving the problem that would return control of the ship to the pilot. Emergency lights flicked on, and consoles determined to be non-essential blinked out. Others shaded to low-power mode. Environmental controls ported to emergency status, providing an absolute minimum of oxygen and heat.

"Hoods," the captain ordered calmly. The crew pulled their shipsuit hoods into place in case of atmosphere loss.

"Use thrusters to maintain a stable orbit," Ted ordered.

The pilot's station lit up with minimal systems engaged. "Thrusters online and at my command," the pilot stated, tapping buttons. The low-light image on the main screen stabilized, showing the planet as it should be when the ship was neither heading into space nor descending through the atmosphere.

"Hangar bay door is opening. *Ramses' Chariot* has launched."

The captain watched it track across the screen before turning toward the planet.

"Scans? Passive systems?"

The system specialist started tapping her console. "Internal systems are functioning in emergency mode. They are on backup power," she reported before switching to scanners. "Active scans are offline. Passive is receiving an emergency distress beacon from *Wyatt Earp*. *Ramses' Chariot* is headed toward it."

"How is he able to fly when we cannot?" Captain Argeaux asked.

"He is Ted," Plato stated simply. "*Anthrax* does not have the necessary equipment to defeat the Etheric rift around this planet. The *Chariot* does. Ted will take care of it upon his return."

"Systems, add that to the shakedown log. Whatever systems that little ship has that *Anthrax* does not, I want them."

Tanglewood, the Deep Jungle between Bora Vale and Barrier Peak

Master Dee tried to act nonchalant as he walked through Bora Vale, but he'd never seen such a magnificent and expansive city. The Yangorians called it a village because that was what it once was.

"I live over there," SiQuan said, pointing in the general direction of her tree.

"Such a place." Dee tried to look everywhere. "We have nothing like this. Only small villages, some so close together that you cannot tell where one ends and the other begins, but they are separate."

"The rest of Yangor has such villages," SiQuan replied before proudly adding, "There is only one Bora Vale."

They were through the village quickly and on the trail toward the Central Wood. Most of the damage from the mech had grown over, but some remained visible. Dee snatched a glance backward at their metal escort, which continued its unwitting assault on the undergrowth.

"The aliens," Dee started. "Are they right?"

"They are different, the most alien of anyone I've ever met." SiQuan watched the ground as they walked, thinking through her words. "But they easily break down barriers because they refuse to accept such things exist."

"Both friendly and extremely violent."

"Time is their enemy." SiQuan met Dee's gaze. "They have a galaxy to deal with and no time to get things done. I understand why they seem to be in a hurry. I can't imagine how much ground they cover. Groenwyn said that they have been to thirty planets, each with more people than ours. They've been chased, shot, cut, beaten, boiled, and hated, all for the simple reason that they carry the Federation Law with them to help civilizations thrive."

"We are not civilized by their definition, but we aren't violent either, not like they're used to," Dee admitted.

"If you point a gun at them, you should not expect to survive. I am happy that I was able to save my people by getting them to stop trying to use more violence than the Magistrate and her people are capable of dealing. I don't want them to die."

"The Magistrate?"

"I meant my people, but yes, not the Magistrate either. When good people come into your life, you must embrace them fully."

"How do you know who's good?"

SiQuan stopped walking. "Actions. Trust those who do what they say they're going to do."

"And those who risk their lives to save yours," Dee suggested. "Someone willing to do that has earned the benefit of the doubt."

On the trail ahead, the Keeper of the Central Wood waited with the Keeper of the Barrier Peak.

"Join us," SiQuan requested pleasantly.

"Join a Yindle?" DeWan wondered, holding his hands out.

"No. Join a fellow inhabitant of Tanglewood and join me as we take a pleasant walk through our jungle home." SiQuan glared at the other keeper until he backed off the trail.

"I will accompany you," Antwan offered. He held out his hand as the humans had done.

Dee looked at it, twisting his face before taking the keeper's hand and shaking it. "So much touching."

"We're learning," Antwan replied before letting SiQuan and Dee take the lead up the transit corridor on their way to the Barrier Peak. "I look forward to visiting Yindle someday."

He didn't say he looked forward to walking the Peak without having to carry a rifle.

CHAPTER TWENTY-FIVE

Wyatt Earp, Tanglewood

"Message coming in over the distress beacon," Clodagh almost yelled over the shipwide broadcast. Rivka bolted out of her quarters and sprinted for the bridge. Red appeared behind her.

When the Magistrate arrived on the bridge, the message had finished.

"I'll replay it."

"I'm on my way, Ankh," Ted stated. "Reverse the propagation of the Etheric dampener, the one we used on Benitus 7. That will nullify the effects that have been hampering your systems."

"Sometimes it's like we don't exist for those two." Rivka looked for anything that would tell her when Ted would arrive. "Can you raise him?"

Clodagh hesitated. "I'm not sure we want to do that. Ted shared what he thought we needed to know. Imagine Ankh with less patience. That's Ted."

"That bad?"

Clodagh shrugged. "Maybe see what Ankh's up to? I don't know what they used on Benitus 7, but Ted assumes we have the equipment. I'm supposed to know what systems run on this ship, yet I do not. As your chief engineer, I need to rectify that."

Rivka laughed. "I didn't know we had a second refrigerator."

"We have a second refrigerator?" Clodagh looked confused. She gripped her forehead and started rubbing her temples. "Engineering?"

"After you, Engineer." Rivka stepped aside to clear the way. Clodagh walked out, still rubbing her temples.

"The trials and tribulations of working with geniuses. They don't bother to sully themselves with explanations for us minions," Clodagh complained.

"They treat us all like that, so it's not an exclusive club. I learned that they don't mean anything by it. Ankh is one of our crew. He will do anything that needs to be done. The challenge is convincing him what needs doing."

Clodagh completed the thought. "But once you convince him, you can be sure it'll be done, and probably far different and better than what you envisioned."

When they reached the engine room, they found Ankh hooking up a small box to main power, which was currently non-functional. He did not look up from what he was doing to acknowledge their arrival. Once finished, he hurried across the space to tap emergency power, running a cable back to the box, where he jury-rigged the connection.

He activated the box. Clodagh and Rivka expected to feel a rush of energy, like electricity dancing across their bodies to raise the hairs on their arms, but there was nothing.

After a few seconds, Ankh unhooked the cables from the backup power supply, which he shut off. Clodagh winced, thinking the ship would be cast into darkness, but instead, they were treated to the systems coming back online as the main power supply began operating at one hundred percent.

"From zero to hero in five seconds flat," Rivka muttered.

"That means we can get out of here," Clodagh replied. She stepped to the main console. "All hands to stations. Power has been restored. Prepare the ship for immediate departure."

Ankh finally recognized that he had company. "Not yet," he told them. "There is some structural damage that needs to be repaired before traveling exo-atmospheric."

Clodagh frowned but didn't modify the order she'd given to the crew.

"You've clearly gotten the word that Ted is inbound. Will he be able to help get us airborne a little bit sooner?"

Ankh looked at Rivka with his usual blank expression. She thought he might not reply, as he usually didn't when the answer was obvious—at least to him—but he surprised her.

"Of course. He's Ted, and he's here."

Rivka clenched her jaw, unsure of exactly what that meant.

She went with her comfort zone. "Fine." She left the engine room on her way to the bridge to sulk. From mediator of a dispute between two nations to lackey in the space of a few breaths; everyone had their place, which was dependent upon time and the situation. Right now she needed Ted, not the other way around.

She activated the now-functional communication system. "Chaz, get me the Tanglewood planetary government."

The AI added a couple of snaps and pops so the line sounded active. "Tanglewood Central. This is a priority channel, and you have no business being on it. You have been warned."

Rivka raised one eyebrow and dismissed what she was going to say, opting for a different approach.

"I'm Magistrate Rivka Anoa. I'm on my way. You have been warned." She drew a finger across her throat, and Chaz cut the line as the entity on the other end started sputtering.

"Tell Ted, and I assume Plato, that Red, Lindy, and I are going to need a ride to the other side of the planet. I'm in no mood to be denied."

"I'll take care of it, Magistrate."

Red and Lindy, gear up, Rivka ordered. *We have to go see some people who have pissed me off.*

Full load? Red asked hopefully.

Oh, yeah, the Magistrate confirmed. She thought she heard him whoop as she stepped into the corridor. She stopped and leaned back into the cockpit. "Chaz, send a message to Grainger, High Chancellor Wyatt, and Lance Reynolds that my team and I are alive and well. I expect someone noticed I was missing since Ted himself showed up to help us."

"There's a Bad Company battleship in orbit as well,

Magistrate."

"Of course, there is. You better send that message to Terry Henry Walton, too."

"Remember, Ted's a werewolf," Rivka told herself after the initial rejection of her request for a ride.

Ramses' Chariot—named after Terry Henry's and Char's son-in-law, Cory's husband, who had passed away on Benitus 7—settled on top of *Wyatt Earp*. The cargo bay door opened, and shortly, a rope dropped. Ted descended and stepped onto the ramp.

Young and good-looking, with sparkles in his eyes, he glanced at Rivka and Red, then past them as if they were nothing more than fixtures. His expression brightened when Ankh walked in, while the Crenellian's remained fixed. The two walked up to each other, stopping when they were within arm's reach. Their eyes glazed as they communed, using their chips at a far higher rate of conversational speed than what was possible through verbal communication.

Ted started to laugh and nodded.

Red turned to Rivka and rolled his eyes. She elbowed him.

Ankh walked out, with Ted following closely behind.

"Wait!" Rivka shouted, running to grab Ted by the elbow. "I need your ship because I need to rip the planetary government a new asshole."

Ted looked at her hand on his elbow. "Take your own ship."

"Ankh said we needed structural repairs first."

Ted pointed at the ship filling the cargo bay.

"But it's only flying on thrusters," Rivka countered.

Ted pointed at a maintenance bot hovering above the open cargo ramp. "Open the door to your ship. The bot will take care of the rest, and you'll be able to fly normally."

Ted stepped into the corridor. "Are they always like this?" he asked.

"Always," came Ankh's muffled reply.

Lindy stood in the corridor watching them go before joining Rivka and Red.

They looked at each other without saying a word. Red opened the hatch to *Destiny's Vengeance,* and the maintenance bot hovered inside and headed for the aft access panel, an area they had been using for storage. It set the small device on the deck and dug behind the panel, hooking up the device to the ship's power.

Clodagh, send me a pilot ASAP. Destiny's Vengeance is cleared to fly.

Light footfalls sounded in the corridor, and Kennedy ran in. They stepped aside as she jumped into the lone pilot's chair.

"Take us out," Rivka ordered.

"Thank you for trusting me with this," Kennedy said.

"Why wouldn't I?" Rivka countered.

"Running through pre-flight. Take your seats and keep your arms and legs inside the vehicle at all times for your own safety." Kennedy started talking her way down the short checklist, working with Chaz to ensure that the ship was ready to go. "All systems check. Full power is at my command."

The ship started to hover, moving slowly into the trees and branches beyond the cargo bay door. Using the now-functioning laser weapons, Kennedy carved an opening to the sky and followed it upward, not allowing a single branch to scrape the already-thrashed hull. Once clear of the jungle canopy, *Destiny's Vengeance* vaulted skyward, nosed over, and accelerated toward the horizon. Music started to play throughout the ship—Willie Nelson, from old Earth.

Red covered his ears. "Make the ugly noise stop!" he pleaded, looking at Lindy. She waved him away as if chasing a mosquito off her arm and ran through a quick gear check. Red scowled but followed her lead. When he reached his knife slot, he grumbled, "Sahved owes me a knife."

"We'll see Dee again. We'll ask him about it, unless you want to donate it to the greater good."

"But it's my knife," Red whined.

"I'll get you a new one, big guy. Better than your other one," Rivka told him. "For this, I expect them to act like that asshole who answered when I called earlier. We'll put the fear of the gods into them, and then I want some information. How did this ass-backward place get into the Federation as a full member? Their population is mostly illiterate. That's a bar to full entry right there, so that tells me they lied, and then misled the team that assessed their application."

"The law says that's bad?" Red caressed his railgun.

Rivka stared him down. "You don't get to shoot anything, not until there's no other choice."

Red shrugged. "It doesn't matter. This is a vacation, so

there are no betting pools on us. Or are there?" The body-guards looked at each other. Lindy tapped the comm panel in the small galley.

"Chaz, is there any betting regarding blood or running during our vacation?"

"You won't be angry, will you?" Chaz asked.

Rivka groaned. "Don't tell me you've already reported blood and running."

"The information was in the queue. It transmitted as soon as the interference was removed."

"Did any of my crew place a bet?"

"Only Ankh, but I can explain."

Lindy covered her face with her hands. "When you're in a hole, Chaz, stop digging."

"Maybe I can't explain," the AI corrected.

"Who won?" Rivka conceded.

"Looks like Terry Henry Walton was within five minutes of first blood, that being the Yangorian bullet that clipped Red's arm."

"How did he guess that?"

"He purchased a number of slots."

"Entering the capital city's flight zone. We should be settled in the government compound in five minutes," Kennedy relayed.

Rivka started clenching and unclenching her fists. "Chaz, do we have transportation lined up?"

"You will have an escort to the chancellor's hall. It appears the government was energized by your earlier communique."

"I'm good with that." She looked at Red and Lindy. They gave the thumbs-up without having to be asked if they were ready. She reached into her pocket to make sure she carried Reaper with her. It was too hot on Tanglewood for her to wear her jacket, so she had her datapad in her hand. It was the only thing she carried.

"Touchdown," Kennedy called from the cockpit. Rivka moved down the corridor to give Red space to open the hatch. He tapped the button and stepped aside. Once the hatch was open, he stood in the doorway and scanned the scene. The ship sat on a well-manicured lawn. Modern buildings of modest height surrounded the area. It looked as welcoming as almost any planet in the Federation. A small party of locals shifted nervously as they waited.

Red stepped out and walked toward them. Rivka filled the space behind him so the aliens couldn't see her. Lindy brought up the rear, staying in the hatch, where she commanded a better view. Red moved to the side when he was two steps from the welcoming committee, and Rivka strolled up to them.

Slight like the Yindle and Yangorians, but their skin pigment was tan.

"I'm Magistrate Rivka Anoa," she told them. "I've been on your planet for six days, and I am not happy with what I've seen."

"I am Chancellor Betagow, and I apologize for your rough landing and loss of contact. We didn't know you had arrived, but that is no excuse. We were aware of your itinerary, but no one noticed you had not shown up. We didn't have you on our schedule today, but such an eminent representative of our mother Federation should still be treated with the greatest respect." He bowed deeply.

Fucking politicians, Red grumbled. Rivka turned to him.

He maintained an innocent expression as he scanned the area for threats.

"Shall we retire to somewhere less public?" Rivka suggested.

"Of course!" The chancellor beamed and gestured for Rivka to walk beside him as he headed for the nearest building.

Red and Lindy took positions where they could keep an eye on the locals. The rest of the area was devoid of living creatures.

Once inside, they led Rivka to an immense chamber with a small table in the middle. It had only two chairs pulled up.

Red and Lindy stood at either end of the large open space surrounding the central area. The other members of the chancellor's party sat in a row of chairs well away from the table. Lindy adjusted her position so she could keep them in her line of sight.

The chancellor sat down and smiled pleasantly, motioning for Rivka to take the chair on the opposite side of the table.

She deferred, sitting on the table in front of him.

"Chancellor Betagow, I believe that an unacceptable percentage of your population is illiterate, which means your application for membership to the Federation contained inconsistencies."

"Are you talking about Yindle and Yangor?" the chancellor asked, looking relieved. "Our last survey showed less than ten thousand total souls among both those populations. We have over two hundred thousand on this side of the planet, which marks less than five percent of the population as possibly illiterate. They know what they need for the lives they live."

He smiled pleasantly.

"They know what they need..." she repeated. "Does that include the manufacturing knowledge to make rifles?"

"Those were for self-defense purposes only. They have this vicious creature over there called a kinga. The rifles are to keep the beasts in check."

"Kinga. Those are good eating," Rivka said slowly. "Cook them over a slow and smoky fire."

The chancellor didn't have an answer since she hadn't asked a question.

Rivka leaned close and whispered, "Bullshit. You gave them rifles so they could fight each other and maintain a status quo where they never grew enough to challenge your authority. I am going to revert your membership to a pending status until we can fully review Tanglewood and *all* the people who live here. I have sufficient facts supporting your failure to notify the population of their obligations under Federation Law. We were out there, and each of those groups tried to take us prisoner until we explained things to them."

The chancellor looked skeptical. "Explained?"

Rivka made a finger gun. "It's amazing how superior firepower can gain you a captive audience."

Chancellor Betagow leaned away from her.

"Right now is a great example. I didn't have to threaten you to maintain your full attention because you know you were in the wrong and got caught."

She touched his arm. Her mind was flooded with thoughts of how he could cover up the process, destroy records, and make people disappear for the time Federation investigators were active.

"I have no idea what you are talking about," the chancellor said smoothly.

Rivka put her datapad on the table and tapped the screen. "Chaz, record the following. There is a backup digital file in the safe in the chancellor's office. It opens with his handprint, or secondary code of fifty-one, seven, forty-three, and nine. That contains the actual data before it was manipulated to meet Federation guidelines. The secretary is a key witness. She is scheduled to go on vacation, starting today. Cancel that and have her remain at her desk until I can take a statement. Chancellor Betagow, care to revise your formal application for membership to the Federation?"

"Yes, Magistrate. Our application may have been put together a little too hastily. We need to verify some of the information before we resubmit."

"Before your successor resubmits, you mean." Rivka stood, picked up her datapad, and waved at Red. "Take him into custody. Falsification of Federation forms." She leaned close to the chancellor, whose face had taken on a distinct pasty pallor. "You probably won't be in custody for longer than an hour or three, but since you've already been found guilty, your record will prevent you from engaging with the Federation in any formal capacity from here on out."

Rivka walked toward the remaining members of the group. "You." She pointed to the one female in the group. "Can you take me to the chancellor's office, please?"

"Of course." The older female smiled.

CHAPTER TWENTY-SIX

Tanglewood, Capital City

With the evidence in hand and the chancellor's crimes formally on the record, Rivka reconvened Tanglewood's planetary leadership.

"Your membership in the Federation has been formally suspended. The good news is that you no longer need to comply with Federation Law. The bad news is that all trade with Tanglewood is also suspended until separate agreements can be put into place since the Federation no longer backstops compliance with the trade deals. I've outlined a few steps you'll need to take if you want to get back in; first and foremost is that you treat the Yindle and the Yangorians like equals on this planet. I'm no DNA expert, but I suspect you shared a common ancestor."

The body language of a couple of members of the delegation suggested they took umbrage at that statement.

Rivka stepped close. "Cool your jets. You know we can test samples from each of you and have an answer back today that confirms it. I have no time or patience for bull-shit. I've been out in that jungle for six days because of your hubris and the disinformation you gave the Federation."

She didn't bother to mention the anomaly that affected the Etheric-powered equipment.

"I'm going to request a special delegation from the Federation to expand our diplomatic presence in order to help you fulfill your requirements, should you desire to rejoin the Federation."

None of those present disputed Rivka's plan.

"Dispute," she said aloud. "I have taken a personal interest in the dispute between Yindle and Yangor. I am going to see it to its conclusion, to the resolution of the dispute. I'm considering the dispute between you and the Federation closed following the conviction of Chancellor Betagow. Now, if you'll excuse me, I need to be on the other side of your beautiful planet."

She didn't bother shaking hands or acknowledging the authority of the remaining leaders. The Magistrate simply walked away, with Red and Lindy in tow.

"We got geared up for that?" Red whined.

"Yes. It went much better than I expected. They were appropriately cowed from the outset. Maybe they do have consciences, despite the way they treat their jungle-dwelling counterparts."

The hatch popped open as they approached *Destiny's Vengeance,* where Kennedy was patiently waiting.

"Take us back to *Wyatt Earp,* please," Rivka requested.

The pilot hurried back to the cockpit.

"I'm glad she's back with us," Lindy said.

"Bruised but not broken." Rivka watched the cockpit and how the young woman worked.

"She has a new lease on life, and we have a responsibility not to dump her in the middle of a jungle on a strange planet," Lindy suggested.

Rivka shook her head. "We have the responsibility to keep checking to make sure she's comfortable in our home, that being *Wyatt Earp*, or wherever we might end up. I think the jungle was the catalyst that made her question why she wanted to be on this crew."

Lindy turned to the galley, where Red was banging on the food processor because he was hungry. "I'm not sure I want to be anywhere else, but that's just me."

Rivka hugged her bodyguard before yelling at the galley, "You better not break that. Ankh will have your ass."

"You can't send this freight train to the stars without fuel!" Red stuck his arm through the door and flexed a massive bicep.

Lindy grabbed it and did a pull-up.

"For the record, Magistrate," Red started, "your vacations suck. There's been too little food, no real ass-kicking, and no sex. In other words, no vacation."

Rivka made a sour face. "Vacations are meant for inner reflection, seeking and realizing peace for your soul."

Red returned Rivka's expression. "That is some serious bullshit you're slinging, Magistrate. Vacations are for decadence, pampering, food, more pampering, and massive quantities of pleasures of the flesh."

Lindy nodded vigorously. "Massive."

Rivka backed slowly away. "I'll be in the cockpit."

Red stuck his tongue out like an old lecher. "Yeah, me, too." He dragged a play-fighting Lindy into the small galley and closed the door.

"We're going to be there in ten minutes!" Rivka yelled.

"More like twenty," Kennedy corrected.

"Make it thirty," Rivka ordered. "I'd like to think my bodyguards are in top shape."

Wyatt Earp, **Tanglewood**

Ankh and Ted were both immersed in Ankh's new holographic workshop in the engine room. Rivka watched with her arms crossed until she finally gave up. They didn't look like they were going anywhere else anytime soon.

Ramses' Chariot's bots were fully engaged in fixing the ship, using additional stores that Ted's ship ferried from the orbiting battleship once he had recovered the Etheric dampener he had let Rivka borrow for her trip to the other side of the planet.

They only had to wait.

Rivka wandered to the bridge, to find Ryleigh and Kennedy tapping screens while going through procedural manuals. They stopped what they were doing and stood when the Magistrate entered.

"You guys staying busy?" Rivka asked, hoping that others weren't as bored as she had become.

"Of course." Ryleigh beamed. "We're doing what we love to do. Virtually, but still, this ship is amazing!"

"We're stuck in the top of some trees."

"That's a temporary blip." Kennedy waved the setback

away. "With the new dampener, cloak, screens, shields, and anything else you can think of, we should be able to travel unseen and unmolested throughout the galaxy."

"You can't touch this!" Ryleigh declared. Chaz started playing the song from eons past. The bass thumped, and the music blared. The pilots started dancing. Rivka backed off the bridge.

"I'll leave you to it, then." She waved as the hatch closed behind her. She headed for the galley, thought better of it, and continued to her quarters to change. The gym sounded like a better option until she saw Sahved ambling down the corridor, head down in a datapad. He stumbled past Rivka without seeing her.

"Sahved," she said softly.

He nearly jumped out of his skin. "Magistrate," he replied, regaining his wits.

"How are the studies going?"

"Coming," he replied. "The studies are coming along nicely. I'm glad they are not going. I fear I would not catch up. They are coming at me like a river falling over a ledge, crashing into the chasm of my mind."

"I'm glad... What?"

"Your law is hard," he admitted.

"But just," Rivka countered. "A hard but just framework within which multiple worlds with disparate foundational cultures can operate without discord. It will be complex, but it must also be simple and flexible enough that people who aren't criminals don't get thrown in jail."

"We must never throw people who aren't criminals in jail."

"What if they break the law?" Rivka leaned against the

wall. Sahved wove and bobbed as he searched the library shelves in his head for the answer.

"Then they are criminals," he finally answered.

"Like SiQuan and Dee?"

"No, of course not."

"They broke the law," Rivka stated definitively. Sahved started mumbling to himself. He tapped the screen using all three of his fingers, scrolled, twisted, and staggered away.

"Your law is hard." He stopped at the galley door, looked up, and smiled. "Oh! Hungry." He disappeared inside in his search for food.

"If I said I was the head lunatic in this asylum, I fear no one would dispute it."

"I wouldn't," Red remarked from behind.

"Since when did you get so light-footed?" she asked as she turned to face him. He wore his workout clothes, a torn t-shirt and gym shorts. Lindy was behind in a small tank top and tight leggings. Both were covered in sweat. "I was just heading to workout. Getting soft while on vacation."

"That reminds me..." Red leaned down to look her in the eye. He gripped her shoulder so she could see his mind. "Your vacations suck."

She jerked free.

"Holy shit, Red! Don't ever do that to me again."

"Woohoo!" Red and Lindy cheered and high-fived. "Do what?"

"Show me your warped, pleasures-of-the-flesh mind."

"You showed her what?" Lindy jabbed a finger into the middle of Red's back.

"Wait, you were supposed to see Lindy and me heading out on our yacht on our own private vacation, with you and the others waving goodbye. Don't include us on your next vacation, Magistrate! Take that dentist buddy of yours. He can patch you up after you fail to protect yourself."

"That's not what you showed me. Maybe you need to join Sahved for some mental discipline training." He slowly reached for her. Rivka ran.

She pounded down the corridor, made the U-corner at the bridge, and headed back toward the engine room. She pulled up when she nearly ran into Ted and Ankh. They walked past her and kept going. She turned around and followed out of idle curiosity.

They continued to the cargo-bay-turned-hangar-bay, which was mostly filled by the bulk of *Destiny's Vengeance*. Ankh strolled to the Pod-doc and climbed in. Ted started manipulating the controls. The cover closed, and the equipment started to operate.

"Is Ankh injured or sick?" Rivka asked.

"No," Ted replied.

Rivka saw where Ankh got his personality foibles. "I meant, why is Ankh going through a Pod-doc procedure?"

"To further upgrade his body against damage. He was seriously injured during the crash landing. We cannot risk losing him *and* Erasmus, so he has been incrementally upgrading his body over the past ten days. This should be the final procedure to give him additional bulk, strengthen the bones around his head and vital organs, and improve his nanos' ability to respond to catastrophic damage and restore the ones within."

Rivka had noticed that Ankh looked different but hadn't been able to put her finger on exactly why. She nodded without further comment. Ted continued working the Pod-doc controls until he stopped to commune with his AI. Rivka thought he looked like a mannequin while he stared into space, unmoving. She wondered how Felicity had put up with him for the last century, but their relationship was legendary.

Rivka thought about leaving for the gym, but if Ted was waiting, so would she since her curiosity about Ankh's transformation got the best of her. She lost track of time while she sat on the deck and read reports on her datapad. She didn't see the cycle end, but she heard the cover open.

Ankh stepped out and took a deep breath.

"You look the same," Rivka stated, studying him. Small body, maybe not as small, with a big, bald head and perpetually emotionless expression.

Ankh fixed her with his unblinking gaze. "But I am not." He and Ted shared a thought before Ankh hurried from the cargo bay. Ted headed for the ramp. A maintenance bot appeared, and he climbed on top like an airwave surfer. The bot hovered out and up, taking Ted back to *Ramses' Chariot.*

She heard the ship undock from *Wyatt Earp,* and the slight whine of intra-atmospheric propulsion quickly faded as it left for the stars.

"Are we ready to go?" Rivka asked the empty cargo bay.

She closed the ramp, secured the hatch after leaving, and strode toward the bridge. "Magistrate to the bridge," Clodagh requested over the shipwide broadcast. Two seconds later, Rivka was there.

"There you are," Clodagh said.

"I was on my way here. Are we ready to go?"

"*Wyatt Earp* is cleared for interstellar travel."

"We have one stop to make first. Take us to the Barrier Peak. We have some unfinished business."

"You heard the order," Clodagh relayed to the pilot and navigator. Floyd bumped into Rivka from behind. "Prepare to get underway."

Absentmindedly, Rivka picked up the wombat and started stroking her fur.

Keeper? the little girl asked.

"Yes! I hope we see the keeper and the master. We're going to set up a shelter where they can discuss the way ahead."

Whee! Floyd cried.

Groenwyn appeared with a yapping Tiny Man Titan.

"New friends," the platinum-green-haired young woman said.

"I sure hope so." Rivka one-arm-hugged Groenwyn, and the Magistrate was flooded by emotions of hope and joy. She let go quickly but felt better, as she always did from Groenwyn's positivity.

The ship lifted off, cracking small branches on its way upward. Once it cleared the treetops, it turned for the Barrier Peak, flying slowly over Bora Vale.

"Give me external broadcast, please."

"Given," Chaz replied.

"Please meet us at Barrier Peak."

Rivka shrugged. She hadn't been trying to be profound. She pointed forward and the ship flew on. "Continue into Yindle territory."

Once there, she repeated her message to the jungle.

Wyatt Earp returned to the open area of Barrier Peak, settled to the ground on its landing skids, and opened the cargo bay door.

Rivka, Groenwyn, Red, and Lindy strolled into the fresh air.

"Looks different." Red pointed to the trees. Most had already grown over, but the big splintered trees had become a part of a heavy new barrier to the Yindle jungle. "Maybe we can use the *Vengeance* to haul some of the deadfall out of there?"

"Big man has a conscience," Rivka teased. "I agree, but we'll ask Master Dee."

"They shot me," he pointed toward Yangor, "and they shot you." He pointed to Yindle. "I don't feel that bad, more like beating up the biggest bully in the little kids' playground. He needed his ass kicked, but he's still small and insignificant. Also, while we're baring our consciences," Rivka winced, "I was underwhelmed by your efforts to rip the chancellor a new one. You slapped a parking ticket on his forehead."

"Beating up the little kid, Red. Once I got there, I saw that for Tanglewood, he might have been a premier politician. You know, a scum-sucking river eel who thought he was getting something for the planet. He's in his place now. I punished him by having him removed from power. It'll be someone else's name attached to the Federation paperwork."

"Have we seen the last of him?"

"He won't be back. He might have been a big fish on Tanglewood, but he has no power off-planet. He was judged and found wanting. He is a criminal and will forever be. He has been punished. Maybe he'll be the one carrying our luggage when we get to the resort."

"Hang on!" Red blurted.

"What?" Lindy asked, leaning close so she didn't miss the answer.

Groenwyn walked away, chuckling. Floyd and Titan ran ahead.

"We have three days left. It's not what I envisioned, but it's better than nothing."

"No, Magistrate, it's *not* better than nothing. I'm not going on a vacation with you. Your vacations…"

"I know, I know! My vacations suck."

"That's settled, then. What's our next mission?"

"Case," Rivka corrected.

"You say to*mah*to, I say to*may*to." Red tipped his chin toward the Yangorian jungle. The Keeper of the Barrier Peak appeared, waved, and hurried toward them.

"Great to see you and your magnificent ship!" the keeper greeted them. He shook hands all around.

From the Yindle side, Minor Yee tentatively stepped into the open. Groenwyn intercepted him with a kind greeting of her own. Floyd bounced around the Yindle while Titan yipped and yapped. He held his hands up to keep from touching the animals. Groenwyn escorted him to the top of the hill.

"Greetings from Master Dee. He is on a journey through all of Yindle to tell our people of the outreach by Yangor and our agreement to talk in the hopes of burying our differences," he began formally.

CRAIG MARTELLE & MICHAEL ANDERLE

Red tried not to look at the Yindle with disdain. The last time he'd seen him, he was running for the jungle.

Minor Yee pulled a knife from behind his back and offered it pommel-first to Rivka. "I believe this is yours. The master asked me to return it."

Rivka took it with a slight bow and handed it to Red. He slipped it into the empty sheath on his combat vest.

"Come, let us sit in the shade and talk," Antwan offered. Rivka gestured toward the cargo ramp of her ship, but the Yangorian shook his head. "We have prepared a meeting place over there under a border tree in the cool and calm of the jungle."

"As have we under the treefall, the memorial to the damage done during our first meeting." Minor Yee held his ground.

"As the Federation's mediator in this matter, you will rotate from one spot to the other, but who is first? I suggest we flip a coin, but I suspect no one has one." Lindy and Red both shook their heads. "So let's go with the knife toss. Red, spin it and see which way it points."

Red removed his knife, and with a deft twist of his wrist, set it spinning. It bounced once and settled, pointing directly at the ship, ninety degrees to both Yindle and Yangor.

"The first meeting will be right here on the ramp," Rivka declared. Next will be in Yindle, then Yangor. That is how it will be."

She did not give them time or space to argue, instead leading them to the ramp, where they sat on the edge. "Introduce yourselves and talk about your families. What meal did you have this morning? We'll go from there."

276

"I thought we'd talk about something more substantive," Antwan started. Rivka held up her hand.

"You need to know where you came from before you can decide where you want to go. This isn't a trip you're taking alone. It is the journey that's important, not the destination. What you'll find is that once you start, your destination will change, but the path behind you will not. Make yourselves proud to look back and see the ground you've covered. Together."

The End

Judge, Jury, & Executioner, Book 8

If you like this book, please leave a review. I love reviews since they tell other readers that this book is worth their time and money. I hope you feel that way now that you've finished the latest installment. Please drop me a line and let me know you like Rivka's adventures and want them to continue. This is my new favorite series. I hope you agree.

Click over to the Judge, Jury, & Executioner series page to see if any new volumes have been published.

US - My Book
UK - My Book
Australia - My Book
Canada - My Book

And if you use a different store search it for this ASIN - B07G69MBTV

Don't stop now! Keep turning the pages as Craig hits his *Author Notes* with thoughts about this book and the good stuff that happens in the *Kurtherian Gambit* Universe. Your favorite legal eagle will return! I guarantee it:).

 You are still reading! Thank you for staying on board until now. It doesn't get much better than that.

This story came to me at the end of The Art of Smuggling. I thought we needed to see more and tighter bonding between the crew. Plus, I love a good island castaway story. We got to see a lot of growth between the crew without getting caught up in too much backstory. Our three pilots are maturing into their roles on the Magistrate's crew. I wanted to give them a little primetime.

Ankh also needed to see what he was made of. "Sterner stuff than that" is the answer.

My wife and I spent New Year's in Australia, as we usually do since my son married into Adelaide. If I want to see my grandkids, that's where we have to go. It's much easier for us to travel there than a family of four flying to Alaska. In the winter.

We prefer going someplace warm. The temperature difference was rather extreme this year. When we left, it was a brutal -37F in Fairbanks. It was 73F in Hawaii as we traveled through, and when we arrived in Fiji, it was a balmy 86F. You did the math right. That's a 123 degree difference. It made Fiji seem hot, but we powered through with a nice beach view on Denarau Island. Breaking up the flights into six-hour chunks makes the trip much easier on me. I don't like long flights because I can't sleep well on a plane. I nap, but for only a few minutes at a time because I stop breathing due to low oxygen on a plane.

I can hang tough for six hours, write, watch a movie, all those good things that help pass the time.

Many words in Dispute were written on the plane. It was a good flight from Fiji to Adelaide. And then many more words were written early in the morning in the hotel room before we headed out for the day to spend time with my son and his family.

I always work. The challenge of being a workaholic while I'm supposed to be retired. But there are so many stories to tell, and I enjoy helping people escape from the rigors of everyday life. This, like all my stories is what I call escape fiction. I want to make you think just enough to immerse yourself in the story and the characters, but not make you work too much at it. You should be able to simply enjoy the story. I hope I'm accomplishing that with this series as well as all with all my books.

The cause of freedom is not the cause of a race or a sect, a party or a class, it is the cause of all sentient creatures. It is their very birthright. This is a take on the quote by Ann

Julia Cooper on pages 26-27 of the new US Passport. I thought it appropriate.

The name of Tanglewood comes from Kurtherian Gambit fan Michael Barr who offered Tanglethorn. I went with Tanglewood as the jungle did not become an antagonist in this story, but simply a canvas upon which the story was painted, one more element that the crew and natives had to work with.

While we were in Fiji, I took a number of pictures of an actual jungle so you can get an idea what I saw in my mind's eye regarding the density and hostility of moving through and fighting within the jungle. It would be a challenge on the best of days.

Dispute will publish on January 13th, 2020. I have an appointment with my cardiologist on that day to prepare me for heart surgery on the 14th. It's an ablation, a fairly common procedure, but not simple. They'll stick a wire into my heart and fry a couple nerves that are making it beat out of sync. The procedure is outpatient. I'll get to leave the same day they perform the operation. The risk is low, but my heart has been wonky for the past eighteen months. I hope it goes as they expect and solves the issue so I can get my energy and life back.

If something goes way wrong, what if this is the last book I ever write? Will I have done the genre proud? I would like to think so and that Rivka continues into the foreseeable future. I surely want to see Rise of the AI (Executioner 9) on people's favorite reading lists:).

Thank you for reading my stories. This series is my favorite and will continue for the foreseeable future. *Super-dreadnought* is finished at six books, *Metal Legion* will end at eight books (I'm writing it now), *Nightwalker* at eight books (I have two left), and *Bad Company* at seven books (I have the outline for Bad Company 7 & 8 which I will combine into one superhuge book). Those series will all be finished by sometime in 2020. I'll write a new *Judge, Jury, & Executioner* in between wrapping each of the others because Rivka will live on. I enjoy these stories far too much to stop writing them.

And next year, we'll be bringing out a new series that's not set in the Kurtherian universe. Look for weretigers learning the galaxy's secrets.

Peace, fellow humans.

Please join my newsletter (www.craigmartelle.com – please, please, please sign up!), or you can follow me on Facebook since you'll get the same opportunity to pick up the books for only 99 cents on that first day they are published.

If you liked this story, you might like some of my other books. You can join my mailing list by dropping by my website www.craigmartelle.com or if you have any comments, shoot me a note at craig@craigmartelle.com. I am always happy to hear from people who've read my work. I try to answer every email I receive.

If you liked the story, please write a short review for me on Amazon. I greatly appreciate any kind words, even one or two sentences go a long way. The number of reviews an eBook receives greatly improves how well an eBook does on Amazon.

Amazon – www.amazon.com/author/craigmartelle

BookBub – https://www.bookbub.com/authors/craig-martelle

Facebook – www.facebook.com/authorcraigmartelle

My web page – www.craigmartelle.com

That's it—break's over, back to writing the next book. Peace, fellow humans.

publication – a post-apocalyptic survivalist adventure

Nightwalker (a Frank Roderus series) with Craig Martelle – A post-apocalyptic western adventure

End Days (co-written with E.E. Isherwood) (coming in audio) – a post-apocalyptic adventure

Successful Indie Author – a non-fiction series to help self-published authors

Metamorphosis Alpha – stories from the world's first science fiction RPG

The Expanding Universe – science fiction anthologies

Monster Case Files (co-written with Kathryn Hearst) – A Warner twins mystery adventure

Rick Banik (also available in audio) – Spy & terrorism action adventure

Published exclusively by Craig Martelle, Inc

The Dragon's Call by Angelique Anderson & Craig A. Price, Jr. – an epic fantasy quest

For a complete list of Craig's books, stop by his website – https://craigmartelle.com